René Vallery-Radot

Louis Pasteur - His Life and Labours

Outlook

René Vallery-Radot

Louis Pasteur - His Life and Labours

1. Auflage | ISBN: 978-3-73262-204-7

Erscheinungsort: Frankfurt am Main, Deutschland

Erscheinungsjahr: 2018

Outlook Verlag GmbH, Frankfurt.

Reproduction of the original.

René Vallery-Radot

Louis Pasteur - His Life and Labours

Outlook

LOUIS PASTEUR
HIS LIFE AND LABOURS

BY HIS SON-IN-LAW

TRANSLATED FROM THE FRENCH
BY
LADY CLAUD HAMILTON

WITH AN INTRODUCTION
BY JOHN TYNDALL

NEW YORK
D. APPLETON AND COMPANY
1, 3, AND 5 BOND STREET
1886.

PREFACE.

In the *salon* of a distinguished man, or of a great writer, there is often to be found a person who, without being either a fellow-worker or a disciple, without even possessing the scientific or literary qualities which might explain his habitual presence, lives nevertheless in complete familiarity with the man whom all around him call 'dear master.' Whence comes this intimate one? who is he? what is his business? He is only known as a friend of the house. He has no other title, and he is almost proud of having no other. Stripped of his own personality, he speaks only of the labours and the success of his illustrious friend, in the radiance of whose glory he moves with delight.

The author of this work is a person of this description. Intimately connected with the life of M. Pasteur, and a constant inmate of his laboratory, he has passed happy years near this great investigator, who has discovered a new world—the world of the infinitely little. Since the first studies of M. Pasteur on molecular dissymmetry, down to his most recent investigations on hydrophobia, on virulent diseases, and on the artificial cultures of living contagia, which have been converted by such cultures into veritable vaccines —passing by the intermediate celebrated experiments on spontaneous generation, fermentation, the diseases of wine, the manufacture of beer and vinegar, and the diseases of silkworms—the author of these pages has been able, if not to witness all, at least to follow in its principal developments this uninterrupted series of scientific conquests.

'What a beautiful book,' he remarked one day to M. Pasteur, 'might be written about all this!'

'But it is all in the Comptes-rendus of the Academy of Sciences.'

'It is not for the readers of the Comptes-rendus that such a book needs to be written, but for the great public, who know that you have done great things, but who know it only vaguely, by the records of journals, or by fragments of biography. The persons are few who know the history of your discoveries. What was your point of departure? How have you arrived at such and such principles, and at the consequences which flow from these principles? What is the connection and rigorous bond of your method? These are the things which it would be interesting to put together in a book which would have some chance of enduring as an historic document.'

'I could not waste my time in going back upon things already accomplished.'

'No; but my desire is that someone else should consecrate his time to the work. And listen,' added this friend, with audacious frankness—'do you know by whom, in my opinion, this book ought to be written? By a man who, without having been in any way trained to follow in your footsteps, is animated by the most lively desire to understand the course which you have pursued; who, while living at your side, has been each day impregnated with your method and your ideas; who, having had the happiness of comprehending your life and its achievements, does not wish to confine the pleasure thus derived to himself alone.'

'Where, then,' interrupted Pasteur with a kindly smile, not without a tinge of irony, 'is this man, at once so happy, and so impatient to share his happiness with others?'

'He is now pleading his cause before you. Yes, I would gladly attempt such a work. I have seen your efforts and observed your success. The experiments which I have not witnessed you have always freely explained to me, with that gift of clearness which Vauvenargues called the "polish" of masters.[1] Initiated by affection, I would make myself initiator by admiration. It would be the history of a learned man by an ignorant one. My ignorance would save me from dwelling too strictly or too long on technical details. With the exposition of your doctrine I would mingle some fragments of your biography. I would pass from a discovery to an anecdote, and so arrange matters as to give the book not only the character of a familiar scientific conversation, which would hardly be more than the echo of what I have learnt while near you, but also to make it a reflex of your life.'

'You should postpone that until I am no longer here.'

'Why so? Why, before assigning to them their places, should we wait till those whose names will endure have disappeared from the scene? No; it is you, living, that I wish to paint—you, in full work, in the midst of your laboratory. And, in addition to all other considerations, I would add, that your presence in the flesh will be the guarantee of my exactitude.'

July 1883.

INTRODUCTION.

In the early part of the present year the French original of this work was sent to me from Paris by its author. It was accompanied by a letter from M. Pasteur, expressing his desire to have the work translated and published in England. Responding to this desire, I placed the book in the hands of the Messrs. Longman, who, in the exercise of their own judgment, decided on publication. The translation was confided, at my suggestion, to Lady Claud Hamilton.

The translator's task was not always an easy one, but it has, I think, been well executed. A few slight abbreviations, for which I am responsible, have been introduced, but in no case do they affect the sense. It was, moreover, found difficult to render into suitable English the title of the original: '*M. Pasteur, Histoire d'un Savant par un Ignorant.*' A less piquant and antithetical English title was, therefore, substituted for the French one.

This filial tribute, for such it is, was written, under the immediate supervision of M. Pasteur, by his devoted and admiring son-in-law, M. Valery Radot. It is the record of a life of extraordinary scientific ardour and success, the picture of a mind on which facts fall like germs upon a nutritive soil, and, like germs so favoured, undergo rapid increase and multiplication. One hardly knows which to admire most—the intuitive vision which discerns in advance the new issues to which existing data point, or the skill in device, the adaptation of means to ends, whereby the intuition is brought to the test and ordeal of experiment.

In the investigation of microscopic organisms—the 'infinitely little,' as Pouchet loved to call them—and their doings in this our world, M. Pasteur has found his true vocation. In this broad field it has been his good fortune to alight upon a crowd of connected problems of the highest public and scientific interest, ripe for solution, and requiring for their successful treatment the precise culture and capacities which he has brought to bear upon them. He may regret his abandonment of molecular physics; he may look fondly back upon the hopes with which his researches on the tartrates and paratartrates inspired him; he may think that great things awaited him had he continued to labour in this line. I do not doubt it. But this does not shake my conviction that he yielded to the natural affinities of his intellect, that he obeyed its truest impulses, and reaped its richest rewards, in pursuing the line that he has chosen, and in which his labours have rendered him one of the most conspicuous scientific figures of this age.

With regard to the earliest labours of M. Pasteur, a few remarks supplementary to those of M. Radot may be introduced here. The days when angels whispered into the hearkening human ear, secrets which had no root in man's previous knowledge or experience, are gone for ever. The only revelation—and surely it deserves the name—now open to the wise arises from 'intending the mind' on acquired knowledge. When, therefore, M. Radot, following M. Pasteur, speaks with such emphasis about 'preconceived ideas,' he does not mean ideas without antecedents. Preconceived ideas, if out of deference to M. Pasteur the term be admitted, are the vintage of garnered facts. We in England should rather call them inductions, which, as M. Pasteur truly says, inspire the mind, and shape its course, in the subsequent work of deduction and verification.

At the time when M. Pasteur undertook his investigation of the diseases of silkworms, which led to such admirable results, he had never seen a silkworm; but, so far from this being considered a disqualification, M. Dumas regarded his freedom from preconceived ideas a positive advantage. His first care was to make himself acquainted with what others had done. To their observations he added his own, and then, surveying all, came to the conclusion that the origin of the disease was to be sought, not in the worms, not in the eggs, but in the moths which laid the eggs. I am not sure that this conclusion is happily described as 'a preconceived idea.' Every whipster may have his preconceived ideas; but the divine power, so largely shared by M. Pasteur, of distilling from facts their essences—of extracting from them the principles from which they flow—is given only to a few.

With regard to the discovery of crystalline facets in the tartrates, which has been dwelt upon by M. Radot, a brief reference to antecedent labours may be here allowed. It had been discovered by Arago, in 1811, and by Biot, in 1812 and 1818, that a plate of rock-crystal, cut perpendicular to the axis of the prism, possessed the power of rotating the plane of polarisation through an angle, dependent on the thickness of the plate and the refrangibility of the light. It had, moreover, been proved by Biot that there existed two species of rock-crystal, one of which turned the plane of polarisation to the right, and the other to the left. They were called, respectively, right-handed and left-handed crystals. No external difference of crystalline form was at first noticed which could furnish a clue to this difference of action. But closer scrutiny revealed upon the crystals minute facets, which, in the one class, were ranged along a right-handed, and, in the other, along a left-handed spiral. The symmetry of the hexagonal prism, and of the two terminal pyramids of the crystal, was disturbed by the introduction of these spirally-arranged facets. They constituted the outward and visible sign of that inward and invisible molecular structure which produced the observed action, and difference of action, on polarised light.

When, therefore, the celebrated Mitscherlich brought forward his tartrates and paratartrates of ammonia and soda, and affirmed them to possess the same atoms, the same internal arrangement of atoms, and the same outward crystalline form, one of them, nevertheless, causing the plane of polarisation to rotate, while the other did not, Pasteur, remembering, no doubt, the observations just described, instituted a search for facets like those discovered in rock-crystal, and which, without altering chemical constitution, destroyed crystalline identity. He first found such facets in the tartrates, while he subsequently proved the neutrality of the paratartrate to be due to the equal admixture of right-handed and left-handed crystals, one of which, when the paratartrate was dissolved, exactly neutralised the other.

Prior to Pasteur the left-handed tartrate was unknown. Its discovery, moreover, was supplemented by a series of beautiful researches on the compounds of right-handed and left-handed tartaric acid; he having previously extracted from the two tartrates, acids which, in regard to polarised light, behaved like themselves. Such was the worthy opening of M. Pasteur's scientific career, which has been dwelt upon so frequently and emphatically by M. Radot. The wonder, however, is, not that a searcher of such penetration as Pasteur should have discovered the facets of the tartrates, but that an investigator so powerful and experienced as Mitscherlich should have missed them.

The idea of molecular dissymmetry, introduced by Biot, was forced upon Biot's mind by the discovery of a number of liquids, and of some vapours, which possessed the rotatory power. Some, moreover, turned the plane of polarisation to the right, others to the left. Crystalline structure being here out of the question, the notion of dissymmetry, derived from the crystal, was transferred to the molecule. 'To produce any such phenomena,' says Sir John Herschel, 'the individual molecule must be conceived as unsymmetrically constituted.' The illustrations employed by M. Pasteur to elucidate this subject, though well calculated to give a general idea of dissymmetry, will, I fear, render but little aid to the reader in his attempts to realise *molecular* dissymmetry. Should difficulty be encountered here at the threshold of this work, I would recommend the reader not to be daunted by it, or prevented by it from going further. He may comfort himself by the assurance that the conception of a dissymmetric molecule is not a very precise one, even in the mind of M. Pasteur.

One word more with regard to the parentage of preconceived ideas. M. Radot informs us that at Strasburg M. Pasteur invoked the aid of helices and magnets, with a view to rendering crystals dissymmetrical at the moment of their formation. There can, I think, be but little doubt that such experiments were suggested by the pregnant discovery of Faraday published in 1845. By both helices and magnets Faraday caused the plane of polarisation in perfectly neutral liquids and solids to rotate. If the turning of the plane of polarisation be a demonstration of molecular dissymmetry, then, in the twinkling of an eye, Faraday was able to displace symmetry by dissymmetry, and to confer upon bodies, which in their ordinary state were inert and dead, this power of rotation which M. Pasteur considers to be the exclusive attribute of life.

The conclusion of M. Pasteur here referred to, which M. Radot justly describes as 'worthy of the most serious consideration,' is sure to arrest the attention of a large class of people, who, dreading 'materialism,' are ready to welcome any generalisation which differentiates the living world from the dead. M. Pasteur considers that his researches point to an irrefragable physical barrier between organic and inorganic nature. Never, he says, have you been able to produce in the laboratory, by the ordinary processes of chemistry, a dissymmetric molecule—in other words, a substance which, in a state of solution, where molecular forces are paramount, has the power of causing a polarised beam to rotate. This power belongs exclusively to derivatives from the living world. Dissymmetric *forces*, different from those of the laboratory, are, in Pasteur's mind, the agents of vitality; it is they that build up dissymmetric molecules which baffle the chemist when he attempts to reproduce them. Such molecules trace their ancestry to life alone. 'Pourrait-on indiquer une séparation plus profonde entre les produits de la nature vivante, et ceux de la nature minérale, que cette dissymmétrie chez les uns, et son absence chez les autres?' It may be worth calling to mind that molecular dissymmetry is the *idea*, or *inference*, the observed rotation of the plane of polarisation, by masses of sensible magnitude, being the *fact* on which the inference is based.

That the molecule, or unit brick, of an organism should be different from the molecule of a mineral is only to be expected, for otherwise the profound distinction between them would disappear. And that one of the differences between the two classes of molecules should be the possession, by the one, of this power of rotation, and its non-possession by the other, would be a fact, interesting no doubt, but not surprising. The critical point here has reference to the power and range of chemical processes, apart from the play of vitality. Beginning with the elements themselves, can they not be so combined as to produce organic compounds? Not to speak of the antecedent labours of Wöhler and others in Germany, it is well known that various French investigators, among whom are some of M. Pasteur's illustrious colleagues of the Academy, have succeeded in forming substances which were once universally regarded as capable of being elaborated by plants and animals alone. Even with regard to the rotation of the plane of polarisation, M. Jungfleisch, an extremely able pupil of the celebrated Berthelot, affirms that the barrier erected by M. Pasteur has been broken down; and though M. Pasteur questions this affirmation, it is at least hazardous, where so many supposed distinctions between organic and inorganic have been swept away, to erect a new one. For my part, I frankly confess my disbelief in its permanence.

Without waiting for new facts, those already in our possession tend, I think, to render the association which M. Pasteur seeks to establish between dissymmetry and life insecure. Quartz, as a crystal, exerts a very powerful twist on the plane of polarisation. Quartz dissolved exerts no power at all. The molecules of quartz, then, do not belong to the same category as the crystal of which they are the constituents; the former are symmetrical, the latter is dissymmetrical. This, in my opinion, is a very significant fact. By the act of crystallisation, and without the intervention of life, the forces of molecules, possessing planes of symmetry, are so compounded as to build up crystals which have no planes of symmetry. Thus, in passing from the symmetrical to the dissymmetrical, we are not compelled to interpolate new forces; the forces extant in mineral nature suffice. The reasoning which applies to the dissymmetric crystal applies to the dissymmetric molecule. The dissymmetry of the latter, however pronounced and complicated, arises from the composition of atomic forces which, when reduced to their most elementary action, are exerted along straight lines. In 1865 I ventured, in reference to this subject, to define the position which I am still inclined to maintain. 'It is the compounding, in the organic world, of forces belonging equally to the inorganic that constitutes the mystery and the miracle of vitality.'[2]

Add to these considerations the discovery of Faraday already adverted to. An electric current is not an organism, nor does a magnet possess life; still, by their action, Faraday, in his first essay, converted over one hundred and fifty symmetric and inert aqueous solutions into dissymmetric and active ones.[3]

Theory, however, may change, and inference may fade away, but scientific experiment endures for ever. Such durability belongs, in the domain of molecular physics, to the experimental researches of M. Pasteur.

The weightiest events of life sometimes turn upon small hinges; and we now come to the incident which caused M. Pasteur to quit a line of research the abandonment of which he still regrets. A German manufacturer of chemicals had noticed that the impure commercial tartrate of lime, sullied with organic matters of various kinds, fermented on being dissolved in water and exposed to summer heat. Thus prompted, Pasteur prepared some pure, right-handed tartrate of ammonia, mixed with it albuminous matter, and found that the mixture fermented. His solution, limpid at first, became turbid, and the turbidity he found to be due to the multiplication of a microscopic organism, which found in the liquid its proper aliment. Pasteur recognised in this little organism a *living ferment*. This bold conclusion was doubtless strengthened, if not prompted, by the previous discovery of the yeast-plant—the alcoholic ferment—by Cagniard-Latour and Schwann.

Pasteur next permitted his little organism to take the carbon necessary for its growth from the pure paratartrate of ammonia. Owing to the opposition of its two classes of crystals, a solution of this salt, it will be remembered, does not turn the plane of polarised light either to the right or to the left. Soon after fermentation had set in, a rotation to the left was noticed, proving that the equilibrium previously existing between the two classes of crystals had ceased. The rotation reached a maximum, after which it was found that all the right-handed tartrate had disappeared from the liquid. The organism thus proved itself competent to select its own food. It found, as it were, one of the tartrates more digestible than the other, and appropriated it, to the neglect of the other. No difference of chemical constitution determined its choice; for the elements, and the proportions of the elements, in the two tartrates were identical. But the peculiarity of structure which enabled the substance to rotate the plane of polarisation to the right, also rendered it a fit aliment for the organism. This most remarkable experiment was successfully made with the seeds of our common mould, *Penicillium glaucam*.

Here we find Pasteur unexpectedly landed amid the phenomena of fermentation. With true scientific instinct he closed with the conception that ferments are, in all cases, living things, and that the substances formerly regarded as ferments are, in reality, the food of the ferments. Touched by this wand, difficulties fell rapidly before him. He proved the ferment of lactic acid to be an organism of a certain kind. The ferment of butyric acid he proved to be an organism of a different kind. He was soon led to the fundamental conclusion that the capacity of an organism to act as a ferment depended on its power to live, without air. The fermentation of beer was sufficient to suggest this idea. The yeast-plant, like many others, can live either with or without free air. It flourishes best in contact with free air, for it is then spared the labour of wresting from the malt the oxygen required for its sustenance. Supplied with free air, however, it practically ceases to be a ferment; while in the brewing vat, where the work of fermentation is active, the budding *torula* is completely cut off by the sides of the vessel, and by a deep layer of carbonic acid gas, from all contact with air. The butyric ferment not only lives without air, but Pasteur showed that air is fatal to it. He finally divided microscopic organisms into two great classes, which he named respectively *ærobies* and *anærobies*, the former requiring free oxygen to maintain life, the latter capable of living without free oxygen, but able to wrest this element from its combinations with other elements. This destruction of pre-existing compounds and formation of new ones, caused by the increase and multiplication of the organism, constitute the process of fermentation.

Under this head are also rightly ranked the phenomena of putrefaction. As M. Radot well expresses it, the fermentation of sugar may be described as the putrefaction of sugar. In this particular field M. Pasteur, whose contributions to the subject are of the highest value, was preceded by Schwann, a man of great merit, of whom the world has heard too little.[4] Schwann placed decoctions of meat in flasks, sterilised the decoctions by boiling, and then supplied them with calcined air, the power of which to support life he showed to be unimpaired. Under these circumstances putrefaction never set in. Hence the conclusion of Schwann, that putrefaction was not due to the contact of air, as affirmed by Gay-Lussac, but to something suspended in the air which heat was able to destroy. This something consists of living organisms which nourish themselves at the expense of the organic substance, and cause its putrefaction.

The grasp of Pasteur on this class of subjects was embracing. He studied acetic fermentation, and found it to be the work of a minute fungus, the *mycoderma aceti*, which, requiring free oxygen for its nutrition, overspreads the surface of the fermenting liquid. By the alcoholic ferment the sugar of the grape-juice is transformed into carbonic acid gas and alcohol, the former exhaling, the latter remaining in the wine. By the *mycoderma aceti* the wine is, in its turn, converted into vinegar. Of the experiments made in connection with this subject one deserves especial mention. It is that in which Pasteur suppressed all albuminous matters, and carried on the fermentation with purely crystallisable substances. He studied the deterioration of vinegar, revealed its cause, and the means of preventing it. He defined the part played by the little eel-like organisms which sometimes swarm in vinegar casks, and ended by introducing important ameliorations and improvements in the manufacture of vinegar. The discussion with Liebig and other minor discussions of a similar nature, which M. Radot has somewhat strongly emphasized, I will not here dwell upon.

It was impossible for an inquirer like Pasteur to evade the question—Whence come these minute organisms which are demonstrably capable of producing effects on which vast industries are built and on which whole populations depend for occupation and sustenance? He thus found himself face to face with the question of spontaneous generation, to which the researches of Pouchet had just given fresh interest. Trained as Pasteur was in the experimental sciences, he had an immense advantage over Pouchet, whose culture was derived from the sciences of observation. One by one the statements and experiments of Pouchet were explained or overthrown, and the doctrine of spontaneous generation remained discredited until it was revived with ardour, ability, and, for a time, with success, by Dr. Bastian.

A remark of M. Radot's on page 103 needs some qualification. 'The great interest of Pasteur's method consists,' he says, 'in its proving unanswerably that the origin of life in infusions which have been heated to the boiling point is solely due to the solid particles suspended in the air.' This means that living germs cannot exist *in the liquid* when once raised to a temperature of 212° Fahr. No doubt a great number of organisms collapse at this temperature; some indeed, as M. Pasteur has shown, are destroyed at a temperature 90° below the boiling point. But this is by no means universally the case. The spores of the hay-bacillus, for example, have, in numerous instances, successfully resisted the boiling temperature for one, two, three, four hours; while in one instance *eight hours'* continuous boiling failed to sterilise an infusion of desiccated hay. The knowledge of this fact caused me a little anxiety some years ago when a meeting was projected between M. Pasteur and Dr. Bastian. For though, in regard to the main question, I knew that the upholder of spontaneous generation could not win, on the particular issue touching the death temperature he might have come off victor.

The manufacture and maladies of wine next occupied Pasteur's attention. He had, in fact, got the key to this whole series of problems, and he knew how to use it. Each of the disorders of wine was traced to its specific organism, which, acting as a ferment, produced substances the reverse of agreeable to the palate. By the simplest of devices, Pasteur, at a stroke, abolished the causes of wine disease. Fortunately the foreign organisms which, if unchecked, destroy the best red wines are extremely sensitive to heat. A temperature of 50° Cent. (122° Fahr.) suffices to kill them. Bottled wines once raised to this temperature, for a single minute, are secured from subsequent deterioration. The wines suffer in no degree from exposure to this temperature. The manner in which Pasteur proved this, by invoking the judgment of the wine-tasters of Paris, is as amusing as it is interesting.

Moved by the entreaty of his master, the illustrious Dumas, Pasteur took up the investigation of the diseases of silkworms at a time when the silk- husbandry of France was in a state of ruin. In doing so he did not, as might appear, entirely forsake his former line of research. Previous investigators had got so far as to discover vibratory corpuscles in the blood of the diseased worms, and with such corpuscles Pasteur had already made himself intimately acquainted. He was therefore to some extent at home in this new investigation. The calamity was appalling, all the efforts made to stay the plague having proved futile. In June 1865 Pasteur betook himself to the scene of the epidemic, and at once commenced his observations. On the evening of his arrival he had already discovered the corpuscles, and shown them to others. Acquainted as he was with the work of living ferments, his mind was prepared to see in the corpuscles the cause of the epidemic. He followed them through all the phases of the insect's life—through the eggs, through the worm, through the chrysalis, through the moth. He proved that the germ of the malady might be present in the eggs and escape detection. In the worm also it might elude microscopic examination. But in the moth it reached a development so distinct as to render its recognition immediate. From healthy moths healthy eggs were sure to spring; from healthy eggs healthy worms; from healthy worms fine cocoons: so that the problem of the restoration to France of its silk-husbandry reduced itself to the separation of the healthy from the unhealthy moths, the rejection of the latter, and the exclusive employment of the eggs of the former. M. Radot describes how this is now done on the largest scale, with the most satisfactory results.

The bearing of this investigation on the parasitic theory of communicable diseases was thus illustrated: Worms were infected by permitting them to feed for a single meal on leaves over which corpusculous matter had been spread; they were infected by inoculation, and it was shown how they infected each other by the wounds and scratches of their own claws. By the association of healthy with diseased worms, the infection was communicated to the former. Infection at a distance was also produced by the wafting of the corpuscles through the air. The various modes in which communicable diseases are diffused among human populations were illustrated by Pasteur's treatment of the silkworms. 'It was no hypothetical, infected medium—no problematical pythogenic gas—that killed the worms. It was a definite organism.'[5] The disease thus far described is that called *pébrine*, which was the principal scourge at the time. Another formidable malady was also prevalent, called *flacherie*, the cause of which, and the mode of dealing with it, were also pointed out by Pasteur.

Overstrained by years of labour in this field, Pasteur was smitten with paralysis in October 1868. But this calamity did not prevent him from making a journey to Alais in January 1869, for the express purpose of combating the criticisms to which his labours had been subjected. Pasteur is combustible, and contradiction readily stirs him into flame. No scientific man now living has fought so many battles as he. To enable him to render his experiments decisive, the French Emperor placed a villa at his disposal near Trieste, where silkworm culture had been carried on for some time at a loss. The success here is described as marvellous; the sale of cocoons giving to the villa a net profit of twenty-six millions of francs.[6] From the Imperial villa M. Pasteur addressed to me a letter, a portion of which I have already published. It may perhaps prove usefully suggestive to our Indian or Colonial authorities if I reproduce it here:—

'Permettez-moi de terminer ces quelques lignes que je dois dicter, vaincu que je suis par la maladie, en vous faisant observer que vous rendriez service aux Colonies de la Grande-Bretagne en répandant la connaissance de ce livre, et des principes que j'établis touchant la maladie des vers à soie. Beaucoup de ces colonies pourraient cultiver le mûrier avec succès, et, en jetant les yeux sur mon ouvrage, vous vous convaincrez aisément qu'il est facile aujourd'hui, non-seulement d'éloigner la maladie régnante, mais en outre de donner aux récoltes de la soie une prospérité qu'elles n'ont jamais eue.'

The studies on wine prepare us for the 'Studies on Beer,' which followed the investigation of silkworm diseases. The sourness, putridity, and other maladies of beer Pasteur traced to special 'ferments of disease,' of a totally different form, and therefore easily distinguished from the true *torula* or yeast-plant. Many mysteries of our breweries were cleared up by this inquiry. Without knowing the cause, the brewer not unfrequently incurred heavy losses through the use of bad yeast. Five minutes' examination with the microscope would have revealed to him the cause of the badness, and prevented him from using the yeast. He would have seen the true *torula* overpowered by foreign intruders. The microscope is, I believe, now everywhere in use. At Burton-on-Trent its aid was very soon invoked. At the conclusion of his studies on beer M. Pasteur came to London, where I had the pleasure of conversing with him. Crippled by paralysis, bowed down by the sufferings of France, and anxious about his family at a troubled and an uncertain time, he appeared low in health and depressed in spirits. His robust appearance when he visited London, on the occasion of the Edinburgh Anniversary, was in marked and pleasing contrast with my memory of his aspect at the time to which I have referred.

⸻

While these researches were going on, the Germ Theory of infectious disease was noised abroad. The researches of Pasteur were frequently referred to as bearing upon the subject, though Pasteur himself kept clear for a long time of this special field of inquiry. He was not a physician, and he did not feel called upon to trench upon the physician's domain. And now I would beg of him to correct me if, at this point of the Introduction, I should be betrayed into any statement that is not strictly correct.

In 1876 the eminent microscopist, Professor Cohn of Breslau, was in London, and he then handed me a number of his 'Beiträge,' containing a memoir by Dr. Koch on Splenic Fever (*Milzbrand, Charbon,* Malignant Pustule), which seemed to me to mark an epoch in the history of this formidable disease. With admirable patience, skill, and penetration, Koch followed up the life history of *bacillus anthracis,* the contagium of this fever. At the time here referred to he was a young physician holding a small appointment in the neighbourhood of Breslau, and it was easy to predict, as I predicted at the time, that he would soon find himself in a higher position. When I next heard of him he was head of the Imperial Sanitary Institute of Berlin. Koch's recent history is pretty well known in England, while his appreciation by the German Government is shown by the rewards and honours lately conferred upon him.

Koch was not the discoverer of the parasite of splenic fever. Davaine and Rayer, in 1850, had observed the little microscopic rods in the blood of animals which had died of splenic fever. But they were quite unconscious of the significance of their observation, and for thirteen years, as M. Radot informs us, strangely let the matter drop. In 1863 Davaine's attention was again directed to the subject by the researches of Pasteur, and he then pronounced the parasite to be the cause of the fever. He was opposed by some of his fellow-countrymen; long discussions followed, and a second period of thirteen years, ending with the publication of Koch's paper, elapsed, before M. Pasteur took up the question. I always, indeed, assumed that from the paper of the learned German came the impulse towards a line of inquiry in which M. Pasteur has achieved such splendid results. Things presenting themselves thus to my mind, M. Radot will, I trust, forgive me if I say that it was with very great regret that I perused the disparaging references to Dr. Koch which occur in the chapter on splenic fever.

After Koch's investigation, no doubt could be entertained of the parasitic origin of this disease. It completely cleared up the perplexity previously existing as to the two forms—the one fugitive, the other permanent—in which the contagium presented itself. I may say that it was on the conversion of the permanent hardy form into the fugitive and sensitive one, in the case of *bacillus subtilis* and other organisms, that the method of sterilising by 'discontinuous heating' introduced by me in February 1877 was founded. The difference between an organism and its spores, in point of durability, had not escaped the penetration of Pasteur. This difference Koch showed to be of paramount importance in splenic fever. He, moreover, proved that while mice and guinea-pigs were infallibly killed by the parasite, birds were able to defy it.

And here we come upon what may be called a hand-specimen of the genius of Pasteur, which strikingly illustrates its quality. Why should birds enjoy the immunity established by the experiments of Koch? Here is the answer. The temperature which prohibits the multiplication of *bacillus anthracis* in infusions is 44° Cent. (111° Fahr.). The temperature of the blood of birds is from 41° to 42°. It is therefore close to the prohibitory temperature. But then the blood globules of a living fowl are sure to offer a certain resistance to any attempt to deprive them of their oxygen—a resistance not experienced in an infusion. May not this resistance, added to the high temperature of the fowl, suffice to place it beyond the power of the parasite? Experiment alone could answer this question, and Pasteur made the experiment. By placing its feet in cold water he lowered the temperature of a fowl to 37° or 38°. He inoculated the fowl, thus chilled, with the splenic fever parasite, and in twenty-four hours it was dead. The argument was clinched by inoculating a chilled fowl, permitting the fever to come to a head, and then removing the fowl, wrapped in cotton-wool, to a chamber with a temperature of 35°. The strength of the patient returned as the career of the parasite was brought to an end, and in a few hours health was restored. The sharpness of the reasoning here is only equalled by the conclusiveness of the experiment, which is full of suggestiveness as regards the treatment of fevers in man.

Pasteur had little difficulty in establishing the parasitic origin of fowl cholera; indeed, the parasite had been observed by others before him. But by his successive cultivations, he rendered the solution sure. His next step will remain for ever memorable in the history of medicine. I allude to what he calls 'virus attenuation.' And here it may be well to throw out a few remarks in advance. When a tree, or a bundle of wheat or barley straw, is burnt, a certain amount of mineral matter remains in the ashes—extremely small in comparison with the bulk of the tree or of the straw, but absolutely essential to its growth. In a soil lacking, or exhausted of, the necessary mineral constituents, the tree cannot live, the crop cannot grow. Now contagia are living things, which demand certain elements of life just as inexorably as trees, or wheat, or barley; and it is not difficult to see that a crop of a given parasite may so far use up a constituent existing in small quantities in the body, but essential to the growth of the parasite, as to render the body unfit for the production of a second crop. The soil is exhausted, and, until the lost constituent is restored, the body is protected from any further attack of the same disorder. Such an explanation of non-recurrent diseases naturally presents itself to a thorough believer in the germ theory, and such was the solution which, in reply to a question, I ventured to offer nearly fifteen years ago to an eminent London physician. To exhaust a soil, however, a parasite less vigorous and destructive than the really virulent one may suffice; and if, after having by means of a feebler organism exhausted the soil, without fatal result, the most highly virulent parasite be introduced into the system, it will prove powerless. This, in the language of the germ theory, is the whole secret of vaccination.

The general problem, of which Jenner's discovery was a particular case, has been grasped by Pasteur, in a manner, and with results, which five short years ago were simply unimaginable. How much 'accident' had to do with shaping the course of his enquiries I know not. A mind like his resembles a photographic plate, which is ready to accept and develop luminous impressions, sought and unsought. In the chapter on fowl cholera is described how Pasteur first obtained his attenuated virus. By successive cultivations of the parasite he showed, that after it had been a hundred times reproduced, it continued to be as virulent as at first. One necessary condition was, however, to be observed. It was essential that the cultures should rapidly succeed each other—that the organism, before its transference to a fresh cultivating liquid, should not be left long in contact with air. When exposed to air for a considerable time the virus becomes so enfeebled that when fowls are inoculated with it, though they sicken for a time, they do not die. But this 'attenuated' virus, which M. Radot justly calls 'benign,' constitutes a sure protection against the virulent virus. It so exhausts the soil that the really fatal contagium fails to find there the elements necessary to its reproduction and multiplication.

Pasteur affirms that it is the oxygen of the air which, by lengthened contact, weakens the virus and converts it into a true vaccine. He has also weakened it by transmission through various animals. It was this form of attenuation that was brought into play in the case of Jenner.

The secret of attenuation had thus become an open one to Pasteur. He laid hold of the murderous virus of splenic fever, and succeeded in rendering it, not only harmless to life, but a sure protection against the virus in its most concentrated form. No man, in my opinion, can work at these subjects so rapidly as Pasteur without falling into errors of detail. But this may occur while his main position remains impregnable. Such a result, for example, as that obtained in presence of so many witnesses at Melun must surely remain an ever-memorable conquest of science. Having prepared his attenuated virus, and proved, by laboratory experiments, its efficacy as a protective vaccine, Pasteur accepted an invitation from the President of the Society of Agriculture at Melun, to make a public experiment on what might be called an agricultural scale. This act of Pasteur's is, perhaps, the boldest thing recorded in this book. It naturally caused anxiety among his colleagues of the Academy, who feared that he had been rash in closing with the proposal of the President.

But the experiment was made. A flock of sheep was divided into two groups, the members of one group being all vaccinated with the attenuated virus, while those of the other group were left unvaccinated. A number of cows were also subjected to a precisely similar treatment. Fourteen days afterwards, all the sheep and all the cows, vaccinated and unvaccinated, were inoculated with a very virulent virus; and three days subsequently more than two hundred persons assembled to witness the result. The 'shout of admiration,' mentioned by M. Radot, was a natural outburst under the circumstances. Of twenty-five sheep which had not been protected by vaccination, twenty-one were already dead, and the remaining ones were dying. The twenty-five vaccinated sheep, on the contrary, were 'in full health and gaiety.' In the unvaccinated cows intense fever was produced, while the prostration was so great that they were unable to eat. Tumours were also formed at the points of inoculation. In the vaccinated cows no tumours were formed; they exhibited no fever, nor even an elevation of temperature, while their power of feeding was unimpaired. No wonder that 'breeders of cattle overwhelmed Pasteur with applications for vaccine.' At the end of 1881 close upon 34,000 animals had been vaccinated, while the number rose in 1883 to nearly 500,000.

M. Pasteur is now exactly sixty-two years of age; but his energy is unabated. At the end of this volume we are informed that he has already taken up and examined with success, as far as his experiments have reached, the terrible and mysterious disease of rabies or hydrophobia. Those who hold all communicable diseases to be of parasitic origin, include, of course, rabies among the number of those produced and propagated by a living contagium. From his first contact with the disease Pasteur showed his accustomed penetration. If we see a man mad, we at once refer his madness to the state of his brain. It is somewhat singular that in the face of this fact the virus of a mad dog should be referred to the animal's saliva. The saliva is, no doubt, infected, but Pasteur soon proved the real seat and empire of the disorder to be the nervous system.

The parasite of rabies had not been securely isolated when M. Radot finished his task. But last May, at the instance of M. Pasteur, a commission was appointed by the Minister of Public Instruction in France, to examine and report upon the results which he had up to that time obtained. A preliminary report, issued to appease public impatience, reached me before I quitted Switzerland this year. It inspires the sure and certain hope that, as regards the attenuation of the rabic virus, and the rendering of an animal, by inoculation, proof against attack, the success of M. Pasteur is assured. The commission, though hitherto extremely active, is far from the end of its labours; but the results obtained so far may be thus summed up:—

Of six dogs unprotected by vaccination, three succumbed to the bites of a dog in a furious state of madness.

Of eight unvaccinated dogs, six succumbed to the intravenous inoculation of rabic matter.

Of five unvaccinated dogs, all succumbed to inoculation, by trepanning, of the brain.

Finally, of three-and-twenty vaccinated dogs, not one was attacked with the disease subsequent to inoculation with the most potent virus.

Surely results such as those recorded in this book are calculated, not only to arouse public interest, but public hope and wonder. Never before, during the long period of its history, did a day like the present dawn upon the science and art of medicine. Indeed, previous to the discoveries of recent times, medicine was not a science, but a collection of empirical rules dependent for their interpretation and application upon the sagacity of the physician. How does England stand in relation to the great work now going on around her? She is, and must be, behindhand. Scientific chauvinism is not beautiful in my eyes. Still one can hardly see, without deprecation and protest, the English investigator handicapped in so great a race by short-sighted and mischievous legislation.

A great scientific theory has never been accepted without opposition. The theory of gravitation, the theory of undulation, the theory of evolution, the dynamical theory of heat—all had to push their way through conflict to victory. And so it has been with the Germ Theory of communicable diseases. Some outlying members of the medical profession dispute it still. I am told they even dispute the communicability of cholera. Such must always be the course of things, as long as men are endowed with different degrees of insight. Where the mind of genius discerns the distant truth, which it pursues, the mind not so gifted often discerns nothing but the extravagance, which it avoids. Names, not yet forgotten, could be given to illustrate these two classes of minds. As representative of the first class, I would name a man whom I have often named before, who, basing himself in great part on the researches of Pasteur, fought, in England, the battle of the germ theory with persistent valour, but whose labours broke him down before he saw the triumph which he *fore*saw completed. Many of my medical friends will understand that I allude here to the late Dr. William Budd, of Bristol.

The task expected of me is now accomplished, and the reader is here presented with a record, in which the verities of science are endowed with the interest of romance.

JOHN TYNDALL.

ROYAL INSTITUTION: *December 1884*

RECOLLECTIONS OF CHILDHOOD AND YOUTH.
FIRST DISCOVERIES.

'Come, M. Pasteur! you must shake off the demon of idleness!' It was the night watcher of the College of Besançon, who invariably at four o'clock in the morning entered Pasteur's room and roused him with this vigorous salute, which was accompanied, when necessary, by a sound shaking. Pasteur was then eighteen years of age. In addition to his food and lodging, the royal college paid him twenty-four francs a month. But if his place was a modest one, it sufficed at the time for his ambition: it was the first tie which bound him to the University.

'Ah,' said his father to him frequently, 'if only you could become some day professor in the College of Arbois I should be the happiest man on earth.'

Already, when he resided at Dôle, and when his son was not yet two years old, this father permitted himself to dream thus of the future. What would he have said had it been announced to him that fifty-eight years later, on the façade of the little house in the Rue des Tanneurs, would be placed, in the presence of his living son—laden with honours, laden with glory, passing in the midst of a triumphal procession along the paved town—a plate bearing these words in letters of gold:

HERE WAS BORN LOUIS PASTEUR,
December 27, 1822.

Pausing before this house, Pasteur recalled the image of his father and mother —of those whom he called his dear departed ones—and from the far-off depths of his childhood came so many memories of affection, devotion, and paternal sacrifices that he burst into tears.

The life of his father had been a rough one. An old soldier, decorated on the field of battle, on returning to France, where he had no longer a home, he was obliged to work hard to earn his bread. He took up the trade of a tanner. Soon afterwards, having made the acquaintance of a worthy young girl, he joined his lot with hers, and together they entered courageously on the labours of their married life—he calm, reflective, and more eager, whenever he had a moment of repose, for the society of books than for the society of his neighbours; she full of enthusiasm, her heart and spirit agitated by thoughts above the level of her modest life. Both of them watched with ceaseless solitude over their little Louis, of whom, with mingled pride and tenderness, they used to say, 'We will make of him an educated man.'

In 1825 the Pasteur family quitted Dôle and established themselves at Arbois, where, on the borders of the Cuisance, the father of our hero had bought a small tanyard. At this town, and in this yard, Louis Pasteur spent his childhood. As soon as he was old enough to be received as a half-pay scholar he was sent to the communal college. He, the smallest of all the pupils, was so proud of passing under the great arched doorway of this ancient establishment, that he arrived laden with enormous dictionaries, of which there was no need.

In the midst of his laborious occupations the father of Pasteur took upon himself the task of superintending his son's lessons every evening. This was at first no sinecure. Louis Pasteur did not always take the shortest road either to reach his class or to return to his work at home. Some old friends still living remember having made with the little Pasteur fishing parties, which proved so pleasant that they have been continued to the present day. The boy, moreover, instead of applying himself to his lessons, often escaped and amused himself by making large portraits of his neighbours, male and female. A dozen of these portraits are still to be seen in the houses of Arbois, all bearing his signature. Considering that his age at the time was only thirteen, the accuracy of the drawing is astonishing.

'What a pity,' said an old lady of Arbois a short time since, 'that he should have buried himself in chemistry! He has missed his vocation, for he might by this time have made his reputation as a painter.'

It was not until he reached the third class that Louis Pasteur, beginning to realise the sacrifices which his father imposed upon himself, determined to abandon his fishing implements and his crayons, feeling aroused within him that passion for work which was to form the foundation of his life. The Principal of the college, who followed with watchful interest the progress of a pupil who, in his first effort, had outstripped all his comrades, used to say, 'He will go far. It is not for the chair of a small college like ours that we must prepare him; he must become professor in a royal college. My little friend,' he would add, 'think of the great École Normale.'

The College of Arbois having no professor of philosophy, Pasteur quitted it for Besançon. There he remained for the scholars' year, received the degree of *bachelier ès lettres*, and was immediately appointed tutor in the same college. In the intervals of his duties he followed the course of mathematics necessary to prepare him for the scientific examinations of the École Normale. He must have been already endowed with a singular maturity of character, for the director confided to him the superintendence of the quarters of the older pupils, who during class time were his comrades. In the class room his table was in the midst of them; and never had so young a master so much authority, and at the same time so little need for its exercise.

His first taste for chemistry manifested itself by frequent questions addressed during class time to an old professor named Darlay. This questioning was so often repeated that the good man, quite bewildered, ended by declaring that it was for him to interrogate Pasteur and not for Pasteur to interrogate him. His pupil pressed him no further, but having heard that at Besançon there lived an apothecary who had once distinguished himself by a paper inserted in the 'Annales de Chimie et de Physique,' he sought this man, with a view of ascertaining whether, on holidays, he would consent to give him lessons secretly.

At the examination for the École Normale, Pasteur passed as fourteenth in the list. This rank, however, did not satisfy him. Notwithstanding the censure of his fellow candidates he declared that he would begin a new year of preparation. It was in Paris itself that he chose to work—in one of the silent corners of the city, amid the seclusion of preparatory schools and convents.

In the Impasse des Feuillantines, there lived a schoolmaster, M. Barbet by name, or rather *le père Barbet*, as the Franc-Comtois, with provincial familiarity, used to call him. Pasteur begged to be allowed to enter his institution, not as an assistant, but as a simple pupil. Knowing how slender were the means of his young compatriot, M. Barbet reduced the fees of his pupil by one-third. Such kindness was customary with the *père Barbet*, who did not like to be reminded of his generosity. This, however, gives double pleasure to him who records it.

The year passes, the time of the examination arrives, and Pasteur is received as fourth on the list. Thus at last, in the month of October 1843, he finds himself in that École Normale in which he was destined to take so great a place. Pasteur's taste for chemistry had become a passion which he could now satisfy to his heart's content. Chemistry was at this time taught at the Sorbonne by M. Dumas and at the École Normale by M. Balard. The pupils of the École attended both courses of lectures. Different as were the two professors, both of them exercised great influence on their pupils. M. Dumas, with his serene gravity and his profound respect for his auditory, never allowed the smallest incorrectness to slip into his exposition. M. Balard, with a vivacity quite juvenile, with the excitement of a southerner in the tribune, did not always give his words time to follow his thoughts. It was he who once, showing a little potash to his audience, exclaimed with a fervour which has become celebrated, 'Potash, which—potash, then—potash, in short, which I now present to you.'

The general principles which M. Dumas in his teaching delighted to develop,

the multitude of facts which M. Balard unfolded to his pupils, all answered to
the needs of Pasteur's mind. If he loved the vaster horizons of science, he was
also possessed by the anxious desire for exactitude, and for the perpetual
control of experiment. Each of the lectures of the École Normale and of the
Sorbonne excited in him a profound enthusiasm. One day M. Dumas, while
illustrating the solidification of carbonic acid, begged for the loan of a
handkerchief to receive the carbonic acid snow. Pasteur rushed forward, and,
presenting his handkerchief, received the snow. He returned triumphant, and
running forthwith to the École Normale, repeated the principal experiments
which the illustrious chemist had just exhibited to his audience. He preserved
religiously the handkerchief which had been touched by M. Dumas.

Pasteur usually spent his Sundays with M. Barruel, the assistant of M. Dumas.
He thought of nothing but experiments. For a long time in one of the
laboratories of the École Normale was exhibited a basin—perhaps it is still
shown—containing sixty grammes of phosphorus obtained from bones bought
at the butcher's by Pasteur. These he had calcined, submitted to the processes
known to chemists, and finally reduced, after a whole day's heating, from four
in the morning to nine in the evening, to the said sixty grammes. It was the first
time that the long manipulations required in the preparation of this simple
substance were attempted at the École Normale.

Isolated in laboratory or library, Pasteur's only thought was to search, to learn,
to question, and to verify. As the rule of the school leaves much to individual
initiative, he devoted himself to his work with a joyful heart. This daily liberty
constitutes the charm and the honour of the École Normale. Not only does it
permit but it encourages individual effort; it allows the student to visit at his
will the library, and to consult there the scientific journals and reviews. This
free system of education develops singularly the spirit of research. There is in
it an element of superiority over the École Polytechnique. Influenced by its
military origin, constrained, moreover, by the number of its pupils to impose
on all an exact discipline, and to introduce into their exercises a strict regularity,
the École Polytechnique is, perhaps, less calculated than the École Normale to
awaken in the minds of its pupils a taste for speculative science. It is certain
that Pasteur owed to the freedom of work, and to the facilities for solitary
reading which he there enjoyed, the first occasion for an investigation which
was the starting-point to a veritable discovery.

I.

Unlike the old professor of physics and chemistry at Besançon, one of the
lecturers in the École Normale often took pleasure, not only in answering

Pasteur's questions, but in leading him on to talk over scientific subjects. M. Delafosse, whose memory remains dear to all his pupils, was one of those men who fail to do themselves justice, or who, according to the expression of Cardinal de Retz, do not fulfil all their merit. Not that circumstances have been unfavourable to them, but that an invincible modesty, and a natural nonchalance which finds in that modesty a shield against latent self-reproach, leave them in a sort of twilight in which they are content to dwell. Pupil, and afterwards fellow worker, of the celebrated crystallographer Haüy, M. Delafosse had devoted himself to questions of molecular physics. Pasteur, who had read with enthusiasm the works of Haüy, conversed incessantly with Delafosse about the arrangements of molecules, when an unexpected note from the German chemist Mitscherlich, communicated to the Academy of Sciences, came to trouble all his scientific beliefs. Here is the note:—

'The paratartrate and the tartrate of soda and ammonia have the same chemical composition, the same crystalline form, the same angles, the same specific weight, the same double refraction, and consequently the same inclination of the optic axes. Dissolved in water, their refraction is the same. But while the dissolved tartrate causes the plane of polarised light to rotate, the paratartrate exerts no such action. M. Biot has found this to be the case with the whole series of these two kinds of salts. Here (adds Mitscherlich) the nature and the number of the atoms, their arrangement, and their distances apart are the same in the two bodies.'

Imbued as he was with the teachings of Haüy and Delafosse, and full of the ideas of M. Dumas in molecular chemistry, Pasteur asked himself this question: 'How can it be admitted that the nature and number of the atoms, their arrangement and distances apart, in two chemical substances are the same; that the crystalline forms are equally the same, without concluding that the two substances are absolutely identical? Is there not a profound incompatibility between the identity affirmed by Mitscherlich and the discrepancy of optic character manifested by the two compounds, tartaric and paratartaric, which form the subject of his note?'

This difficulty rested in Pasteur's mind with the tenacity of a fixed idea. Received as *agrégé* of physical science at the end of his third year at the École, and then keeping near his master, M. Balard, he had begun the study of crystals and the determination of their angles and forms, when his nomination to the professorship of physics in the Lycée of Tournon surprised and distressed him. M. Balard repaired immediately to the bureau of the Minister of Education, and spoke of his assistant in terms which caused the nomination to be cancelled. Pasteur remained in the laboratory of the École Normale.

With a view to mastering the science of crystallography, he took for his guide the extensive work of M. de la Provostaye, resolving to repeat all the measurements of angles and all the other determinations of this author with a view to a comparison of their respective results. The work of M. de la Provostaye, who was distinguished by the exactitude of his researches, had for its subject the tartaric and paratartaric acids and their saline compounds.

Two or three years ago, while we were walking together along a road in the Jura, M. Pasteur, after quoting textually the note of Mitscherlich, described to me with enthusiasm the pleasure he had experienced in crystallising tartaric acid and its salts, the crystals of which, he said, rivalled in size and beauty the most exquisite of crystalline forms.

'I should have great difficulty,' I remarked, 'in following you through the labyrinth of tartaric acid, tartrates, and paratartrates. However much your other studies have attracted me, those which had for their starting-point the note of Mitscherlich and the memoir of M. de la Provostaye have appeared to me, whenever I tried to master them, difficult of access. Ah,' I added, 'you would have done well, out of consideration for those who love to speak of your labours, had you made no discoveries in this field.'

Pasteur, with a mixture of indignation and indulgence, replied:—'Is it possible that you have not discerned the grand horizons that lie behind these researches in physics and molecular optics? If I have a regret, it is that I did not follow out this path. Less rough than it at first sight appears, it would, I am convinced, have led to the most important discoveries. By a sudden turn it threw me unexpectedly upon the subject of fermentation, and fermentation led me to the study of diseases; but I still continue to lament that I have never had time to retrace my steps.'

Then, with a simplicity of exposition in which one recognised the teacher who had always endeavoured to place his ideas within the range of his hearers, he said—

'If you picture to yourself all the bodies in nature—mineral, animal, or vegetable, and consider even the objects formed by the hands of man, you will see that they divide themselves into two great categories. The one has a plane of symmetry and the other has not. Take, for instance, a table, a chair, a playing die, or the human body; we can imagine a plane passing through these objects which divides each of them into two absolutely similar halves. Thus, a plane passing through the middle of the seat and of the back of an arm-chair would have, on its right and left, identical parts; in like manner a vertical plane passing through the middle of the forehead, nose, mouth, and chin of an individual, would have similar parts to the right and to the left. All these objects, and a multitude of similar ones, constitute our first category. They have, as mathematicians express it, one or several planes of symmetry.

'But, as regards the repetition of similar parts, it is far from being the case that all bodies are constituted in the manner here described. Consider, for example, your right hand: it is impossible to find for it a plane of symmetry. Whatever be the position of a plane which you imagine cutting the hand, you will never find on the right of this plane exactly the same as you find on its left. The same remark applies to your left hand, to your right ear and to your left ear, to your right eye and to your left eye; to your two arms, your two legs, and your two feet. The human body, taken as a whole, has a plane of symmetry, but none of the parts composing one or the other of its halves has such a plane. The stalk of a plant whose leaves are distributed spirally round its stem has not a plane of symmetry, nor has a spiral staircase such a plane; but a straight one has. You see this?

'It would have been truly extraordinary, would it not, if the various kinds of minerals, such as sea salt, alum, the diamond, rock crystal, and so many others which illustrate the great law of crystallisation, and which clothe themselves in geometric forms, should not present to us examples of the two categories of which we have just been speaking? They do so in fact. Thus a cube, which has the form of a player's die, has a plane of symmetry; it has indeed several planes. The form of the diamond, which is a regular octahedron, has also several planes of symmetry. It is thus also with the great majority of the mineral forms met with in nature or in the laboratory. They have generally one or several planes of symmetry. There are, however, exceptions. Rock crystal, which is found in prisms, often of large volume, in the fissures of certain primitive rocks, has no plane of symmetry. This crystal exhibits certain small facets, distributed in such a manner that in their totality they might be compared to a helix, or spiral, or screw, which are all objects not possessing a plane of symmetry.

'Every object which has a plane of symmetry, when placed before a looking-glass, has an image which is rigorously identical with the object itself. The image can be superposed upon the reality. Place a chair before a mirror; the image faithfully reproduces the chair. The mirror also reproduces the human body considered as a whole. But place before the mirror your right hand and you will see a left hand. The right hand is not superposable on the left, just as the glove of your right hand cannot be fitted to your left, and inversely.'

Then reverting to the beginnings of his studies in crystallography, Pasteur recounted to me briefly that, after having gone through the work of M. de la

Provostaye, he perceived that a very interesting fact had escaped the notice of this skilful physicist. M. de la Provostaye had failed to observe that the crystalline forms of tartaric acid and of its compounds all belong to the group of objects which have not a plane of symmetry. Certain minute facets had escaped him. In other words, Pasteur discerned that the crystalline form of tartaric acid, placed before a mirror, produced an image which was not superposable upon the crystal itself. The same was found to be true of the forms of all the chemical compounds of this acid. On the other hand, he imagined that the crystalline form of paratartaric acid, and of all the compounds of this acid, would be found to form part of the group of natural objects which have a plane of symmetry.

Pasteur was transported with joy by this double result. He saw in it the possibility of reaching by experiment the explanation of the difficulty which the note of Mitscherlich had thrown down as a kind of challenge to science, when it signalised an optical difference between two chemical compounds affirmed to be otherwise rigorously identical. Pasteur reasoned thus:—Since I find tartaric acid and all its tartrates without a plane of symmetry, while its isomer, paratartaric acid, and its compounds have such a plane, I will hasten to prepare the tartrate and the paratartrate of the note of Mitscherlich. I will compare their forms, and in all probability the tartrate will be found dissymmetrical—that is to say, without a plane of symmetry—while the paratartrate will continue to have such a plane. Henceforward the absolute identity stated by Mitscherlich to exist between the forms of these two compounds will have no existence. It will be proved that he has erred, and his note will no longer have in it anything mysterious. As the optic action proper to the tartrates spoken of in his note manifests itself by a deviation of the plane of polarisation to the right, we have here a kind of dissymmetry which has nothing incompatible with the dissymmetry of form. On the contrary, these two dissymmetries can be referred to one and the same cause. In like manner, the absence of dissymmetry in the form of the paratartrate will be connected with the optical neutrality of that compound.

The fulfilment of Pasteur's hopes was only partial. The tartrates of soda and ammonia presented, as did all the other tartrates, the dissymmetry manifested by the absence of any plane of symmetry; that is to say, the crystals of this salt placed before a mirror produced an image which was not superposable upon the crystal. It was like a right hand having its left for an image. With regard to the paratartrates of soda and ammonia, one circumstance struck Pasteur in a quite unexpected manner. Far from establishing in the crystals of this salt the absence of all dissymmetry, he found that they all manifestly possessed it. But, strange to say, certain crystals possessed it in one sense and other crystals in a sense opposite. Some of these crystals, when placed before a mirror, produced the image of the others, and one of the two kinds of crystals corresponded rigorously in form with the tartrate prepared by means of the tartaric acid of the grape. Pasteur continued his reasoning thus:—Since there is no difference between the form of the tartrate derived from the tartaric acid of the grape and one of the two kinds of crystals deposited at the moment of crystallisation of the paratartrate, the simple observation of the dissymmetry proper to each will enable me to separate, by hand, all the crystals of the paratartrate which are identical with those of the tartrate. By ordinary chemical processes I ought to be able to extract a tartaric acid identical with that of the grape, possessing all its physical, mineralogical, and chemical properties—that is to say, a tartaric acid possessing, like the natural tartaric acid of the grape, dissymmetry of form, and exerting an action on polarised light. *Per contra*, I ought to be able to extract from the second sort of crystals, associated with the former in the paratartaric group, an acid which will reproduce ordinary tartaric acid, but possessing a dissymmetry of an inverse kind and exerting an action equally inverse on polarised light.

With a feverish ardour Pasteur hastened to make this double experiment. Imagine his joy when he saw his anticipations not only realised but realised with an exactitude truly mathematical. His delight was so great that he quitted the laboratory abruptly. Hardly had he gone out when he met the assistant of the physical professor. He embraced him, exclaiming, 'My dear Monsieur Bertrand, I have just made a great discovery! I have separated the double paratartrate of soda and ammonia into two salts of inverse dissymmetry, and exerting an inverse action on the plane of polarisation of light. I am so happy that a nervous tremulousness has taken possession of me, which prevents me from looking again through the polariscope. Let us go to the Luxembourg, and I will explain it all to you.'

These results excited in a high degree the attention of the Academy of Sciences, where sat, at the time now referred to, Arago, Biot, Dumas, De Senarmont, and Balard. It might be said without exaggeration that the Academy was astounded. At the same time there were many members who were slow to believe in this discovery. Charged with drawing up the report, M. Biot began by requiring from Pasteur the verification of each point which he had announced. To this verification M. Biot brought his habitual precision, which was associated with a kind of suspicious scepticism.

In one of his lectures Pasteur thus described his interview with M. Biot:—'He made me come to his house, where he put into my hands some paratartaric acid which he had carefully studied himself, and found perfectly neutral as regards polarised light. It was not in the laboratory of the École Normale, it was in his own kitchen, and in his presence, that I was to prepare this double salt with soda and ammonia procured by himself. The liquor was left slowly to evaporate, and at the end of ten days, when it had deposited thirty or forty grammes of crystals, he begged me to go over to the Collège de France to collect the crystals and to extract from them specimens of the two kinds, which he proposed to have placed, the one on his right hand, the other on his left, desiring me to declare if I was ready to re-affirm, that the crystals to the right would turn the plane of polarisation to the right and the others to the left. This declaration made, he said that he would charge himself with the rest of the inquiry. M. Biot then prepared the solutions in well-measured proportions, and at the moment of observing them in the polarising apparatus he invited me again to come into his study. He placed first in the apparatus the most interesting solution, that which ought to deviate to the left. Without even making any measurements, he saw, by the mere inspection of the colours of the ordinary and extraordinary images of the analyser, that there was a strong deviation to the left. Visibly moved, the illustrious old man took my arm and said, "My dear child, I have loved science so well throughout my life that this makes my heart beat."'

The emotion of M. Biot was all the more profound because he had been himself the first to discover the rotation of the plane of polarisation by chemical substances, and had, for more than thirty years, affirmed that the study of these substances and of their action in regard to rotatory polarisation was, perhaps, the surest means of penetrating into the intimate constitution of bodies. His counsels were received with deference, but they had never been followed out. And now there appeared before the old man, already somewhat discouraged, a youth of twenty-five, who from his first investigation had proved himself a master, who had dissipated the obscurities of the famous German note, and created a new chapter in crystallographic chemistry. The composition and nature of paratartaric acid had been explained, and a new substance, the left-handed tartaric acid, with its truly surprising properties, had been discovered; molecular physics and chemistry had been enriched with new facts and theories of great value.

The first care of Pasteur, after having discovered the left-handed tartaric acid and the constitution of paratartaric acid, was to compare very carefully the properties of the new left-handed acid with those of the right, endeavouring to determine by strict experiment the influence on these properties of the internal atomic arrangements of the two acids. Although we are unable to picture the exact figure of these atomic groupings, there can be no doubt that they are formed of the same elementary particles, that they are, moreover, dissymmetrical, and that, in short, the dissymmetry of the one group is the same as that of the other, but in an inverse sense. If, for example, the arrangement of the atoms of the right-handed tartaric acid present the exterior appearance of an irregular pyramid, the arrangement of the atoms of the left-handed tartaric acid ought, of necessity, to present the form of a pyramid irregular in the inverse sense.

II.

Nominated assistant professor of chemistry at Strasburg, Pasteur followed up with enthusiasm these curious studies. To interrupt them for an instant it required nothing less than his engagement with Mademoiselle Marie Laurent, daughter of the Rector of the Academy. It is even asserted that on the very morning of his marriage it was necessary to go to his laboratory and remind him of the event that was to take place on that day. But if Pasteur was thus guilty of an absent-mindedness worthy of La Fontaine, he proved as a husband so different from La Fontaine that Madame Pasteur, when reminded of this lapse of memory, receives the reminder with an indulgent smile.

But to return to the laboratory: Under the same conditions of weight, temperature, and quantity of solvent, Pasteur placed successively, in presence of the two acids, all the substances capable of combining with them. In this way he obtained right-handed and left-handed tartrates of potash, of soda, of ammonia, of lime, and of all the oxides properly so called. He applied himself to the compounds—and they are numerous—which deposit themselves in liquids under well-determined crystalline forms. Without entering into the details of these long and patient studies, it may be stated generally that Pasteur proved that whatever could be done with one of the tartaric acids could be repeated rigorously, under similar conditions, with the other, the resultant products manifesting constantly the same properties, with the single difference already exhibited by the two acids—that in the one case the deviation of the plane of polarisation was to the right, while in the other it was to the left. With regard to all their other properties, both chemical and physical, the identity was absolute. Solubility, simple refraction by solutions, double refraction by crystals, the action of heat in producing decomposition, &c., the similitude extended to the most perfect identity.

The Academy of Sciences, which shows by the rarity of its reports the importance which it attaches to them, gave for the second time an account of these new researches. M. Biot was again the reporter. It was with a sort of coquetry that Pasteur brought from Strasburg perfectly labelled specimens of the magnificent crystallisations of the double series of right-handed and left-handed tartrates. By means of models he was able to render the forms of these crystals visible at a distance.

M. Biot undertook to bring the subject before the Academy. On the morning of the day when he was to read his report he spent several hours in conversation with Pasteur. M. Biot became so excited during the discussion that Madame Biot, with the solicitude peculiar to the wives of Academicians, requested Pasteur to change the subject of conversation.

The members of the Academy shared the enthusiasm of M. Biot. Arago moved that the report be inserted in the collected *mémoires* of the Academy. This was an exceptional honour. Arrived for the most part at the end of their own careers, these learned men observed with pleasure the incipient ray which had not yet become a glory but which was the precursorthereof.

'My young friend,' said M. Biot to Pasteur, when presenting him to Mitscherlich somewhere about that time, 'you may boast of having done something great, in having discovered what had escaped such a man as this.'

'I had studied,' replied Mitscherlich, not without a shade of regret, addressing himself to Pasteur, 'I had studied with so much care and perseverance, in their smallest details, the two salts which formed the subject of my note to the Academy, that, if you have established what I was unable to discover, you must have been guided to your result by a preconceived idea.'

Mitscherlich was right, and this preconceived idea might have been formulised thus: A dissymmetry in the internal molecular arrangement of a chemical substance ought to manifest itself in all its external properties which are themselves capable of dissymmetry.

If this theoretic conception was correct, Pasteur might expect to find that all the substances in which M. Biot had observed the power of rotating the plane of polarisation would possess the crystalline dissymmetry revealed by the absence of superposability. The result was in great part conformable to those previsions. The substances which acted upon polarised light, as liquids or solutions, were generally found by Pasteur to produce dissymmetric crystals. Some of them, however, notwithstanding their power of crystallisation, exhibited, when crystallised, no dissymmetric face. This difficulty did not deter Pasteur. It gave him, on the contrary, the opportunity of showing that when a theory had in so many cases proved itself correct, an apparent objection must not be assumed insuperable without first sounding it to the bottom. May it not be, he reasoned, that the absence of dissymmetry in substances which have the molecular rotatory power is not an accident; and may it not be possible, by changing the conditions of the crystallisation, to make the dissymmetry appear?

Then, in order to modify the crystalline forms of substances which did not show themselves to be spontaneously dissymmetrical, Pasteur employed a method which had been often tried before, though its principles could not be explained or its effects foreseen. In imitation of Romé de Lisle, Leblanc, and Beudant, he varied the nature of his solvents; he introduced into the solution, sometimes an excess of acid or of base, sometimes foreign matters incapable of acting chemically upon those which were to be modified; he even employed sometimes impure mother liquids. On each occasion new facets were thus produced, and these new facets showed the kind of dissymmetry which the optical character demanded. Although he had to limit his researches to those substances which, by their ready crystallisation and the beauty of their forms, lent themselves best to this class of proofs, the results were so far in accord with the previsions of theory, that no reasonable doubt could exist as to the necessary correlation between dissymmetry and the power to deviate polarised light.

By these researches Pasteur was led to a conclusion, which is worthy of the most serious consideration, regarding the difference which exists between mineral species and artificial products on the one side, and the organic products which can be extracted from vegetables or animals on the other. All mineral or artificial products—for brevity let us say all the products of inorganic nature—have a superposable image, and are therefore not dissymmetrical, while vegetable and animal products—in other words, products formed under the influence of life—have an image not superposable; that is to say, they are atomically dissymmetrical, this dissymmetry expressing itself externally in the power of turning the plane of polarisation. If any exceptions exist they are more apparent than real. Pasteur himself pointed out some of them, while demonstrating at the same time that it is easy to explain why all trace of dissymmetry disappears when substances which, like rock crystal, have an external dissymmetry are subjected to the process of solution.

An apparent contradiction to this law of demarcation between artificial products and those of animal and vegetable life is presented by the existence in living creatures of substances like oxalic acid, formic acid, urea, uric acid, creatine, &c. None of these products exert an action on polarised light or show any dissymmetry in the form of their crystals. But it is necessary to observe that these products are the result of secondary actions. Their formation is evidently governed by the laws which determine the constitution of the artificial products of our laboratories, or of the mineral kingdom properly so called. In living beings they are the products of excretion rather than substances essential to vegetable or animal life. When, on the other hand, we consider the most primordial substances of vegetables and animals—those whereof it may be justly said that they are born under the directive influence of *becoming* life, such as cellulose, fecula, albumen, fibrine, &c.—they are found to possess the power of acting, on polarised light, a characteristic necessary and sufficient to establish their internal dissymmetry, even when, through the absence of crystallising power, they fail to manifest this dissymmetry outwardly.

It is, therefore, true to say that the products of inorganic nature, whether mineral or artificial, have never yet presented molecular dissymmetry. It may also be affirmed that the substances which exert the greatest influence in vital manifestations, which are present and active in the seed and in the egg at the moment of the marvellous start of animal and vegetable life, all present molecular dissymmetry.

Would it be possible to indicate a more profound distinction between the respective products of living and of mineral nature, than the existence of this dissymmetry on the part of the one and its absence on the part of the other? Is it not strange that not one of these thousands and thousands of artificial products of the laboratory, the number of which is each day augmented, should manifest either the power of turning the plane of polarisation or non-superposable dissymmetry? No doubt natural dissymmetric substances—gum, sugar, tartaric and malic acids, quinine, strychnine, essence of turpentine, &c. —may be employed in forming new compounds which remain dissymmetric, though they are artificially prepared; but it is evident that all these new products do but inherit the original dissymmetry of the substances from which they are derived. When chemical action becomes more profound, all dissymmetry disappears, and is never seen to reappear in the successive ulterior products.

What can be the causes of so great a difference? M. Pasteur has often expressed to me the conviction that it must be attributed to the circumstance that the molecular forces which operate in the mineral kingdom, and which are brought into play every day in our laboratories, are forces of the symmetrical order; while the forces which are present and active at the moment when the grain sprouts, when the egg develops, and when, under the influence of the sun, the green matter of the leaves decomposes the carbonic acid of the air and utilises in divers ways the carbon of this acid, the hydrogen of the water, and the oxygen of these two products—are of the dissymmetric order, probably depending on some of the grand, dissymmetric, cosmic phenomena of our universe. While expounding this opinion before the Academy of Sciences, Pasteur, on one occasion, expressed himself thus:—

'The universe is a dissymmetric whole. I am inclined to think that life, as manifested to us, must be a function of the dissymmetry of the universe or of the consequences that follow in its train. The universe is dissymmetrical; for, placing before a mirror the group of bodies which compose the solar system, with their proper movements, we obtain in the mirror an image not superposable on the reality. Even the motion of solar light is dissymmetrical. A luminous ray never strikes in a straight line, and at rest, the leaf wherein organic matter is created by vegetable life. Terrestrial magnetism, the opposition which exists between the north and south poles of a magnet, the opposition presented to us by positive and negative electricity, are all the resultants of dissymmetric actions and motions.'

At the moment when Pasteur, entering upon the labours which form the principal subject of this book, abandoned the study of molecular physics and chemistry which had previously occupied him, all his thoughts were directed to the search of means suited to render evident the influence of these causes and these phenomena. At Strasburg he had procured powerful magnets with the view of comparing the actions of their poles, and, if possible, of introducing by their aid, among the forms of crystals, a manifestation of dissymmetry. At Lille, where he was nominated Dean of the Faculty of Sciences in 1854, he had contrived a piece of clockwork intended to keep a plant in continual rotary motion, first in one direction and then in the other. 'All this was gross,' he said to me one day; 'but, further than this, I had proposed, with the view of influencing the vegetation of certain plants, to invert, by means of a heliostat and a reflecting mirror, the motion of the solar rays which should strike them from the birth of their earliest shoots, and in this direction there was more to be hoped for.' He never spoke of these attempts, because he had not had the time to follow them to the issues of which he dreamed; but to this day he remains persuaded that the barrier which exists between the mineral and organic kingdoms—and which is revealed to our eyes by the impossibility of producing, in the reactions of the laboratory, dissymmetric organic substances—can never be crossed until we have succeeded in introducing among these reactions influences of the dissymmetric order. According to Pasteur, success in this direction would give access to a new world of substances, and probably also of organic transformations. As we have succeeded in finding the inverse of right-handed tartaric acid, we may hope to obtain some day all the immediate principles inverse to those now known to us. Who could say what vegetable and animal species would become if it were possible to replace, in the living cells, cellulose, albumen, and their congeners, by their isomers with an inverse action? Certainly the thing is not easy, and Pasteur would be the last person to deceive himself as to the difficulty of the problem. His latest thought on the matter is this:—When the attempt is made to introduce into living species primordial substances, inverse to those now existing, the great difficulty will be to master the *tendency* (*devenir*[7]) proper to the species, a tendency which is potential in the germ of each of them. In this germ, it is to be feared, the dissymmetry of the dissymmetric primordial substances which it embraces will always manifest itself. Ah! if spontaneous generation were possible; if we could form from mineral matter a living cell, how much more accessible would the problem become! However this may be, we must seek, by all possible means, to produce molecular dissymmetry by the application of forces which have a dissymmetric action. 'We must,' said Pasteur to me on the day when, starting from the note of Mitscherlich, he passed all these things in review, 'we must invoke the action of solenoid or helix. Entangled at present in labours more than sufficient to absorb whatever of ardour and of force still remains to me, I have no longer time to occupy myself with these questions.' But what great things are to be done in following out this order of ideas, and what a route will be opened to young men possessed of that genius of invention which is evoked so often by persistent work!

This complete opposition between artificial mineral products and vegetable and animal ones was to Pasteur a truth so well established that he found frequent opportunity of affirming it under decisive circumstances. One day, a very skilful chemist, M. Dessaignes, who later on became one of the correspondents of the Academy of Sciences, announced that he had transformed fumaric and malic acids into aspartic acid. Pasteur, who some time previously had had occasion to study these same acids, had proved that the two first had no molecular dissymmetry—that is to say, they exercised no optic action. In the state of solution they did not turn the plane of polarised light. Aspartic acid, on the contrary, had presented to him molecular dissymmetry, like asparagine itself. If the observation of M. Dessaignes were true, then bodies which were inert in regard to polarised light, and consequently non-dissymmetric, could be transformed in the laboratory into active dissymmetric bodies. The line of demarcation so well established would be broken. Pasteur, whose experience regarding the note of Mitscherlich had shown him how even the most conscientious observers may fail to seize upon fugitive appearances, when unprompted to seek them by a preconceived idea, doubted at once the accuracy of the facts cited by M. Dessaignes. From Strasburg he started for Vendôme, where M. Dessaignes at that time resided. M. Dessaignes immediately gave Pasteur a small quantity of the aspartic acid which he had prepared by means of fumaric and malic acids. Returning to his laboratory, Pasteur immediately recognised that, despite the very close resemblance of the new acid of M. Dessaignes to that derived from asparagine, the former differed from the latter by the complete absence in its case of molecular dissymmetry.

With regard to other facts of the same kind, announced not only in France, but in Italy, and in England—chiefly the pretended formation of grape tartaric acid from succinic acid, artificial and inert, by Perkin and Duppa—Pasteur testified with absolute certainty of judgment to the existence of phenomenal peculiarities proper to these substances, which he had never seen, and which had, on the other hand, been the object of careful study by observers of great talent.

After these verifications and deductions from theoretic views, Pasteur discovered a surprising connection between the prior researches of chemistry and crystallographic physics and the new and entirely unexpected results of physiological chemistry. This connection, like the thread of Ariadne, conducted him to his recent great discoveries in medical biology. M. Chevreul was right when, some years ago, at the Academy of Sciences, he expressed himself thus:—

'It is by first examining in their chronological order the researches of M. Pasteur, and then considering them as a whole, that we are enabled to appreciate the rigour of judgment of that learned man in forming his conclusions, and the perspicacity of a mind which, strong in the truths which it has already discovered, is carried forward to the establishment of new ones.'

III.

Pasteur had thus established that bodies endowed with internal dissymmetry carried this property, in varying degrees, into their compounds or their derivatives. When two of these bodies whose nature has been revealed by the discovery of right-handed and left-handed tartaric acid, where all is chemically identical—and which are only to be distinguished from each other by their inverse crystallographic form, and by their action on polarised light—enter into combination with a substance which is optically and crystallographically inert, the chemical identity ought, under these new conditions, to be preserved. Everything remains optically and crystallographically comparable. The inert element adds nothing to, and takes away nothing from, the dissymmetric faculties of the active one.

To these curious studies Pasteur soon added a new chapter. He reasoned thus:—If into these compounds I introduce a substance possessing in itself the specific properties of dissymmetry, it is evident that this substance, while entering into these combinations, must preserve its own properties. The active substance would, from the moment of its combination, add something to the properties of the molecular group which acts like itself, and subtract something from the properties of the group which acts in the opposite manner. The resultant effect of these actions, sometimes concordant, sometimes antagonistic, would cease to be alike in absolute quantity. And if this be the necessary condition of similitude as to molecular arrangement, this similitude would cease to exist, and with its disappearance would appear all the differences of chemical and physical properties which constitute its outward manifestations.

The facts were found to harmonise with these logical deductions. After having made dissymmetry intervene as a modifier of chemical affinity, he had a strange and manifest proof of the influence of dissymmetry in the phenomena of life.

It had been long known, through the observations of a manufacturer of chemical products in Germany, that the impure tartrate of lime of commerce, if contaminated with organic matters and permitted to remain under water in summer, would ferment and yield various products. Pasteur caused the ordinary right-handed tartrate of ammonia to ferment in the following manner:—He took some very pure crystalline salt and dissolved it, adding at the same time to the liquid some albuminoid matter, about one gramme to 100 grammes of the tartrate. The liquid placed in a warm chamber fermented. During the process of fermentation the liquid mass, previously limpid, became gradually turbid, in consequence of the appearance of a small organism which played the part of ferment. Pasteur applied this mode of fermentation to the paratartrate of ammonia. He saw that this salt also fermented, depositing the same organism. All appeared as if the course of things was the same as in the case of the right-handed tartrate. But Pasteur, having had the idea of following the course of the operation with the aid of the polariscope, soon detected a profound difference between the two fermentations. In the case of the paratartrate, the liquid, at first inert, gradually assumed a sensible power of deviation to the left, which augmented by degrees and attained a maximum. The fermentation was then suspended; there was no longer any of the right-handed acid in the liquid, which, when evaporated and mixed with its own volume of alcohol, immediately furnished a beautiful crystallisation of left-handed tartrate of ammonia.

From that moment a great new fact was established—namely, that the molecular dissymmetry proper to organic matters intervened in a phenomenon of the physiological order, and did so as a modifier of chemical affinity. The kind of dissymmetry proper to the molecular arrangement of the left-handed tartaric acid was, no doubt, the sole cause of the difference between this acid and the right-handed acid, in regard to the fermentation produced by a microscopic fungus. We shall see later on that organised ferments are almost always microscopic vegetables, which embrace in their constitution cellulose, albumen, &c., identical with these same substances taken from the higher class of vegetables and equally dissymmetric. We can thus understand, that for the nutrition of the ferment and the formation of its principles the chemical changes are more easy with one of the two tartaric acids than with the other.

The opposition of the properties of the two tartaric acids, right and left, at the moment when the conditions of life and nutrition of an organised being intervened, showed themselves still more strikingly in a very curious experiment made by Pasteur. He was the first to prove that mildew could live and multiply on a purely mineral soil, composed, for example, of the phosphates of potash, of magnesia, and an ammoniacal salt of an organic acid. For such a development of vegetable life he employed the seed of *penicillium glaucum*, which is to be found everywhere as common mould, and to which he offered, as its only carbon aliment, paratartaric acid. At the end of a little time the left-handed tartaric acid appeared. Now this left-handed acid could only show itself on the condition that a rigorously equal quantity of the right-handed acid had been decomposed. The carbon of the tartaric acid evidently supplied to the little plant the carbon that was necessary for the formation of its constituents and all their organic accessories. If the microscopic seed of penicillium sown upon this soil was not formed of dissymmetric elements, as is the case with all other vegetable substances, its development, its life, its fructification would accommodate themselves equally well with the left-handed tartaric acid as with the right. The fact that the left-handed tartaric acid is less assimilable than its opposite is due solely and evidently to the dissymmetry of one or other of the primordial substances of the little plant.

Thus for the first time was introduced into physiological studies and considerations the fact of the influence of the molecular dissymmetry of natural organic products.

Pasteur always speaks with enthusiasm of the grand future reserved for researches which have this influence for their object; for molecular dissymmetry is the only sharp line of demarcation which exists between the chemistry of inorganic and that of organic nature.

FERMENTATION.

Arrived at this unexpected turn in the road which he had hitherto pursued, Pasteur paused for an instant. Should he commit himself to the course which abruptly opened before him? His scientific instincts urged him to do so, but the prudence and reserve which show themselves to be the basis of his character, whenever he finds himself called upon to make a choice of which the necessity is not absolutely demonstrated, held him back. Was it not wiser to continue in the domain of molecular physics and chemistry? M. Biot counselled his doing so; the route had been made plain, success awaited him at each step, but an incident connected with the University triumphed over his hesitations.

He had just been nominated, at thirty-two years of age, Dean of the Faculté des Sciences at Lille. One of the principal industries of the Département du Nord is the fabrication of alcohol from beetroot and from corn. Pasteur resolved to devote a portion of his lectures to the study of fermentation. He felt that if he could make himself directly useful to his hearers he would thereby excite general sympathy with, and direct attention to the new Faculté. The young man congratulated himself on this idea, and the man of science rejoiced in it still more. He was filled by the reflections suggested to him by the strangeness of the phenomena which he had just encountered in regard to the molecular dissymmetry of the two tartaric acids, in connection with the life of a microscopic organism. He saw new light thrown upon the obscure problem of fermentation. The part so active performed by an infinitely small organism could not, he thought, be an isolated fact. Behind this phenomenon must lie some great general law.

I.

All that has lived must die, and all that is dead must be disintegrated, dissolved or gasified; the elements which are the substratum of life must enter into new cycles of life. If things were otherwise, the matter of organised beings would encumber the surface of the earth, and the law of the perpetuity of life would be compromised by the gradual exhaustion of its materials. One grand phenomenon presides over this vast work, the phenomenon of fermentation. But this is only a word, and it suggests to the mind simply the internal movements which all organised matter manifests spontaneously after death, without the intervention of the hand of man. What is, then, the cause of the processes of fermentation, of putrefaction, and of slow combustion? How is the disappearance of the dead body or of the fallen plant to be accounted for? What is the explanation of the foaming of the must in the vintage cask? of dough, which, abandoned to itself, rises and becomes sour? of milk, which curdles? of blood, which putrefies? of the heap of straw, which becomes manure? of dead leaves and plants embedded in the earth, which transform themselves into soil?

Many different attempts were made to account for this mystery before science was in a condition to approach it. In our age, and at the time when Pasteur was led to the study of the question, one theory held almost undisputed sway. It was a very ancient theory, to which Liebig, in reviving it, had given the weight of his name. 'The ferments,' said Liebig, 'are all nitrogenous substances—albumen, fibrine, caseine; or the liquids which embrace them, milk, blood, urine—in a state of alteration which they undergo in contact with the air.'

The oxygen of the air was, according to this system, the first cause of the molecular breaking up of the nitrogenous substances. The molecular motions are gradually communicated from particle to particle in the interior of the fermentable matter, which is thus resolved into new products.

These theoretic ideas regarding the part played in fermentation by the oxygen of the air were based upon experiments made in the beginning of the century by Gay-Lussac. In examining the process of Appert for the preservation of animal and vegetable substances—a process which consisted in inclosing these substances in hermetically sealed vessels and heating them afterwards to a sufficiently high temperature—Gay-Lussac had seen, for example, the must of the grape, which had been preserved without alteration during a whole year, caused to enter into a state of fermentation by the simple fact of its transference to another vessel—that is to say, by having been brought for an instant into contact with the oxygen of the air. The oxygen of the air appeared, then, to be the *primum movens* of fermentation.

The illustrious chemists Berzelius and Mitscherlich explained the phenomena of fermentation otherwise. They placed these phenomena in the obscure class known as *phenomena of contact*. The ferment, in their view, took nothing from, and added nothing to, the fermentable matter. It was an albuminoid substance, endowed with a force to which the name *catalytic* was given. The ferment in fact acted by its mere presence.

A very curious observation, however, had been made in France by Cagniard-Latour and in Germany by Schwann. Cagniard-Latour, however, was the first to publish this observation, which was destined to become so fruitful. One of the ferments most in use, and known as early as the leavening of dough or the turning of milk, is the deposit formed in beer barrels, which is commonly called *yeast*. Repeating an observation of the naturalist Leuwenhoeck, Cagniard-Latour saw this yeast, which was composed of cells, multiplying itself by budding, and he proposed to himself the question whether the fermentation of sugar was not connected with this act of cellular vegetation. But as in other fermentations the existence of an organism had not been observed even by the most careful search, the hypothesis of Cagniard-Latour of a possible relation between the organisation of the ferment and the property of being a ferment was abandoned, though not without regret by some physiologists. M. Dumas, for example, recognised that in the budding of the yeast globules there must be some clue to the phenomenon of fermentation. I, however, repeat that as nothing of the kind had been found elsewhere, and as all other fermentations presented the common character of requiring, to put them in train, organic matter in a state of decomposition, the hypothesis of Cagniard-Latour remained a simple incident, instead of having the value of a scientific principle.

Liebig, moreover, carrying general opinion along with him, contended that it is not because of its being organised that yeast is active, but because of its being in contact with air. It is the dead portion of the yeast—that which has lived and is in the course of alteration—which acts upon the sugar.

The new memoirs published on the subject agreed in rejecting the hypothesis of any influence whatever of organisation or of life in the process of fermentation. Books, memoirs, dogmatic teaching, all were favourable to the theoretic ideas of Liebig. If a few rare observers indicated the presence in certain fermentations of living organisms, this presence was, in their opinion, a purely accidental fact, which, instead of favouring the phenomenon of fermentation, was injurious to it.

From his first investigation on lactic fermentation Pasteur was led to take an entirely different view of the matter. In this fermentation he recognised the presence and the action of a living organism, which was the ferment, just as yeast was the ferment of alcoholic fermentation. The lactic ferment was formed of cells, or rather of little rods nipped at their centres, extremely small, being hardly the thousandth part of a millimeter in diameter.[8] It reproduced itself by fission—that is to say, the little rod divided itself at its middle and formed two shorter rods, which became elongated, nipped, in their turn, at their centres, each giving rise, as before, to two rods. Each of these, again, soon divided itself into two, and so on. Why had not this been observed prior to Pasteur? For the simple reason that chemists had never observed the production of lactic fermentation except in complex substances. They mixed chalk with their milk for the purpose of preserving the neutrality of the fermenting medium. They employed substances such as caseine, gluten, animal membranes, all of which, when examined by the microscope, exhibited a multitude of mineral or organic granules, with which the lactic ferment was confounded. Thus the first care of Pasteur, with the view of proving the presence of the ferment and its life, was to replace the cheesy matter and all its congeners by a soluble, nitrogenous body, which would permit of the microscopic examination of all the living cellular products.

In a memoir presented to the Academy of Sciences in 1857 Pasteur stated that there were 'cases where it is possible to recognise in lactic fermentation, as practised by chemists and manufacturers, above the deposit of chalk and the nitrogenous matter, a grey substance which forms a zone on the surface of the deposit. Its examination by the microscope hardly permits of its being distinguished from the disintegrated caseum or gluten which has served to start the fermentation. So that nothing indicates that it is a special kind of matter which had its birth during the fermentation. It is this, nevertheless, which plays the principal part.'

To isolate this substance and to prepare it in a state of purity, Pasteur boiled a little yeast with from fifteen to twenty times its weight of water. He then carefully filtered the liquid, dissolved in it about fifty grammes of sugar to the litre, and added to it some chalk. Taking then, by means of a drawn-out tube, from a good ordinary lactic fermentation a trace of the grey matter of which we have just spoken, he placed it as the seed of the ferment in the limpid saccharine solution. By the next day a lively and regular fermentation had set in, the liquid becoming turbid and the chalk disappearing, and one could distinguish a deposit which progressed continually as the chalk dissolved. This deposit was the lactic ferment.

Pasteur reproduced this experiment by substituting for the water of the yeast a clear decoction of nitrogenous plastic substances. The ferment invariably presented the same aspect and the same multiplication. These results, however, did not yet satisfy Pasteur. He desired more rigour in a subject of such theoretic importance. Might not the partisans of Liebig's theory argue, if not without subtlety yet with a semblance of justice, that the fermentation was not due to the formation and progressive growth of this feeble nitrogenous globular deposit, but rather to the nitrogenous matter dissolved during the decoction of the yeast used in the composition of the liquor? Up to a certain point it might be maintained that the dissolved matters which had been in contact with the oxygen of the air had been thrown into molecular motion, that this motion had been communicated to the fermentable matter, and that the deposit of the pretended organised ferment was but an accident—one of the physical changes or one of the precipitates so frequently observed in the modifications of albuminoid matters. In the observation of Cagniard-Latour and of Schwann as to the life of the yeast, Liebig saw nothing more. 'One cannot deny,' said he, 'the organisation of the yeast or its multiplication by budding, but these living cells are always associated with other dead cells in process of molecular alteration. It is these molecular motions which communicate themselves to the molecules of the sugar, break them up, and cause them to ferment.'

The arguments of Liebig derived great strength from the belief which was shared by all chemists that the cells of yeast perish during fermentation and form lactate of ammonia. On examining this assertion, Pasteur found that not only was there no ammonia formed during alcoholic fermentation, but that even if ammonia were added it disappeared, entering into the formation of new yeast cells. Was not this a proof of the potency of the organised ferment?

Tormented, however, by the idea that, notwithstanding all these facts, the reasonings of Liebig might still find some credit, Pasteur worked earnestly to discover new facts capable of demonstrating that Liebig's theory was absolutely false. He made two crucial experiments, the one relating to the yeast of beer, or of alcohol, and the other relating to the lactic ferment. He introduced into a pure solution of sugar a small quantity of crystallisable salt of ammonia, then some phosphates of potash and magnesia, and he sowed in this medium an imponderable quantity, if we may so express it, of fresh cells of yeast. The cells thus sown multiplied, and the sugar fermented. In other words, the phosphorus, the potassium, the magnesium of the mineral salts, united to form the substances which compose the ferment. By this experiment, so simple and yet so demonstrative, the power of the organisation of the ferment was once for all established. The contact theory of Berzelius had no longer any meaning, since it was evident that the fermentable matter here furnished to the ferment one of its essential elements, namely, carbon. Liebig's theory of communicated molecular motion, originating in a nitrogenous albuminoid substance, had no better claim, since such substances had been discarded. The whole process took place between the sugar and a ferment germ which owed its life and development to nutritive matters, the most important of which was the fermentable substance. Fermentation, in short, was simply a phenomenon of nutrition. The ferment augmented in weight, feeding upon the sugar, and its vitality was such that it contrived to build up the complex materials of its own organisation by means of sugar and purely mineral elements.

In a second experiment, Pasteur demonstrated that, notwithstanding their smallness and the possibility of confounding them with the amorphous granules of caseine and gluten, the little particles of lactic ferment were indeed alive, and that they, and they only, were the cause of lactic fermentation. He mixed with some water, sweetened with sugar, a small quantity of a salt of ammonia, some alkaline and earthy phosphates, and some pure carbonate of lime obtained by precipitation. At the end of twenty-four hours the liquid began to get turbid and to give off gas. The fermentation continued for some days. The ammonia disappeared, leaving a deposit of phosphates and calcareous salt. Some lactate of lime was formed, and at the same time one could notice the deposition of the little lactic ferment. The germs of the lactic ferment had, in this case, been derived from particles of dust adhering to the substances themselves, of which the mixtures were made, or to the vessels used, or from the surrounding air. The chapter on spontaneous generation will render this clear.

It suffices here to state that the results of this second experiment were absolutely conclusive, and that the theories of contact force or of communicated motion, which up to that time had reigned in science, were completely overthrown.

II.

The light shed by these experiments quickly extended its sphere; and Pasteur lost no time in discovering a new ferment, that of butyric acid. Having shown the absolute independence which exists between the ferment of butyric acid and the others, he found, contrary to the general belief, that the lactic ferment is incapable of giving rise to butyric acid, and that there exists a butyric fermentation having its own special ferment. This ferment consists of a species of vibrio. Little transparent cylindrical rods, rounded at their extremities, isolated or united in chains of two or three, or sometimes even more, form these vibrios. They move by gliding, the body straight, or bending and undulating. They reproduce themselves by fission, and to this mode of generation their frequent arrangement in the form of a chain is due.

Sometimes one of the little rods, with a train of others behind it, agitates itself in a lively manner as if to detach itself from the rest. Often, also, the little rod, after being broken off, holds on still to its chain by a mucous transparent thread.

These little infusoriæ may be sown like the yeast of beer or the lactic ferment. If the medium in which they are sown is suitable for their nourishment, they will multiply to infinity; but the character most essential to be observed is, that they may be sown in a liquid which contains only ammonia and crystallisable substances, together with the fermentable substances, sugar, lactic acid, gum, &c. The butyric fermentation manifests itself as these little organisms multiply. Their weight sensibly increases, though it is always minute in comparison with the quantity of butyric acid produced; this is found to be the case in all other fermentations.

This experiment no doubt resembles those made with the alcoholic and lactic ferments. But it is distinguished from them by one circumstance eminently worthy of attention. The butyric ferment, by its motions and by its mode of generation, furnishes the irrefutable proof of its organisation and of its life. This ferment, moreover, presented to Pasteur a new and unexpected peculiarity. The vibrios live and multiply without the smallest supply of air or of free oxygen. Not only, indeed, do they live without air, but the air destroys them and arrests the fermentation which they initiate. If a current of pure carbonic acid is made to pass into the liquid where they are multiplying, their life and reproduction do not appear to be at all affected by it. If, on the contrary, instead of the current of carbonic acid we employ one of atmospheric air for only one or two hours, the vibrios fall without movement to the bottom of the vessel, and the butyric fermentation which was dependent on their existence is immediately arrested.

Pasteur designated this new class of organisms by the name of *anaérobies*; that is to say, beings which can live without air. He reserves the designation *aérobies* for all the other microscopic beings which, like the larger animals, cannot live without free oxygen. 'It matters little,' added Pasteur, 'whether the progress of science makes of this vibrio a plant or an animal; it is a living organism, endowed with motion, which is a ferment and which lives without air.'

In meditating upon these facts, and upon the general character of fermentation, Pasteur soon found himself in a position to approach more nearly to the essential nature of these mysterious phenomena. In what way do microscopic organisms provoke the phenomena of fermentation?

The organism eats, if one may say so, one part of the fermentable matter. But how does this phenomenon of nutrition differ so much from that of higher beings? In general, for a given weight of nutritive matter which the animal takes in, it assimilates a quantity of the same order. In fermentation, on the contrary, the ferment, while nourishing itself with fermentable matter, decomposes a quantity great in comparison to its own individual weight. Again, the butyric ferment lives without free oxygen. Is there not, said Pasteur, a hidden relation between the property of being a ferment and the faculty of living without free oxygen? Are not vibrios which imperatively require for their nutrition and multiplication the presence of oxygen gas those which will never have the properties of ferments?

Pasteur then contrived a series of experiments with the view of placing in parallelism these two curious physiological facts: life without air and the characteristics of ferments.

We know how wine and beer are prepared. The must of grapes and the must of beer are placed in wooden vats, or in barrels of greater or less dimensions. Whether the fermentation proceeds from germs taken from the exterior surface of the grapes, or from a small quantity of ferment sown in the must under the form of yeast, as in the fermentation of beer, the life of the ferment, its multiplication, the augmentation of its weight, are so many vital actions which to a certainty cannot borrow from the free oxygen of the external air, or from that originally dissolved in the must, an appreciable quantity of this gas. All the life of the cells of the ferment which multiplies itself indefinitely appears then to take place apart from free oxygen gas. In certain breweries in England the fermenting vats have sometimes a capacity of several thousands of hectolitres; and the fermentation liberates pure carbonic acid, a gas much heavier than atmospheric air, which rests on the surface of the liquid in the vat in a layer thick enough to protect the liquid underneath from any contact with the external air. All this liquid mass, then, is inclosed between the wooden sides of the vat and a deep layer of heavy gas which contains no trace of free oxygen. In this liquid, nevertheless, the life of the cells of the ferment and the production of all its constituents go on for several days with extraordinary activity. Here certainly we have life without air, and the ferment character expresses itself in the enormous difference between the weight of the ferment formed and collected from the vats under the name of yeast, at the end of the operation, and the weight of the sugar which has fermented, transforming itself into alcohol, carbonic acid, and various other products.

Pasteur has studied experimentally that which takes place when, without otherwise changing the conditions of these phenomena, the arrangement is so modified as to permit the introduction of the free oxygen of the atmosphere. It sufficed for this purpose to provoke a fermentation of the must of beer, or the must of grapes, upon shallow glass dishes presenting a large surface, or in a flat-bottomed wooden trough with sides a few centimeters in height, instead of in deep vats as before. In these new conditions the fermentation manifests an activity even more extraordinary than it did in the deep vats. The life of the ferment is itself singularly enhanced, but the proportion of the weight of the decomposed sugar to that of the yeast formed is absolutely different in the two cases. While, for example, in the deep vats, a kilogram of ferment sometimes decomposes seventy, eighty, one hundred, or even one hundred and fifty kilograms of sugar, in the shallow troughs one kilogram of the ferment will be found to correspond to only five or six kilograms of decomposed sugar. These proportions between the weight of the sugar which ferments and the weight of the ferment produced, constitute the measure of what one might call the ferment's character—of that character which distinguishes its mode of life from that of all other existences, great or small, in which the weight of the organising matter and the assimilated alimentary matter are about equal. In other words, the more free oxygen the yeast ferment consumes, the less is its power as a ferment. Such is the case in the shallow troughs where the extended surface is exposed to the contact of the oxygen of the air. The more, on the contrary, the life of the ferment is carried on without the presence of free oxygen, the greater is its power of decomposing and of fermenting the saccharine matter. This is the case in deep casks. The intimate co-relation then between life without air and fermentation appears complete.

The unexpected light which these facts threw upon the cause of the phenomena of fermentation made a forcible impression upon all thinking minds. 'In these infinitely small organisms,' M. Dumas said one day to M. Pasteur before the Academy of Sciences, 'you have discovered a third kingdom—the kingdom to which those organisms belong which, with all the prerogatives of animal life, do not require air for their existence, and which find the heat that is necessary for them in the chemical decompositions which they set up around them.'

The work of Pasteur, demonstrating that fermentation was always dependent on the life of a microscopic organism, continued without interruption. One of the most remarkable of his researches is that which relates to the fermentation of the tartrate of lime. The demonstration of life and of fermentation without free oxygen is in this paper carried to the utmost limits of experimental rigour and precision.

III.

But there is still another class of chemical phenomena where the life without air of microscopic organisms is fully shown. Pasteur proved that in the special fermentation which bears the name of putrefaction the *primum movens* of the putrefaction resides in microscopic vibrios of absolutely the same order as those which compose the butyric ferment. The fermentation of sugar, of mannite, of gums, of lactate of lime, by the butyric vibrio, so closely resembles the phenomena of putrefaction, that one might call these fermentations the putrefaction of sugar and of the other products.

If it has been thought right to call the fermentation of animal matters putrefaction, it is because at the moment of the decomposition of fibrine, of albumen, of blood, of gelatine, of the substance of the tendons, &c., the sulphur, and even the phosphorus, which enter into their composition give rise to putrid odours, due to the evil-smelling gases of sulphur and phosphorus.

The phenomena of putrefaction being then simply fermentations, differing only in regard to the chemical composition of the fermenting matters, Liebig naturally included them in his general theory of the decomposition of organic matters after death. At a period long antecedent to Pasteur's labours it had been established that there existed in putrefying matters fungi or microscopic animalculæ, and the idea had taken shape that these creatures might have an influence in the phenomena. The proofs were wanting, but the notion of a possible relation remained. We may read in his 'Lessons on Chemistry' with what disdain Liebig mentioned these hypothetical opinions.

'Those who pretend to explain the putrefaction of animal substances by the presence of animalculæ,' he wrote, 'reason very much like a child who would explain the rapidity of the Rhine by attributing it to the violent motions imparted to it in the direction of Bingen by the numerous wheels of the mills of Mayence. Is it possible to consider plants and animals as the causes of the destruction of other organisms when their own elements are condemned to undergo the same decompositions as the creatures which have preceded them? If the fungus is the cause of the destruction of the oak, if the microscopic animalcula is the cause of the putrefaction of the dead elephant, I would ask in my turn what is the cause which determines the putrefaction of the fungus or of the microscopic animalcula when life is withdrawn from these two organisms?'

Thirty-two years later, and after Pasteur had accumulated, during more than twenty years, proof upon proof that the theory of Liebig would not stand examination, a physician of Paris, M. Bouillaud, asked, with the insistent voice of a querulous octogenarian: 'Let M. Pasteur then tell us here, in presence of the Académie de Médecine, what are the ferments of the ferments.'

Before replying to this argument, which Liebig and M. Bouillaud believed to be irrefutable, Pasteur, wishing to mark all the phases of the phenomena, expounded in a short preamble the part played by atmospheric oxygen in the destruction of animal and vegetable matters after death. It is easy to understand, indeed, that fermentation and putrefaction only represent the first phase of the return to the atmosphere and to the soil of all that has lived. Fermentations and putrefactions give rise to substances which are still very complex, although they represent the products of decomposition of fermentable matters. When sugar ferments, a large proportion of it becomes gas; but alongside of the carbonic acid gas which is formed, and which is, indeed, a partial return of the sugar to the atmosphere, new substances, such as alcohol, succinic acid, glycerine, and materials of yeast, are produced. When the flesh of animals putrifies, certain products of decomposition, also very complex, are formed with the vapour of water and the other gases of putrefaction. Where, then, does nature find the agents of destruction of these secondary products?

The great fact of the destruction of animal and vegetable matters is accomplished by slow combustion, through the appropriation of atmospheric oxygen. Here, again, one must banish from science the preconceived views which assumed that the oxygen seized directly on the organic matter after death, and that this matter was consumed by purely chemical processes. It is life that presides over this work of death.

If fermentation and putrefaction are principally the work of microscopic anaérobies, living without free oxygen, the slow combustion is found very largely, if not exclusively, to depend upon a class of infinitely small aérobies. It is these last which have the property of consuming the oxygen of the air. It is these lower organisms which are the powerful agents in the return to the atmosphere of all which has lived. Mildew, mould, bacteria, which we have already noticed, monads, two thousand of which would go to make up a millimeter, all these microscopic organisms are charged with the great work of re-establishing the equilibrium of life by giving back to it all that it has formed.

To demonstrate the important part played everywhere by these microscopic organisms, Pasteur made two experiments. He first introduced into vessels air deprived of all dust. This process we shall have occasion to examine in all its details, in connection with the researches on spontaneous generation. In these vessels, containing pure air, were placed the water of yeast with sugar dissolved in it, milk, sawdust—all of which had been deprived by heat of the germs of the lower organisms. The vessels and their contents were then subjected to a temperature of twenty-five to thirty-five degrees Centigrade. In a series of parallel experiments, made under the same conditions and at the same temperature, Pasteur took no steps to prevent the germination of the little seeds of mould suspended in the air, or associated with the substances contained in the vessels, neither did he avoid other infinitely small germs of the class aérobies.

After some time the air of all the vessels of the two series was submitted to analysis, when, behold, a very interesting fact! In the vessels where life had been withdrawn from the organic matters—that is to say, where there were no germs—the air still contained a large proportion of oxygen. In the vessels, on the contrary, where the microscopic organisms had been allowed to develop, the oxygen was totally absent, having been replaced by carbonic acid gas. And, further, for this absorption and total consumption of the oxygen gas a few days had sufficed; while in the vessels without microscopic life there remained, after several years, a considerable quantity of oxygen in a free state, so weak is the proportion of oxygen that the organic matters consume directly and chemically when the infinitely small organisms are absent.

But can these microscopic organisms, after having decomposed or burnt up all these secondary products, be in their turn decomposed?

How, cried M. Bouillaud, repeating his question, can they be destroyed or decomposed? How can their materials, which are of the same order as those of all the living creatures of the earth, be gasified and caused to return to the atmosphere? After having been charged with the transformation of others, whose business will it be to transform them?

A ferment which has finished its work, replied Pasteur, and which for want of aliment cannot continue it, becomes in its turn an accumulation, so to speak, of dead organic matters. Such, for example, would be an accumulation of yeast exposed to the air. Leave this mass to itself in summer temperature, and you will see appear in the interior of the mass anaérobic vibrios and the putrefactions associated with their life when protected from contact with the air. At the same time, on the surface of the entire mass—that is to say, that which finds itself in immediate contact with the oxygen of the air—the germs of bacteria, the seeds of mould will grow, and, by fixing the oxygen, determine the slow combustions which gasify the mass. The ferments of ferments are simply ferments. As long as the aérobic ferments of the surface have at their disposal free oxygen, they will multiply and continue their work of destruction. The anaérobic vibrios perish for want of new matter to decompose, and they form, in their turn, a mass of organic matter which, by and by, becomes the prey of aérobies. The portion of the aérobies which has lived becomes the prey either of new aérobies of different species, or of individuals of their own species, so that from putrefaction to putrefaction, and from combustion to combustion, the organic mass with which we started finds itself reduced to an assemblage of anaérobic and aérobic germs—of those same germs which were mixed up in the original primitive organic substances.

Though a collection of germs becomes again in its turn a collection of organic matter, subject to the double action of the phenomena of putrefaction and of combustion, there need be no anxiety as to their ultimate destruction; in the final analysis they represent life under its eternal form, for life is the germ, and the germ is life.

Thus in the destruction of that which has lived, all reduces itself to the simultaneous action of these three great natural phenomena—fermentation, putrefaction, and slow combustion. A living organism dies—animal, or plant, or the remains of one or the other. It is exposed to the contact of the air. To the life which has quitted it succeeds life under other forms. In the superficial parts, which the air can reach, the germs of the infinitely small aérobies hatch and multiply themselves. The carbon, the hydrogen, and the nitrogen of the organic matters are transformed by the oxygen of the air, and under the influence of the life of these aérobies, into carbonic acid, vapour of water, and ammonia gas. As long as organic matter and air are present, these combustions will continue. While these superficial combustions are going on, fermentation and putrefaction are doing their work in the interior of the mass by the developed germs of the anaérobies, which not only do not require oxygen for their life, but which oxygen actually kills. Little by little, at length, by this work of fermentation and slow combustion, the phenomenon is accomplished. Whether in the free atmosphere, or under the earth, which is always more or less impregnated with air, all animal and vegetable matters end by disappearing. To arrest these phenomena an extremely low temperature is required. It is thus that in the ice of the Polar regions antediluvian elephants have been found perfectly intact. The microscopic organisms could not live in so cold a temperature. These facts still further strengthen all the new ideas as to the important part performed by these infinitely small organisms, which are, in fact, the masters of the world. If we could suppress their work, which is always going on, the surface of the globe, encumbered with organic matters, would soon become uninhabitable.

ACETIC FERMENTATION.
THE MANUFACTURE OF VINEGAR.

Soon afterwards Pasteur came upon a most curious illustration of the 'fixation' of atmospheric oxygen by a microscopic organism—the transformation of wine into vinegar. As its name indicates, vinegar is nothing else than wine turned sour. Everybody has remarked that wine, left to itself, in circumstances which occur daily, is frequently transformed into vinegar. This is noticed more particularly when bottles, having been uncorked, are left in a half-empty condition. Sometimes, however, wine turns sour even in corked bottles. In this case we may be sure that the bottles have been standing upright, and that corks more or less defective have permitted the air to penetrate into the wine. The presence of air, in fact, is indispensable to the chemical act of transforming wine into vinegar. How does this air intervene? And what is the little microscopic creature which, in conjunction with the air, becomes the agent of this fermentation?

In a celebrated lecture given at Orleans at the request of the manufacturers of vinegar in that town, Pasteur, after having stated the two foregoing scientific questions, proceeded to examine the difference between wine and vinegar. What takes place in the fermentation of the juice of the grape which yields the wine? The sugar of this juice disappears, giving place to carbonic acid gas, which is exhaled during fermentation, and to alcohol, which remains in the fermented liquid. Formerly, chemists gave the name of 'spirit' to all volatile matters which could be collected from distillation. Now, when we distil wine and condense the vapour in a worm surrounded by cold water, we collect the spirit of wine at the extremity of the worm—this, when the water with which it is mixed during distillation is withdrawn from it, we designate by the name of alcohol. Vinegar contains no alcohol. When distilled it yields water and a spirit. But this spirit is acid, with a very pungent odour, and not inflammable like spirit of wine. Separated from the water which had accompanied it during the distillation, this spirit takes the name of acetic acid. This is the form in which it is used in smelling bottles—in those bottles of English salts the vapour of which is so penetrating.

In the formation of vinegar in contact with air the alcohol disappears, and is replaced by acetic acid. The air has thus given up something to the wine. Atmospheric air every one knows to be a mixture of nitrogen and oxygen, the nitrogen in the proportion of four-fifths of the total volume, and the oxygen of one-fifth. Well, in the transformation of wine into vinegar the nitrogen remains inactive. It is the oxygen alone which enters into combination with the alcohol. You ask for the proof of this? Take a bottle of wine turned sour, a bottle which at the same time is stopped hermetically; if the oxygen of the air contained in the bottle has combined with the alcohol, then, instead of air, there will be nothing in the bottle but nitrogen gas. Turn the bottle upside down and open it in a basin of water. The water of the basin will rush into the bottle to fill the partial vacuum created by the disappearance of the oxygen. The volume of water which enters the bottle is precisely equal to a fifth part of the total original volume of the air which the bottle contained at the time when it was closed. Moreover, it is easy to show that the gas which remains in the bottle has the properties of nitrogen gas. A lighted match is extinguished in it as if plunged into water, and a bird dies immediately in it of asphyxia.

If we confine our knowledge to what has gone before, it would seem that alcohol diluted with water and exposed to the air ought to furnish acetic acid. It is not so, however. Pure water alcoholised to the degree of ordinary wines may remain for whole years in contact with the air, without the least acetification. In this difference between natural wine and pure water alcoholised, and exposed to contact with air, we touch upon a vital point in the phenomena of fermentation. The celebrated theory of Liebig, which Pasteur was destined to overthrow, might be thus summed up:—If pure alcoholised water cannot become sour in contact with air, as is the case with wine, it is because the pure alcoholised water lacks the albuminoid substance which exists in the wine in a state of chemical alteration, and which is a ferment capable of causing the oxygen of the air to combine with the alcohol. And the proof, according to Liebig, that things act rigorously thus is, that if you add to the mixture of water and alcohol a little flour, or a little meat-juice, or even a minute quantity of any vegetable juice, the acetic fermentation arises, as if by compulsion. In other words, by the addition of a small quantity of any nitrogenised substance in process of alteration, you cause the union of the oxygen of the air with the alcohol.

There is doubtless always in the wine, when it turns sour, a necessary intermediary, producing the fixation of the oxygen of the air; since in no circumstances can pure alcohol, diluted to any degree whatever with pure water, transform itself into vinegar. But this necessary intermediary is not, as the German theory would have it, a dead albuminoid substance; it is a plant, and of all plants one of the simplest and most minute, which has been known from time immemorial under the name of flower of vinegar. This little fungus is invariably present on the surface of a wine which is being transformed into vinegar. Liebig was not ignorant of this, but he regarded it as a simple coincidence. Do we not know, said he, that whenever an infusion of organic matter is exposed to the air it becomes covered with a cryptogamic vegetation, or is invaded by a crowd of animalculæ? Is not vinegar a vegetable infusion? Vinegar affords a refuge to the flower of vinegar, just as it gives refuge to what are called the little eels of vinegar.

We can appreciate here the uncertainties of pure observation. The great art—and no one practised it better than Pasteur—consists in instituting decisive experiments which leave no room for an inexact interpretation of facts. These decisive proofs of the true part played by the little microscopic fungus, by this flower of vinegar, this mycoderma aceti, are thus formulated by Pasteur. It is but another example of the method which he used in alcoholic, lactic, and tartaric fermentations. The theories of Berzelius, of Mitscherlich, and of Liebig were destined again to receive the rudest shocks by the demonstration of these rigorous facts.

Let us place a little wine in a bottle, then hermetically seal it, and leave it to itself. In these conditions the wine becomes sour. But if we take the precaution of putting the bottle into hot water, so that the wine and the air in the bottle may be heated for some instants to a temperature of 60° Centigrade, and if, after cooling, we leave the bottle to itself, the wine in these conditions will never become transformed into vinegar. The heating, however, must have left intact the albuminoid or nitrogenous substances contained in the wine. These, then, cannot constitute the ferment of the vinegar. Can it be maintained that by heating the wine to 60° we have altered the albuminoid matter, which is, on this account, no longer able to act as a ferment, or, in other words, no longer able to determine the union of the oxygen of the air with the alcohol? This hypothesis falls to pieces before the following experiment. Open the bottle, blow into it with bellows, so that the once heated wine shall come into contact with ordinary air, and the acetification of the wine will take place.

But the master experiment is the following. We have seen that pure alcoholised water never turns sour unless some albuminoid matter is introduced into it. Pasteur saw that this albuminoid matter might be completely suppressed and replaced by saline crystallisable substances, alkaline and earthy phosphates, to which has been added a little phosphate of ammonia. In these conditions, especially if the alcoholised water be acidulated by small quantities of pure acetic acid, one actually sees the mycoderm developing, and the alcohol transforming itself into acetic acid. It is not possible to demonstrate in a more convincing manner that the albuminoid matters of the wine are not in this case the acetic ferment. These albuminoid matters, however, contribute to the acetic fermentation, but only as being an aliment to the mycoderma aceti, and notably a nitrogenous aliment. The true and only ferment of vinegar is the little fungus; it is the great agent of the phenomenon; it, indeed, accomplishes all.

Is there not a great charm in seeing an obscure subject clearly illuminated by facts well understood and well interpreted? If in a bottle containing wine and air and raised to a temperature of 50° or 60° the wine never turns sour, it is because the germs of the mycoderma aceti, which the wine and the air hold in suspension, are deprived of all vitality by the heat. Placed, however, in contact with ordinary air, this once-heated wine can turn sour; because, though the germs of the mycoderma aceti contained at first in the wine are killed, this is not the case with those derived from the surrounding air. Pure alcoholised water never turns sour, even in contact with ordinary air, and with whatever germs this air may carry, or that may be found in the dust of the vessels which receive it. The reason is that these germs cannot become fertile because of the absence of their indispensable food. Wine in bottles well filled and laid flat do not acetify; this is because the mycoderm cannot multiply for lack of oxygen. Without doubt the air constantly penetrates through the pores of the cork, but always in such feeble quantities that the colouring matters of the wine, and other more or less oxydisable constituents, take possession of it without leaving the smallest quantity for the germs of the mycoderm which are generally suspended in the wine. When the bottle is upright the conditions are quite altered. The desiccation of the cork renders it much more permeable to the air, and the germs of the mycoderm on the surface of the liquid, if any exist there, are enveloped by air.

Thus, to recapitulate in a few words the principles which have just been established; it is easy to see that the formation of vinegar is always preceded by the development, on the surface of the wine, of a little plant formed of strangulated particles, of an extreme tenuity, and the accumulation of which sometimes takes the form of a hardly visible veil, sometimes of a wrinkled film of very slight thickness, and greasy to the touch, because of the various fatty matters which the plant contains.

This cryptogam has the singular property of condensing considerable quantities of oxygen and of provoking the *fixation* of this gas upon the alcohol, which is thereby transformed into acetic acid. The little mycoderm is not less exacting than larger vegetables. It must have its appropriate aliments. Wine offers them in abundance: nitrogenous matters, the phosphates of magnesia and of potash. The mycoderm thrives, moreover, in warm climates. To cultivate it in temperate regions like ours it is well to warm artificially the places where it is cultivated. But if wine contains within itself all the elements necessary to the life of the little mycoderm, this life is further promoted by rendering the wine more acid through the addition of acetic acid.

What, then, can be more simple than to produce vinegar from wine—a manufacture which justly makes the reputation of the town of Orleans? Take some wine, and after having mixed with it one-fourth or one-third of its volume of vinegar already formed, sow on its surface the little plant which does the work of acetification. It is only necessary to skim off, by means of a wooden spatula, a little of the mycodermic film from a liquid covered with it, and to transfer it to the liquid to be acetified. The fatty matters which it contains render the wetting of it difficult. Thus, when we plunge into the liquid the spatula covered with the film, the latter detaches itself and spreads out over the surface instead of falling to the bottom. When we operate in summer, or in a room heated to 15° or 25° Centigrade in winter, in twenty- four or forty-eight hours at most, the mycoderm covers the whole liquid, so easy and rapid is its development. After some days all the wine has become vinegar.

On one occasion, in a discussion which he was holding at the Academy of Sciences, Pasteur, wishing to affirm the prodigious activity of the life and multiplication of this little organism, expressed himself thus:—

'I would undertake in the space of twenty-four hours to cover with mycoderma aceti a surface of vinous liquid as large as the hall in which we are here assembled. I should only have to sow in it the day before almost invisible particles of newly-formed mycoderma aceti.'

Let the reader try to imagine the millions upon millions of little mycoderma particles which would come to life in that one day.

But how is the mycoderm seed to be obtained in the first instance? Nothing more simple. The mycoderma aceti is one of those little so-called 'spontaneous' productions which are sure to appear of themselves on the surface of liquids or infusions suitable to their development. In wine, in vinegar, or suspended in air, everywhere around us, in our towns, in our houses, there exist germs of this little plant. If we wish to procure some fresh mycoderm it is only necessary to put a mixture of wine and vinegar into a warm place. In a few days, generally, if not always, there appear here and there little greyish patches scattering the light instead of regularly reflecting it, as does the surrounding liquid. These specks go on increasing progressively and rapidly. This is the mycoderma aceti raised from the seeds which the wine or the added vinegar contained, or which the air deposited; just as we see a field covered with divers weeds by seeds naturally distributed in the earth, or which have been brought to it by the wind or by animals. Even in this last circumstance the comparison holds good, for after you have put wine or vinegar in a warm place there soon appear, whence we know not, little reddish flies, so commonly seen in vinegar manufactories, and in all places where vegetable matter is turning sour. With their feet, or with their probosces, these flies transport the seed.

At Orleans the process for the manufacture of vinegar is very simple. Barrels ranged over each other have on each of their vertically-placed bottoms a circular opening some centimeters in diameter, and a smaller hole adjacent, called *fausset*, for the air to pass in and out when the large opening is closed, either by the funnel, through which the wine is introduced, or by the syphon, which is used for drawing off the vinegar. These barrels, of which the capacity is 230 litres, are half filled. The manual labour consists in keeping up a suitable temperature in the vessel, and in drawing from it every eight days about eight or ten litres of vinegar, which are replaced by eight or ten litres of wine.

A barrel in which this give-and-take of wine and vinegar goes on is technically called a 'mother.' The starting of a 'mother' is not a rapid process. We begin by introducing into the barrel 100 litres of very good and very limpid vinegar; then two litres only of wine are added. Eight days after, three litres of wine are added, a week later four or five, until the barrel contains about 180 to 200 litres. Then for the first time vinegar is drawn off in sufficient quantity to bring back the volume of the liquid to about 100 litres. At this moment the labours of the 'mother' begin. Henceforward ten litres of vinegar may be drawn off every eight days, to be replaced by ten litres of wine. This is the maximum that a cask can yield in a week. When the casks work badly, as is often the case, it is necessary to diminish their production.

This Orleans system has many drawbacks. It requires three or four months to prepare what is called a 'mother,' which must be nourished with wine *very* regularly once a week under penalty of seeing it lose all its power. Then it is necessary to continue the manufacture at all times, whether the vinegar be required or not. To reconstitute a 'mother,' one must begin from the very beginning, a process which involves a loss of three or four months' time. Lastly—a condition which is at times very inconvenient—a 'mother' cannot be transported from one place to another, or even from one part of the same locality to another. The 'mother,' in fact, must rest immovable.

Pasteur advised the suppression of the 'mothers.' He recommended an apparatus, which is simply a vat, placed in a chamber the temperature of which can be raised to 20° or 25° Centigrade. In these vats vinegar already formed is mixed with wine. On the surface is sown the little plant which converts the wine into vinegar. The mode of sowing it has been already explained. The acetification begins with the development of the plant.

A great merchant of Orleans, who had from the first adopted Pasteur's process, and who had won the prize offered by the 'Society for the

Encouragement of National Industry' for a manufactory perfected after these principles, has stated that at the end of nine or ten days, sometimes even in eight, all the acetified wine is converted into vinegar. From a hundred litres of wine he drew off ninety-five litres of vinegar. After the great rise of temperature observed at the moment of the formation of the vinegar, and which is caused by the chemical union of the alcohol and the oxygen of the air, the vinegar is allowed to cool. It may then be drawn from the vat, introduced into barrels, refined, and straightway delivered, fit for consumption. When the vat is quite emptied, and well cleaned, a new mixture is made of vinegar and wine, the little plant is sown as before, and the same facts are reproduced in the second as in the first operation.

In the vessels where vinegar is preserved, whether in the manufactories, in private houses, or in grocers' shops, it often happens that the liquid becomes turbid, and impoverished in an extraordinary manner; it even ends in putrefaction, if a remedy be not promptly applied. Pasteur has pointed out the cause of these phenomena. After the alcohol has become acetic acid by the combustive action of the mycoderm, the question remains, what becomes of the mycoderm? Most frequently it falls to the bottom of the vessel, having no more work to accomplish. This is a phase of the manufacture which must be watched with care. It is shown by the experiments of Pasteur that the mycoderma aceti can live on vinegar already formed, maintaining its power of fixing the oxygen on certain constituents of the liquid. In this case the acetic acid itself is the seat of the chemical action—in other words, the oxygen unites with the carbon of the acetic acid, and transforms it into carbonic acid, and as the acetic acid has a composition which can be represented by carbon and water, it follows that if the combustion is allowed to take its course, instead of vinegar we have eventually nothing but water mixed with a small proportion of nitrogenous and mineral matters, and the remains of the mycoderm. We have thus an ordinary organic infusion exempt from all acidity, and one which could not be better fitted to become the prey of the vibrios of putrefaction or of the aérobic mucors. By these mucors, moreover, which form a film on the surface of the liquid after the mycoderm has fallen, the anaérobic vibrios, protected from the action of the air, can come into active existence. Here we find ourselves in presence of one of those double phenomena, of putrefaction in the deeper parts of the liquid, and of combustion at the surface which is in contact with the air. Nothing is more prejudicial to the quality of the vinegar than the setting in of this combustion after the vinegar has been formed, and when it contains no more alcohol. The first materials of the vinegar upon which the oxygen transmitted by the mycoderm fixes are, in fact, the ethereal and aromatic constituents which give to vinegar its chief value.

Another cause of the deterioration of the quality of vinegar, which is sometimes very annoying to the manufacturer, consists in the frequent presence of little eel-like organisms, very curious when viewed with a strong magnifier. Their bodies are so transparent that their internal organs can be easily distinguished. These eel-like creatures multiply with extraordinary rapidity. Certainly there is not a single barrel of vinegar manufactured by the Orleans system which does not contain them in alarming numbers. Prior to Pasteur's investigations, the ignorance regarding these organisms was such that they were actually considered necessary to the production of the vinegar; whereas they are, on the contrary, most inimical to it, and must, if possible, be got rid of. This is, moreover, rendered desirable by the repugnance which is naturally felt to using a liquid defiled by the presence of such animalcules—a repugnance which becomes almost insurmountable to anyone who has once seen through a microscope the swarms contained in a drop of vinegar. The mischief wrought by these little beings in the manufacture of vinegar results from the fact that they require air to live. The effect can easily be perceived by filling to the brim a bottle of vinegar, corking it, and then comparing it with a similar bottle half filled with the same vinegar, and left uncorked in contact with the air. In the first bottle, the motions of the eel-like creatures become gradually slower, until after a few days they cease to multiply and fall lifeless to the bottom of the vessel. In the second bottle, on the contrary, they continue to swarm and move about. This need of oxygen is further demonstrated by the fact that, if the vinegar reaches a certain depth in the bottle, life is suspended in the lower parts, and the little eel-like organisms, in order to breathe more freely, form a crawling zone in the upper layers of the liquid.

Connecting these observations with the other fact that the vinegar is formed by the action of the mycodermic film on its surface, we can understand at once that the mycoderm and the little eels continually carry on a struggle for existence, since both of these living things—the one animal the other vegetable—imperiously demand the same aliment, oxygen. They live, moreover, in the same superficial layers, a circumstance which gives rise to very curious phenomena. When, for one reason or another, the film of mycoderm is not formed, or when there is any delay in its production, the little eels invade in such great numbers the upper layers of the liquid that they absorb all the oxygen. The little plant has in consequence great difficulty in developing itself or even in beginning its life. Reciprocally, when the work of acetification is active, and when the mycoderm has occupied the upper layers, it gradually drives away the eels, which take refuge, not deep down, where they would perish, but against the moist sides of the barrel or the vat. There they form a thick whitish scum all in motion. It is a very curious spectacle. Here their enemy, the mycoderm, can no longer injure them to the same extent, since they are surrounded with air; and here they wait with impatience for the moment when they can again take their place in the liquid, and, in their turn, fight against the mycoderm. In Pasteur's process, where the vats are very often cleansed, it is easy to keep them free from these little animalcules; they have not time to multiply to a hurtful extent. Indeed, if the operation be well conducted, they do not make their appearance at all.

Nearly all Pasteur's publications have had from the moment of their appearance to undergo the severest criticism. Their novelty caused them to clash with the prejudices and errors current in science. His researches on fermentation provoked lively opposition. Liebig did not accept without recrimination a series of researches which concurred in upsetting the theory he had enunciated and defended in all his works. After having kept silence for ten years, he published, at Munich, where he was professor, a long memoir entirely directed against Pasteur's results. In 1870, on the eve of the war, Pasteur, who was at that time returning from a scientific journey into Austria, determined to pass by Munich, with the view of attempting to convince his distinguished adversary. Liebig received him with great courtesy, but, hardly recovered from an illness, he alleged his convalescence as a reason for declining all discussion.

Then followed the Franco-German war. Hardly was it terminated when Pasteur brought before the Academy of Sciences at Paris a defence of what he had published, as a sort of challenge to his illustrious opponent. The memoir of Liebig was filled with the most skilful arguments.

'I pondered it for nearly ten years before producing it,' he wrote. Pasteur, putting aside all subtleties of argument, went straight to the two objections of the German chemist which lay at the root of the discussion.

It may be remembered that one of the most decisive proofs by which Pasteur overthrew Liebig's theory resulted from the experiments in which by the aid of mineral bodies and fermentable matter he produced a special living ferment for each definite fermentation. By removing all nitrogenous organic matter, which in Liebig's theory constitutes the ferment, Pasteur established, at one and the same time, the life of the ferment and the absence of all action of albuminoid matter in process of alteration. Liebig here formally contested the fact that Pasteur had been able to produce yeast and alcoholic fermentation in a sweetened mineral medium by sowing therein an infinitesimal quantity of yeast. It is certain that, ten years previously, when Pasteur announced the production of yeast life and alcoholic fermentation under such conditions, his experiment was one so difficult to perform that it sometimes happened to Pasteur himself to be unable to reproduce it. The cells of yeast sown in the sweetened mineral medium found themselves often associated with other microscopic organisms, which were singularly hurtful to the life of the yeast. Pasteur was at this period far from being familiarised with the delicacy which such experiments require, and he did not yet know all the precautions indicated later on, which were indispensable to success. Though in his original memoir of 1860 Pasteur had pointed out the difficulties of his experiment, these difficulties existed nevertheless. Liebig took hold of them with skill, exaggerated them; saw, so to speak, nothing but them; and declared that the results announced never could have been obtained. But in 1871 the fundamental experiment of Pasteur, on the life of yeast in a sweetened mineral medium, had become a trifle for him. He knew exactly how to form media deprived of all foreign germs, how to prepare pure yeast, and how to prevent the introduction of new germs, which could develop in the liquids and hinder the life of the yeast.

'Choose,' said he to Liebig, 'from the members of the Academy one or several, and ask them to decide between you and me. I am ready to prepare before you and before them, in a sweetened mineral medium, as much yeast as you can reasonably ask for, and with substances provided by yourself.'

Liebig's second objection had reference to acetic fermentation. The process of acetification known as that of 'beech shavings' is widely practised in Germany and even in France. It consists in causing alcohol diluted with water and with the addition of some *millièmes* of acetic acid to trickle slowly into barrels or vats filled with shavings of beech, either massed together without order or disposed in layers after having been rolled up like the spring of a watch. Openings formed in the sides of the barrel, and in a double bottom upon which the shavings rest, permit the access of the air, which rises into the barrel as it would in a chimney, and yields all or part of its oxygen to the alcohol to convert it into acetic acid. All writers prior to Pasteur, and Liebig in particular, maintained that the shavings acted like porous bodies in the same manner as finely divided platinum. The acetic acid, they said, was formed by a direct oxidation, without any other influence than the porosity of the wood. This view of the subject was rendered plausible by the fact that in many manufactories the alcohol employed is that of distillation, which contains no albuminoid substances. Moreover, the duration of the shavings is in a sense indefinite.

According to Pasteur, the shavings perform only a passive part in the manufacture. They promote the division of the liquid and cause a considerable augmentation of the surface exposed to the air. They moreover serve as a support for the ferment, which is still, according to him, the mycoderma aceti, under the mucous form proper to it when submerged.

Certainly appearances were far from being favourable to this view. When the shavings of a barrel which has been in work for several months or even for several years are examined, they are found to be extraordinarily clean. It might be said that they had just been carefully washed. Pasteur has shown that this is but a deceptive appearance, and that in reality these shavings are partly or wholly covered with a mucous film of mycoderma aceti of excessive tenuity. It is necessary to scrape the surface of the wood with a scalpel and examine the scrapings with the microscope to be assured of the presence of this pellicle.

Liebig, who somewhere speaks, not without a certain contempt, of the microscope, denied formally the exactitude of these assertions.

'With diluted alcohol, which is used for the rapid manufacture of vinegar,' he wrote, 'the elements of nutrition of the mycoderm are excluded, and the vinegar is made without its intervention.' He asserted also in his memoir of 1869 that he had consulted the head of one of the principal manufactories of vinegar in Germany, that in this manufactory the diluted alcohol did not receive during the whole course of its transformation any foreign addition, and that beyond the air and the surfaces of wood and charcoal—for charcoal is sometimes associated with the beech shavings—nothing can act upon the alcohol. Liebig added that the director of the manufactory did not believe at all in the presence of the mycoderm, and that finally he, Liebig, in examining the shavings which had been used for twenty-five years in the manufactory, saw no trace of mycoderm on their surface.

The argument appeared conclusive. How, in fact, could we understand the production of a plant containing within itself nitrogen and mineral elements which was nevertheless to be nourished by water and alcohol.

'You do not take into account,' replied Pasteur, 'the nature of the water which serves to dilute your alcohol. This water, like all ordinary waters, even the purest, contains salts of ammonia and mineral matters which are capable of nourishing the plant. Finally, you have not rightly examined with the microscope the surface of the shavings, otherwise you would have seen the little particles of the mycoderma aceti united, in some cases, to a thin film which can even be lifted up. I propose to you, moreover, to send to the Academic Commission charged with the decision of the debate, some shavings that you have obtained yourself in the manufactory at Munich, and in the presence of its director. I will undertake to prove before the members of the commission the presence of the mycoderm on the surface of these shavings.'

Liebig did not accept this challenge. To-day the question is decided.

THE QUESTION OF SPONTANEOUS GENERATION.

'All dry bodies,' said Aristotle, 'which become damp, and all damp bodies which are dried, engender animal life.' Bees, according to Virgil, are produced from the corrupted entrails of a young bull. At the time of Louis XIV. we were hardly more advanced. A celebrated alchemist doctor, Van Helmont, wrote: 'The smells which rise from the bottom of morasses produce frogs, slugs, leeches, grasses, and other things.' But most extraordinary of all was the true recipe given by Van Helmont for producing a pot of mice. It suffices to press a dirty shirt into the orifice of a vessel containing a little corn. After about twenty-one days, the ferment proceeding from the dirty shirt modified by the odour of the corn effects the transmutation of the wheat into mice. Van Helmont, who asserted that he had witnessed the fact, added with assurance:

'The mice are born full grown; there are both males and females. To reproduce the species it suffices to pair them.'

'Scoop out a hole,' said he again, 'in a brick, put into it some sweet basil, crushed, lay a second brick upon the first so that the hole may be perfectly covered. Expose the two bricks to the sun, and at the end of a few days the smell of the sweet basil, acting as a ferment, will change the herb into real scorpions. An Italian naturalist, Redi, was the first to subject this question of spontaneous generation to a more attentive examination. He showed that maggots in meat are not spontaneously generated, but that they are the larvæ of flies' eggs. To prevent the production of maggots, Redi showed that it was only necessary to surround the meat with fine gauze before exposing it to the air. As no flies could alight upon meat thus protected, there were no eggs deposited, and consequently neither larvæ nor maggots. But at the moment when the doctrine of spontaneous generation began to lose ground by the limitation of its domain, the discovery of the microscope brought to this doctrine new and formidable support. In presence of the world of animalculæ, the partisans of spontaneous generation raised a note of triumph. 'We may have been mistaken,' they said, 'as to the origin of mice and maggots, but is it possible to believe that microscopic organisms are not the outcome of spontaneous generation? How can we otherwise explain their presence and rapid multiplication in all dead animal or vegetable matter in process of decomposition?'

Buffon lent the authority of his name to the doctrine of spontaneous generation. He even devised a system to explain this hypothesis. In 1745 two ecclesiastics entered upon an eager controversy for and against this question. While the English Catholic priest Needham adopted the theory of spontaneous generation, the Italian priest Spallanzani energetically opposed it; but while in the eyes of the public the Italian remained master of the dispute, his success was more apparent than real, more in word than in deed.

The problem was again brought forward in a more emphatic manner in 1858. M. Pouchet, director of the Museum of Natural History at Rouen, in addressing the Academy of Sciences, declared that he had succeeded in demonstrating in a manner absolutely certain the existence of microscopic living organisms, which had come into the world without germs, and consequently without parents similar to themselves.

How came Pasteur to throw himself into this discussion, at first sight so far removed from his other occupations? The results of his researches on fermentation led him to it as a sort of duty. He was carried on by a series of logical deductions. Let us recall to mind, for example, the experiment in which Pasteur exposed to the heat of the sun water sweetened with sugar and mixed with phosphates of potash and magnesia, a little sulphate of ammonia, and some carbonate of lime. In these conditions the lactic fermentation was often seen to develop itself—that is to say, the sugar became lactic acid, which combined with the lime of the carbonate to form lactate of lime. This salt crystallises in long needles, and ends sometimes by filling the whole vase, while a little organised living thing is at the same time produced and multiplied. If the experiment is carried on further, another fermentation generally succeeds to this one. Moving vibrios make their appearance and multiply, the lactate of lime disappears, the fluidity returns to the mass, and the lactate finds itself replaced by butyrate of lime. What a succession of strange phenomena! How did life appear in this sweetened medium, composed originally of such simple elements, and apparently so far removed from all production of life? This lactic ferment, these butyric vibrios, whence do they come? Are they formed of themselves? or are they produced by germs? If the latter, whence do the germs come? The appearance of living organised ferments had become for Pasteur the all-important question, since in all fermentations he had observed a correlation between the chemical action set up and the presence of microscopic organisms. Prior to the establishment of the facts already mentioned, these difficulties did not exist. The theory of Liebig was universally accepted.

Thus the question as to the origin of microscopic organisms and the part played by them in fermentation was imposed as a necessity on Pasteur. He could not proceed further in his researches without having solved this question.

In the month of October, 1857, Pasteur was called to Paris. After having been made dean at an incredibly early age, he was now, at the age of thirty-five, entrusted with the scientific studies at the École Normale Supérieure. But if the position was flattering, it did not give to Pasteur what he most desired. As he had no Professor's chair, he had no laboratory. In those days science, and the higher education in science, were at a discount. It was the period when Claude Bernard lived in a small damp laboratory, when M. Berthelot, though known through his great labours, was still nothing more than an assistant in the Collège de France.

At the time here referred to, the Minister of Public Instruction said to Pasteur, 'There is no clause in the budget to grant you 1,500 francs a year to defray the expense of experiments.' Pasteur did not hesitate to establish a laboratory at his own expense in one of the garrets of the École Normale. We can readily imagine the modesty of such an establishment in such a place. Dividing his time between his professional duties and his laboratory experiments, Pasteur never went out but to talk over his daily researches with M. Biot, M. Dumas, M. de Senarmont, and M. Balard. M. Biot especially was his habitual confidant. The day when M. Biot learned that Pasteur proposed to study the obscure question of spontaneous generation, he strongly dissuaded him from entangling himself in this labyrinth. 'You will never escape from it,' said he, 'you will only lose your time;' and when Pasteur attempted some timid observations with the view of showing that in the order of his studies it was indispensable for him to attack this problem, M. Biot grew angry. Although endowed, as Sainte-Beuve has said, with all the qualities of curiosity, of subtlety, of penetration, of ingenious exactitude, of method, and of perspicuity, with all the qualities, in short, essential and secondary, M. Biot treated the project of Pasteur as a presumptuous adventure.

Bolder than M. Biot, but with a circumspection always alive, M. Dumas declared to Pasteur, without, however, further insisting upon the point, that he would not advise anyone to occupy himself too long with such a subject. M. de Senarmont alone took the part of Pasteur, and said to M. Biot:

'Let Pasteur alone. If there is nothing to be found in the path which he has entered upon, do not be alarmed, he will not continue in it. But,' added he, 'I should be surprised if he found nothing in it.'

M. Pouchet had previously stated the problem with precision:

'The opponents of spontaneous generation assert that the germs of microscopic organisms exist in the air, which transports them to a distance. What, then, will these opponents say if I succeed in inducing the generation of living organisms, while substituting artificial air for that of the atmosphere?'

Pouchet then devised this ingenious experiment. He filled a bottle with boiling water, hermetically sealed it with the greatest care, and plunged it upside down into a basin of mercury. When the water was quite cold he uncorked the bottle under the metal, and introduced into it half a litre of pure oxygen gas, which is as necessary to the life of the smallest microscopic organism as it is to that of the larger animals and vegetables. Up to this time there was nothing in the vessel but pure water and oxygen. Pouchet then introduced a minute bunch of hay which had been enclosed in a corked bottle, and exposed in a stove for a long time to a temperature of more than 100 degrees. At the end of eight days a mouldiness was developed in this infusion of hay. 'Where does this come from?' cried M. Pouchet triumphantly. Certainly not from the oxygen, which had been prepared from a chemical compound at the temperature of incandescence. The water had been equally deprived of germs, since at the boiling temperature all germs would have been destroyed. The hay also could not have contained them, for it had been taken from a stove heated to 100 degrees. As it was urged, however, that certain organisms could resist this temperature, M. Pouchet heated the hay from 200 to 300 degrees, or to any temperature that might be desired.

Pasteur came to disturb the triumph of M. Pouchet.

In a lecture which he gave at the Sorbonne in 1864, before a large assembly composed of savants, philosophers, ladies, priests, and novelists—Alexandre Dumas was in the first row—all showing eager interest in the problems to be dealt with in the lecture, Pasteur thus criticised the experiment of Pouchet: 'This experiment is irreproachable, but irreproachable only on those points which have attracted the attention of its author. I will demonstrate before you that there is a cause of error which M. Pouchet has not perceived, which he has not in the least suspected, which no one before him suspected, but which renders his experiment as completely illusory as that of Van Helmont's pot of dirty linen. I will show you where the mice got in. I will prove to you, in short, that it is the mercury which carries the germs into the vessels, or, rather, not to go beyond the demonstrated fact, the dust which is suspended in the air.'

To render visible this floating dust, Pasteur caused the hall to be darkened, and pierced the obscurity by a beam of light. There then appeared, dancing and twirling in the beam, thousands of little particles of dust.

'If we had time to examine them well,' continued Pasteur, 'we should see them, though agitated with various movements, falling downwards more or less quickly. It is thus that all objects become covered with dust—the furniture, the table, the mercury in this basin. Since this mercury was taken from the mine, how much dust must have fallen upon it, to say nothing of all that has been intimately mixed up with it during the numerous manipulations to which it has been subjected in the laboratory? It is not possible to touch this mercury, to place the hand in it, or a bottle, without introducing into the interior of the basin the dust which lies on its surface. You will now see what takes place.'

Projecting, in the darkness, the beam of light upon the basin of mercury, the liquid metal shone forth with its usual brilliancy. Pasteur then sprinkled some dust upon the mercury, and, plunging a glass rod into it, the dust was seen to travel towards the spot where the rod entered the mercury, and to penetrate into the space between the glass and the metal.

'Yes,' exclaimed Pasteur with a voice which gave evidence of the sincerity of his conviction, 'yes, M. Pouchet had removed the germs from the water and from the hay, but he had neglected to remove the dust from the surface of the mercury. This is the cause of his error; this is what has vitiated his whole arrangement.'

Pasteur then instituted experiments exactly similar to those of Pouchet, but taking care to remove every cause of error which had escaped the latter. He employed a glass bulb with a long neck, which he bent, and connected with a tube of platinum placed in a furnace, so that it could be heated nearly to redness. In the bulb he placed some very putrescible liquids—urine for example. When the furnace which surrounded the platinum tube was in action, Pasteur boiled the liquid for some minutes, then he allowed it to cool, keeping the fire around the platinum tube still active. During the cooling of the bulb the external air was introduced, after having first travelled through the red-hot platinum tube. The liquid was thus placed in contact with air whose suspended germs were all burnt up.

In an experiment thus carried out, the urine remains unchanged—it undergoes only a very slight oxidation, which darkens its colour a little—but it exhibits no kind of putrefaction. If it be desired to repeat this experiment with alkaline liquids, such as milk, the temperature must be raised a little above the boiling point—a condition easily realised with the apparatus just described. It is only necessary to connect with the free extremity of the platinum tube a glass tube bent at right angles, and to plunge the latter to a depth of some centimeters into a basin of mercury. In these circumstances ebullition goes on under a pressure greater than that of the atmosphere, consequently at a temperature higher than 100 degrees Centigrade.

It remained, however, to be proved that the floating dust of the air embraces the germs of the lower organisms. Through a tube stopped with cotton wool, Pasteur, by means of an aspirator, drew ordinary air. In passing through the wool it was filtered, depositing therein all its dust. Taking a watch-glass, Pasteur placed on it a drop of water in which he steeped the cotton wool stopper and squeezed out of it, upon a glass slide, a drop of water which contained a portion of the intercepted dust. He repeated this process until he had extracted from the cotton nearly all the intercepted dust. The operation is simple and easily executed. Placing the glass slide with a little of the soiled liquid under a microscope, we can distinguish particles of soot, fragments of silk, scraps of wool, or of cotton. But, in the midst of this inanimate dust, living particles make their appearance—that is to say, organisms belonging to the animal or vegetable kingdom, eggs of infusoria, and spores of cryptogams. Germs, animalculæ, flakes of mildew, float in the atmosphere, ready to fall into any appropriate medium, and to develop themselves at a prodigious rate.

But are these apparently organised particles which are found thus associated with amorphous dust indeed the germs of microscopic living beings? Granting the experiment devised by Pasteur to verify that of Pouchet to be irreproachable, is Pasteur's interpretation of it rigorously true? In presence of the problem of the origin of life, all hypotheses are possible as long as the truth has not been clearly revealed. Truly, it might be argued, if fermentation be caused by germs, then the air which has passed through a red-hot platinum tube cannot provoke fermentation, or putrefaction, or the formation of organisms, because the germs of these last, which were suspended in the air, have lost all vitality. But what right have you to speak of germs? How do you know that the previous existence of germs is necessary to the appearance and development of microscopic organisms? May not the prime mover of the life of microscopic organisms be some appropriate medium started into activity by magnetism, electricity, or even ozone? Now, by the passing of the air through your red-hot platinum tube these active powers are destroyed, and the sterility of your bulb of urine has nothing surprising in it.

The partisans of spontaneous generation had often employed this apparently formidable reasoning, and Pasteur thought it necessary to strengthen the proof that the cotton wool through which his air had filtered was really charged with germs.

By an ingenious method he sowed the contents of the cotton wool in the same liquids that had been rendered sterile by boiling. The liquids became fertile, even more fertile than if they had been exposed to the free contact of atmospheric air. Now, what was there in the dust contained in the cotton wool? Only amorphous particles of silk, cotton, starch; and, along with these, minute bodies which, by their transparency and their structure, were not to be distinguished from the germs of microscopic organisms. The presence of imponderable fluids could not here be pleaded.

Nevertheless, fearing that determined scepticism might still attribute to the cotton wool an influence of some sort on account of its being an organised substance, Pasteur substituted for the stoppers of cotton wool stoppers of asbestos previously heated to redness. The result was the same.

Wishing still further to dispose of the hypothesis that, in ordinary air, an unknown something existed which, independent of germs, might be the cause of the observed microscopic life, Pasteur began a new series of experiments as simple as they were demonstrative. Having placed a very putrescible infusion—in other words, one very appropriate to the appearance of microscopic organisms—in a glass bulb with a long neck, by means of the blowpipe, he drew out this neck to a very small diameter, at the same time bending the soft glass to and fro, so as to form a sinuous tube. The extremity of this narrow tube remained open. He then boiled his liquid for some minutes until the vapour of the water came out in abundance through the narrow open tube. In these conditions the liquid in the bulb, however putrescible, is preserved indefinitely without the least alteration. One may handle it, transport it from place to place, expose it to every variety of climate, place it in a stove with a temperature of thirty or forty degrees, the liquid remains as clear as it was at first. A slight oxidation of the constituents of the liquid, is barely perceptible. In this experiment the ordinary air, entering suddenly at the first moment, finds in the bulb a liquid very near the boiling temperature; and when the liquid is so far cooled that it can no longer destroy the vitality of the germs, the entrance of the air is correspondingly retarded, so that the germs capable of acting upon the liquid, and of producing in it living organisms, are deposited in the bends of the still moist tube, not coming into contact with the liquid at all.

If, after remaining for weeks, months, or even years, in a heated chamber, the sinuous neck of the bulb is snipped off by a file in the vertical part of the stem, after twenty-four or forty-eight hours there begin to appear mildew, mucors, bacteria, infusoria, exactly as in the case of infusions recently exposed to the contact of ordinary air.

The same experiments may be repeated with slightly alkaline liquids, such as milk, the precaution being taken of raising them to a temperature higher than that of 100 degrees Centigrade.

The great interest of Pasteur's method consists in its proving unanswerably that the origin of life, in infusions which have been heated to the boiling point, is solely due to the solid particles suspended in the air. Of gas, electricity, magnetism, ozone, things known or unknown, there is nothing in ordinary atmospheric air which, apart from these solid particles, can cause the fermentation or putrefaction of the infusions.

Lastly, to convince the most prejudiced minds, and to leave no contradiction standing, Pasteur showed one of these bulbs with the sinuous neck which he had prepared and preserved for months and years. The bulb was covered with dust. 'Let us,' said he, 'take up a little of this outside dust on a bit of glass, porcelain, or platinum, and introduce it into the liquid; the following day you will find that the infusion, which up to this time remained perfectly clear, has become turbid, and that it behaves in the same manner as other infusions in contact with ordinary air.'

If the bulb be tilted so as to cause a little drop of the clear infusion to reach the extremity of the bent part of the neck where the dust particles are arrested, and if this drop be then allowed to trickle back into the infusion, the result is the same—turbidity supervenes and the microscopic organisms are developed. Finally, if one of those bulbs which have stood the test of months and years without alteration be several times shaken violently, so that the external air shall rush into it, and if it be then placed once more in the stove, life will soon appear in it.

In 1860 the Academy of Sciences had offered a prize, the conditions ofwhich were stated in the following terms:

'To endeavour by well-contrived experiments to throw new light upon the question of spontaneous generation.' The Academy added that it demanded precise and rigorous experiments equally well studied on all sides; such experiments, in short, as should render it possible to deduce from them results free from all confusion due to the experiments themselves. Pasteur carried away the prize, and no one, it will be acknowledged, deserved it better than he. Nevertheless, to his eyes, the subject was still beset with difficulties. In the hot discussions to which the question of spontaneous generation gave rise, the partisans of the doctrine continually brought forward an objection based on an opinion already referred to, and first enunciated by Gay-Lussac. As already known to the reader, Gay-Lussac had arrived at the conclusion that, in Appert's process, one condition of the preservation of animal and vegetable substances consisted in the exclusion of oxygen.

Even this proposition was soon improved upon, and it became a current opinion in science that the smallest bubble of oxygen or of air which might come in contact with a preserve would be sufficient to start its decomposition. The partisans of spontaneous generation—the heterogenists—thenceforward threw their objections to Pasteur into this form:

'How can the germs of microscopic organisms be so numerous that even the smallest bubble of air contains germs capable of developing themselves in every organic infusion? If such were the case the air would be encumbered with organic germs.' M. Pouchet said and wrote that they would form a thick fog, as dense as iron.

But Pasteur showed that the interpretation of Gay-Lussac's experiment, with respect to the possible alteration of preserves by a small quantity of oxygen gas, was quite erroneous. If, after a certain time, an Appert preserve contains no oxygen, this is simply because the oxygen has been gradually absorbed by the substances of the preserve, which are always more or less chemically oxidisable. But in reality it is easy to find oxygen in these preserves. Pasteur did not fail to perceive that the interpretation given to Gay-Lussac's experiment was wrong in another particular. He proved the fallacy of the assumption that the smallest quantity of air was always capable of producing microscopic organisms.

More thickly spread in towns than in the country, the germs become fewer in proportion as they recede from human habitations. Mountains have fewer than plains, and at a certain height they are very rare.

Pasteur's experiments to prove these facts were extremely simple. He took a series of bulbs of about a quarter of a litre in capacity, and, after having half filled the bulbs with a putrescible liquid, he drew out the necks by means of the blowpipe, then he caused the liquid to boil for some minutes, and during the ebullition, while the steam issued from the tapering ends of the bulbs, he sealed them with the lamp. Thus prepared, the bulbs can be easily transported. As they are empty of air—that which they originally contained having been driven out with the steam—when the sealed end of a bulb is broken off, the air rushes into the tube, carrying with it all the germs which this air holds in suspension. If it is closed again immediately afterwards by a flame, and if the vessels are then left to themselves, it is easy to recognise those in which a change occurs. Now, Pasteur established that, in whatever place the operation might be carried on, a certain number of bulbs would escape alteration. They must not, however, be opened in a room after dusting the furniture or sweeping the floor, for in this case all the bulbs would become altered because of the great quantity of germs raised by the dusting and remaining suspended in the air.

Pasteur started for Arbois with a series of bulbs. Some he opened in the country far from all habitations; others he opened at the foot of the mountains which form the first range of the Jura; a series of twenty-four bulbs was opened upon Mount Poupet, at 850 meters above the level of the sea; and, lastly, twenty others were transported to the Montanvert, near the Mer de Glace, at an elevation of 2,000 meters. He afterwards brought his whole collection back to Paris, and in the month of November, 1860, deposited them on the table at the Academy of Sciences.

Of the twenty bulbs first opened in the country, eight contained organised productions. Of the twenty opened on the heights of the Jura, five only were altered, and of the twenty opened upon the Montanvert during a strong wind which blew from the glacier, one alone was altered.

If a similar series of experiments were made in a balloon, it would be found that the air of the higher atmosphere is absolutely free from germs. Care would, however, be necessary to prevent the introduction of dust particles, which the rigging and the aëronauts themselves might carry with them.

But we have not yet related all. So far, all these conclusive experiments had been made only on organic liquids, very putrescible it is true, but which had all been subjected to boiling or even to temperatures higher than 100 degrees Centigrade. The partisans of spontaneous generation might then be justified in saying that if the precaution had been taken of putting into contact with pure air natural organic liquids in a state compatible with the operations of animal and vegetable life, the results would have been different. Under such conditions, life would have appeared spontaneously in the production of microscopic organisms. None of Pasteur's opponents had formulated this argument; but Pasteur himself, who had within him an adversary always present, always on the alert, prepared to yield only to accumulated proofs, saw this objection. He was not satisfied until he had succeeded in completely refuting it. Having by means of ingenious experimental arrangements deprived some air of all living germs, he placed in contact with this pure air the most putrescible liquids, particularly venous blood, arterial blood, and urine. He took these liquids directly from the veins, the arteries, and the bladders of animals in full health. No alteration was produced. In due time a chemical absorption of small quantities of oxygen took place, but neither fermentation nor putrefaction, nor the smallest development of bacteria, of vibrios, or of mould. After this, Pasteur was able legitimately to exclaim in his celebrated lecture at the Sorbonne:

'There is not one circumstance known at the present day which justifies the assertion that microscopic organisms come into the world without germs or without parents like themselves. Those who maintain the contrary have been the dupes of illusions and of ill-conducted experiments, tainted with errors which they know not how either to perceive or to avoid. Spontaneous generation is a chimera.'

Pasteur was not alone in affirming this fixed conviction. With the authority of a judge delivering sentence in court, M. Flourens, permanent Secretary of the Academy of Sciences, pronounced these words before the whole Academy:

'As long as my opinion was not formed I had nothing to say; now it *is* formed and I can speak. The experiments are decisive. If spontaneous generation be a fact, what is necessary for the production of animalculæ? Air and putrescible liquids. Now Pasteur puts together air and putrescible liquids and nothing is produced. Spontaneous generation, then, has no existence. Those who still doubt have failed to grasp the question.'

But some adversaries remained incredulous. When Pasteur had announced the result of his experiments, and brought before the Academy his series of bulbs, Pouchet and Joly declared that if Pasteur had opened his bulbs in the Jura and on the Mer de Glace, they, on their part, had been on the top of the Maladetta, and had proved there the inexactitude of Pasteur's results.

Pasteur asked to be judged by the Academy. 'A commission alone,' said he, 'will terminate the debate.' The commission was named, and the position on both sides was clearly stated.

'I affirm,' said Pasteur, 'that everywhere it is possible to take from the midst of the atmosphere a certain quantity of air which contains neither egg nor spore, and which does not produce organisms in putrescible solutions.'

On his side, M. Joly wrote: 'If one alone of your bulbs remains unaltered we shall loyally acknowledge our defeat.' Lastly, M. Pouchet, as distinct and positive as M. Pasteur, said: 'I affirm that in whatever place I take a cubic decimeter of air, when this air is placed in contact with a fermentable liquid enclosed in a glass vessel hermetically sealed, the liquid will become filled with living organisms.'

This double declaration, which excited at that time all the learned world, took place in the month of January, 1864. Eager to engage in the combat, Pasteur waited impatiently for the order of the Commission that this experiment, which was to decide everything, should be made. But M. Pouchet begged for a postponement, desiring, he said, to wait for the warm season. Pasteur was astonished, but resigned himself to the delay. The Commission and the opponents met on June 15.

The Commission announced, 'that, as the whole dispute turned upon one simple fact, one single experiment ought to be undertaken, which alone would close the discussion.'

The partisans of spontaneous generation wished nevertheless to go through the entire series of their experiments. In vain the Commission tried to persuade them that this would make the judgment as long as the discussion itself had been, that all bore upon one fact, and that this fact could be decided by a single experiment. The heterogenists would not listen to this. M. Pouchet and M. Joly withdrew from the contest.

M. Jamin, an exact and authorised historian of these debates, observed that 'the heterogenists, however they may have covered their retreat, were thereby self-condemned. If they had been sure of the fact—which they were solemnly engaged to prove, under penalty of acknowledging themselves defeated—they would have hastened to demonstrate it, for it would have been the triumph of their doctrine. People do not allow themselves to be condemned by default except in causes in which they have no confidence.'

STUDIES ON WINE.

Having thus solved the problem of spontaneous generation, a problem which was but a parenthesis forced upon his attention, Pasteur returned to fermentation. Guided by his studies on vinegar and other observations of detail, he undertook an inquiry into the diseases of wine. The explanations of the changes which wine was known to undergo rested only on hypothesis. From the time of Chaptal, who was followed by Liebig and Berzelius, all the world believed wine to be a liquid in which the various constituents react upon each other mutually and slowly. The wine was thought to be continually 'working.' When the fermentation of the grape is finished, equilibrium is not quite established between the diverse elements of the liquor. Time is needed for them to blend together. If this reciprocal action be not regular, the wine becomes bad. This was, in other words, the doctrine of spontaneity. Without support from carefully reasoned experiments, these explanations could not satisfy Pasteur, especially at a moment when he had just been proving that there was nothing spontaneous either in the phenomena of fermentation or in animal and vegetable infusions.

Pasteur tried first of all to show that wine does not 'work' as much as it was supposed to do. Wine being a mixture of different substances, among which are acids and alcohol, particular ethers are no doubt formed in it in course of time, and similar reactions perhaps take place between the other constituents of the liquid. But if the exactitude of such facts cannot be denied, based as they are upon general laws, confirmed and extended by recent inquiries, Pasteur thought that a false application was made of them when they were employed to explain the maladies of wine, the changes which occur in it through age—in a word, the alterations, whether good or bad, which wines are subject to. The 'ageing' of wine soon appeared to him to consist essentially in the phenomena of oxidation, due to the oxygen of the air which dissolves and is diffused in the wine. He gave manifest proofs of this. I will only mention one of them. New wine inclosed in a glass vessel hermetically sealed keeps its freshness; it does not 'work,' it does not 'age.' Pasteur demonstrated besides, that all the processes of wine-making are explained by the double necessity of oxygenising the wine to a suitable degree, and of preventing its deterioration. In seeking for the actual causes of injurious alterations, Pasteur, always obedient to a preconceived idea, while carefully controlling it with the utmost rigour of the experimental method, asked himself whether the diseases of wine did not proceed from organised ferments, from little microscopic vegetations? In the observed alterations, he thought, there must be some influences at work foreign to the normal composition of the wine.

This hypothesis was verified. In his hands the injurious modifications suffered by wines were shown to be correlative with the presence and the multiplication of microscopic vegetations. Such growths alter the wine, either by subtracting from it what they need for their nourishment, or, and principally, by forming new products which are the effect of the multiplication of these parasites in the mass of the wine.

Everyone knows what is meant by *acid wine, sharp wine, sour wine*. The former experiments of Pasteur had clearly shown that no wine can become acid, sharp—can, in a word, become vinegar—without the presence of a little microscopic fungus known by the name of *mycoderma aceti*. This little plant is the necessary agent in the condensation of the oxygen of the air, and its fixation on the alcohol of the wine. Chaptal, who published a volume on the art of wine-making, knew of the existence of these mycoderm flowers; but to his eyes they were only 'elementary forms of vegetation,' which had no influence whatever upon the quality of the liquid. Besides the *mycoderma aceti*, which is the agent of acetification, there is another mycoderm called *mycoderma vini*. This one deposits nothing which is hurtful to the wine, and its flowers are developed by preference in new wines, still immature, and preserving the astringency of the first period of their fabrication.

The requirements of the two sorts of flowers are such that even when the flower of vinegar is sown on the surface of a new wine, no development takes place. Conversely, the *mycoderma vini* sown on wines that have grown old in casks or in bottles will refuse to multiply. The *mycoderma vini* produces no alteration in the wine; it does not turn the wine acid. In proportion as the wine grows old the flower tends to disappear, the wine 'despoils' itself, to use a technical expression; physiologically speaking, the wine loses its aptitude to nourish the *mycoderma vini*, which, finding itself progressively deprived of appropriate nourishment, fades and withers. But it is then that the *mycoderma aceti* appears, and multiplies with a facility so much the greater that it draws its first nourishment from the cells of the *mycoderma vini*. The *mycoderma aceti* has played so large a part in the early pages of this book that it is not necessary to go back upon it here.

There is another disease very common among wines when the great heat of summer begins to make itself felt in the vintage tubs. The wine is said to *turn*, to *rise*, to *spurt*. The wine becomes slightly turbid and at the same time flat and piquant. When it is poured into a glass, very small bubbles of gas form like a crown upon the surface. On placing the glass between the eye and the light and slightly shaking it, one can distinguish silky waves shifting about and moving in different directions in the liquid. When the *turned* wine is in a cask, it is not unusual to see the bottom of the cask bulge a little and sometimes a leakage takes place at the joints of the staves. If a little opening is made, the wine spurts out, and that is the reason why the wine is said to spurt.

Authors who have written on the subject of wine attributed this malady to the rising of the lees. They believed that the deposit which always exists in greater or less quantities in the lower part of the cask rises and spreads itself into all the mass of the wine.

Nothing can be more inexact. If this phenomenon is sometimes produced— that is to say, if the deposit rises into the mass of wine—the effect is due to a sudden diminution of the atmospheric pressure, as in times of storm, for example. As the wine is always charged with carbonic acid gas, which it holds in solution from the moment of fermentation, one can conceive that a lowering of barometric pressure would cause the escape of some bubbles of carbonic acid. These bubbles, rising from the lower part of the cask, may disturb a portion of the deposit, which then mixes with the wine and renders it turbid. But the real cause of the disease is quite different. The turbidity is without exception due to the presence of little filaments of an extreme tenuity, about a thousandth part of a millimeter in diameter. Their length is very variable. It is these which, when the wine is agitated, give rise to the silky waves just referred to. Often the deposit of the casks leaves a swarm of these filaments entangled in each other, forming a glutinous mass, which under the microscope is seen to be composed entirely of these little filaments. In acting upon certain constituents of the wine particularly upon the tartar, this ferment generates carbonic acid. The phenomenon of spurting is then produced, because when the cask is closed the internal pressure of the liquid augments. The sparkling and the crown of little gas-bubbles, observed when the turned wine is poured out into a glass, is similarly explained. In a word, the disease of turned wine is nothing else than a fermentation, due to an organised ferment which, without any doubt, proceeds originally from germs existing on the surface of the grapes at the moment of gathering them, or on spoilt grapes such as are found in every vintage. It is very rare not to find this parasite of turned wine in the deposit of the wine at the bottom of the casks, but the parasite is not troublesome unless it multiplies very largely. Pasteur found the means of preventing this multiplication by a very simple remedy, equally applicable to other diseases of wines, such as that of bitterness or greasiness (*maladie de la graisse*).

Many wines acquire with age a more or less bitter taste, sometimes to a degree which renders them unfit for consumption. Red wines, without exception, are subject to this disease. It attacks by preference wines of the best growth, and particularly the finest wines of the Côte-d'Or. It is once more a little filamented fungus which works the change; and not only does it cause in the wine a bitterness which little by little deprives it of all its better qualities, but it forms in the bottles a deposit which never adheres to the glass, but renders the wine muddy or turbid. It is in this deposit that the filaments of the fungus float. If white wines do not suffer from this disease of bitterness, they are exposed, particularly the white wines of Orleans and of the basin of the Loire, to the disease of greasiness. The wines lose their limpidity; they become flat and insipid and viscous, like oil when poured out. The disease declares itself in the casks or in the best-corked bottles. M. Pasteur has discovered that the greasiness of wines is likewise produced by a special ferment, which the microscope shows to be formed of filaments, like the ferments of the preceding diseases, but differing in structure from the other organisms, and in their physiological action on the wine.

In short, according to Pasteur's observations, the deterioration of wines should not in any case be attributed to a natural working of the constituents of the wine, proceeding from a sort of interior spontaneous movement, which would only be affected by variations of temperature or atmospheric pressure. They are, on the contrary, exclusively dependent on the development of microscopic organisms, the germs of which exist in the wine from the moment of the original fermentation which gave it birth. What vast multitudes of germs of every kind must there not be introduced into every vintage tub! What modifications do we not meet with in the leaves and in the fruit of each individual spoilt vine! How numerous are the varieties of organic dust to be found on the stems of the bunches, on the surface of the grapes, on the implements of the grape gatherers! What varieties of moulds and mildews! A vast proportion of these germs are evidently sterilised by the wine, whose composition, being at the same time acid, alcoholic, and devoid of air, is so little favourable to life. But is it to be wondered at that some of these exterior germs, so numerous, and possessing in a more or less marked degree the anaerobic character, should find at certain moments, in the state of the wine, the right conditions for their existence and multiplication?

The cause of these alterations having been found, a mode of preventing the development of all these parasites had still to be sought. Pasteur's first endeavour was to discover some substance which would be antagonistic to the life of these ferments of disease, while harmless to the wine itself, and devoid of any special smell or taste. But in this research success was dependent on too many conditions to be easily attainable. After some fruitless trials, the thought occurred to Pasteur of having recourse to heat. He soon ascertained that, to secure wine from all ulterior changes, it sufficed to raise it, for some instants only, to a temperature of from fifty-five to sixty degrees. His experiments were first directed upon the disease of 'bitterness.' He procured some of the best wines of Burgundy, wines of Beaune, and of Pomard, of different years—1858, 1862, and 1863. Twenty-five bottles were left standing forty-eight hours to allow all the particles suspended in the wine to settle; for, however clear wine may be, it always produces a slight deposit. Pasteur then decanted the wine with minute care, by means of a syphon of slow delivery. This last precaution was necessary to prevent the deposit from being stirred up. When there remained in each bottle only one cubic centimeter of liquid, Pasteur shook the bottle, and then examined with the microscope the residue of each bottle. He perceived in each case distinct filaments of ferment. The wines, however, were not in the least bitter to the taste, but the germs of a possible evil were there—an evil which would have been first detected by the palate when the little fungus had fully developed.

Without uncorking it, Pasteur then heated a bottle of each of these wines. The heating was carried to a temperature of sixty degrees (140° Fahr.). After the cooling of the bottles he laid them by the side of other unheated bottles of the same wines in a cellar, the temperature of which varied in summer between thirteen and seventeen degrees. Every fifteen days Pasteur inspected them. Without uncorking the bottles, he held them up against the light, so that he could see the sediment at the bottom of each bottle, and thus detect the least formation of deposit. In less than six weeks, particularly in the wine of 1863, a very perceptible floating deposit began to form in all the unheated bottles. These deposits gradually augmented, and on examining them with the microscope they were seen to be formed of organised filaments, mixed sometimes with a little colouring matter which had become insoluble. No deposit appeared in the heated bottles.

The idea of heating wines does not belong to Pasteur. Those who love to search into questions of priority will find described in the works of Latin agriculturists various methods for the preservation of wine, based on the employment of heat. To give the wine durability, they sometimes added to the vintage variable quantities of boiled must, reduced to half or two thirds, in which orris, myrrh, cinnamon, white resin, and other ingredients, were infused. But, to cite examples nearer our own time, Appert, whose preserves have become so popular, relates that he sent to St. Domingo some bottles of Beaune which had been previously heated to seventy degrees, and that he compared, on their return into France, two bottles of this wine with a bottle which had remained at Havre, and also with other bottles of the same wine which had remained in his cellar, neither of which had undergone the operation of heating. The superiority of the wine which came from St. Domingo, said Appert, was incontestable. Nothing could equal its delicacy or its perfume. But Appert did not by any means describe the wine of the two bottles which remained in France as either injured or diseased. His remark was based upon an incomplete observation. It simply stated the fact, which indeed was previously known, that a long voyage, added to the employment of heat, had an excellent effect upon the Beaune. This incident had been so completely forgotten, that it was only in 1865 that Pasteur, during the historical researches which preceded his 'Etudes sur le vin,' accidentally met with this story of the bottles of St. Domingo, and hastened to communicate it to the Academy. But in reference to this question of heating, a discussion arose as to priority, which was quite unexpected by him. A Burgundian wine grower, M. de Vergnette, having first proposed the congealing of wines as a protective influence, had afterwards spoken, without much precision, of heat as another means of preservation. On this ground he claimed for himself a great part of the invention of Pasteur's process. 'If, after having subjected some specimens of wines which are to be sent abroad to the ordeal of heating,' said M. de Vergnette, 'one sees that they have been able to resist the action of the heat, then they may safely be shipped. In the contrary case they ought not to be sent.' According to M. de Vergnette, it was to the composition of the wine, its robust condition, and good constitution, that it owed its power of supporting the heating process. Pasteur had no difficulty in demonstrating that these assertions are contradicted by experiment. Wine never changes by the moderate application of heat when air is excluded; and it is precisely when of doubtful soundness that it should be subjected to the process of heating. This operation does not alter it any more than would be the case if it were in a perfectly healthy state. All wines may undergo the action of heat without the least deterioration, and one minute's heating at the proper temperature suffices to insure the preservation of every kind of wine. Thanks to this operation, the weakest wine, the most disposed to turn sour, to become greasy, or to be threatened with bitterness, is insured against injurious change.

Nothing is more simple than to realise the condition of heating in bottles. After having firmly tied down the corks, the bottles are placed in a water- bath. An iron basket is here useful. The water ought to rise up to the wire of the cork. Among these bottles is placed a bottle of water, into which the bulb of a thermometer is plunged. The bath being heated, as soon as the thermometer marks fifty or sixty degrees Centigrade, the basket is withdrawn. The subsequent soundness of the wine is thus insured.

But if Pasteur had overlooked nothing in his efforts to prevent or arrest the evil changes of wine, he still saw that full confidence was not felt in the efficacy of a process which must, it was thought, damage the taste, or the colour, or the limpidity of the wine. After having invited the judgment of people in society, whose preference, if they felt any, was generally for the heated wines, Pasteur wished to have a more decisive opinion. He addressed himself first to wine merchants and others practised in detecting the smallest peculiarities of wines; and afterwards he organised a grand experiment in tasting. On November 16, 1865, a sub-commission, nominated by the representative commission of the wholesale wine-sellers of Paris, repaired to the École Normale and examined a considerable number of specimens. After a series of tastings, which recognised, if not a superiority over the heated wines, at least a shade of imperceptible flavour, which, however, it was admitted, would escape nine-tenths of the consumers, Pasteur, fearing that there remained still in the mind of the majority of the commission a slight prejudice against the operation of heating, and that imagination, moreover, had some share in determining shades of flavour, proposed that at the next sitting there should be no indication which of the samples of wine had been heated and which had not. The commission, having no other desire than to arrive at the truth, at once accepted this proposition.

The resulting uncertainty as to whether the heated or the unheated wines were to be preferred was so absolute as to be comical. It is unnecessary to say that the heated wines had not experienced the least alteration. At a certain point Pasteur, who was astonished at the extraordinary delicacy of the palate of these tasters, employed a little trickery. He offered them two specimens absolutely identical, taken out of the same bottle. There were preferences, very slight it is true, but preferences gravely expressed for one or the other glass. The commission, making allusion in its report to this special tasting experiment, was the first to allow with a good grace that the differences between the heated and non-heated wines were insignificant, imperceptible if they existed, and that the imagination—added the report—was not without considerable influence in the tasting; since the members of the commission had themselves fallen into a little experimental snare.

Thus Pasteur, after having revealed the causes which determine the alterations of wines, had found the means of practically neutralising them. By the application of heat, and without producing any change in the colour or flavour of the wines, he had been able to insure their limpidity, and to render them capable of being indefinitely preserved in well-closed vessels. If these wines, being afterwards exposed too long to the air, were again threatened with alteration, it was because the air brought to them new living germs of those ferments which had been destroyed by the heat. But germs from this source are so trifling compared with those contained in the wine itself, that one may almost say the heating process renders the wine unalterable even after it has been rebottled in contact with the air. Thus, by a series of experiments which left nothing to chance, one of the greatest economic questions of the day was solved. Wines could be kept or transported into all countries without losing their flavour or their perfume. These experiments of the laboratory were destined to have an extensive application; for very soon arrangements were made for heating wine in barrels, the inquiry thereby assuming the proportions of a public benefit.

THE SILKWORM-DISEASE.

The life of the population of certain departments in the South of France hangs on the existence of silkworms. In each house there is nothing to be seen but hurdles, over which the worms crawl. They are placed even in the kitchens, and often in well-to-do families they occupy the best rooms. In the largest cultivations, regular stages of these hurdles are raised one above the other in immense sheds, under roofs of disjointed tiles, where thousands and thousands of silkworms crawl upon the litters which they have the instinct never to leave. Great or small, the silkworm-rearing establishments exist everywhere. When people accost each other, instead of saying 'How are you?' they say 'How are the silkworms?' In the night they get up to feed them or to keep up around them a suitable temperature. And then what anxiety is felt at the least change of weather! Will not the mulberry leaves be wet? Will the worms digest well? Digestion is a matter of great importance to the health of the worms, which do nothing all their lives but eat! Their appetites become especially insatiable during the last days of rearing. All the world is then astir, day and night. Sacks of leaves are incessantly brought in and spread out on the litters. Sometimes the noise of the worms munching these leaves resembles that of rain falling upon thick bushes. With what impatience is the moment waited for when the worms arrive at the last moulting! Their bodies swollen with silk, they mount upon the brambles prepared for them, there they shut themselves up in their golden prisons and become chrysalides. What days of rejoicing are those in which the cocoons are gathered; when, to use the words of Olivier de Serres, the silk harvest is garnered in!

Just as in all agricultural harvests, this ingathering of the silk is exposed to many risks. Nearly always, however, it pays the cultivator for his trouble, and sometimes pays him largely. But in 1849, after an exceptionally good year, and without any atmospheric conditions to account for the fact, a number of cultivations entirely broke down. A disease which little by little took the proportions of an epidemic fell upon the silkworm nurseries. Worms hardly hatched, and worms arrived at the last moulting, were equally stricken in large numbers. It mattered little in what phase the silkworm happened to be: in all it was assailable by the evil.

There is hardly a schoolboy who has not reared in the recesses of his desk some five or six silkworms, feeding them, in default of mulberry leaves, with leaves of lettuce or salsify. Therefore it is hardly necessary to remind my readers how the silkworm is born, grows, and is transformed. Coming out of its egg, which is called a grain, because of its resemblance to a small vegetable seed, the silkworm appears in the first fine days of spring. It does not then weigh more than one or two milligrammes. Little by little its size and its activity augment. The seventh day after its birth it rests on a leaf and appears to sleep. It remains thus for nearly thirty hours. Presently, its head moves, as if it did not belong to the rest of the body, and under the skin of this head appears a second quite new head. Just as if it came out of a case, the silkworm disengages itself from its old withered skin. Here are its front feet, there the false feet (*fausses pattes*), which it carries behind. At length the worm is quite complete. It rests a while and then begins to eat. At the end of a few days new sleep, new skin, new shedding of the skin, then a third, and then a fourth metamorphosis. About eight days after the fourth shedding of its skin, the worm ceases to eat, its body becomes more slender, more transparent; it seeks to leave its litter, it raises its head and appears uneasy. Some twigs of dried heather are then arranged for it to fasten upon; these it climbs, never to descend again. It spins its cocoon and becomes a chrysalis. When the worms of a cultivation have all spun their cocoons, they are smothered in a steam stove, and, after being dried in the sun, they are handed over to the spinners. If it is desired to reserve some of the cocoons for seed, instead of being smothered, they are strung together in chaplets. After about three weeks, the moth comes out of its chrysalis. It pierces the cocoon by means of a liquid which issues from its mouth, and which has the property of so softening the silk that the moth is able to pass through the cocoon. It has hardly dried itself and developed its wings when the males and females pair for several hours. Then the females lay their eggs, of which they can produce from four to six hundred. These are all the phases through which silkworms pass in the space of two months.

In the epidemic which ravaged the silkworm nurseries in 1849 the symptoms were numerous and changeable. Sometimes the disease exhibited itself immediately. Many of the eggs were sterile, or the worms died during the first days of their existence. Often the hatching was excellent, and the worms arrived at their first moulting, but that moulting was a failure. A great number of the worms, taking little nourishment at each repast, remained smaller than the others, having a rather shining appearance and a blackish tint. Instead of all the worms going through the phases of this first moulting together, as is usually the case in a batch of silkworms, they began to present a marked inequality, which displayed itself more and more at each successive moulting. Instead of the worms swarming on the tables, as if their number was uniformly augmenting, empty spaces were everywhere seen; every morning corpses were collected on the litters.

Sometimes the disease manifested itself under still more painful circumstances. The batch would progress favourably to the third, and even to the fourth moulting, the uniform size and the health of the worms leaving nothing to be desired; but after the fourth moulting the alarm of the husbandman began. The worms did not turn white, they retained a rusty tint, their appetite diminished, they even turned away from the leaves which were offered to them. Spots appeared on their bodies, black bruises irregularly scattered over the head, the rings, the false feet, and the spur. Here and there dead worms were to be seen. On lifting the litter, numbers of corpses would be found. Every batch attacked was a lost batch. In 1850 and 1851 there were renewed failures. Some cultivators, discouraged, attributed these accidents to bad eggs, and got their supplies from abroad.

At first everything went as well as could be wished. The year 1853, in which many of these eggs were reared in France, was one of the most productive of the century. As many as twenty-six millions of kilogrammes of cocoons were collected, which produced a revenue of 130,000,000 francs. But the year following, when the eggs produced by the moths of these fine crops of foreign origin were tried, a singular degeneracy was immediately recognised. The eggs were of no more value than the French eggs. It was in fact a struggle with an epidemic. How was it to be arrested? Would it be always necessary to have recourse to foreign seed? and what if the epidemic spread into Italy, Spain, and the other silk cultivating countries?

The thing dreaded came to pass. The plague spread; Spain and Italy were smitten. It became necessary to seek for eggs in the Islands of the Archipelago, in Greece, or in Turkey. These eggs, at first very good, became infected in their turn in their native country; the epidemic had spread even to that distance. The eggs were then procured from Syria and the provinces of the Caucasus. The plague followed the trade in the eggs. In 1864 all the cultivations, from whatever corner of Europe they came, were either diseased or suspected of being so. In the extreme East, Japan alone still remained healthy.

Agricultural societies, governments, all the world was preoccupied with this scourge and its invading march. It was said to be some malady like cholera which attacked the silkworms. Hundreds of pamphlets were published each year. The most foolish remedies were proposed, as quite infallible—from flowers of sulphur, cinders, and soot spread over the worms, or over the leaves of the mulberry, to gaseous fumigations of chlorine, of tar, and of sulphurous acid. Wine, rum, absinthe, were prescribed for the worms, and after the absinthe it was advised to try creosote and nitrate of silver. In 1863 the Minister of Agriculture signed an agreement with an Italian who had offered for purchase a process destined to combat the disease of the silkworms, by which he (the Minister) engaged himself, in case the efficacy of the remedy was established, to pay 500,000 francs as an indemnity to the Italian silk cultivator. Experiments were instituted in twelve departments, but without any favourable result. In 1865 the weight of the cocoons had fallen to four million kilogrammes. This entailed a loss of 100,000,000 francs.

The Senate was assailed by a despairing petition signed by 3,600 mayors, municipal councillors, and capitalists of the silk-cultivating departments. The great scientific authority of M. Dumas, his knowledge of silk husbandry, his sympathy for one of the departments most severely smitten, the Gard, his own native place, all contributed to cause him to be nominated Reporter of the Commission. While drawing up his report the idea occurred to him of trying to persuade Pasteur to undertake researches as to the best means of combating the epidemic.

Pasteur at first declined this offer. It was at the moment when the results of his investigations on organised ferments opened to him a wide career; it was at the time when, as an application of his latest studies, he had just recognised the true theory of the fabrication of vinegar, and had discovered the cause of the diseases of wines; it was, in short, at the moment when, after having thrown light upon the question of spontaneous generation, the infinitely little appeared infinitely great. He saw living ferments present everywhere, whether as agents of decomposition employed to render back to the atmosphere all that had lived, or as direct authors of contagious maladies. And now it was proposed to him to quit this path, where his footing was sure, which offered him an unlimited horizon in all directions, to enter on an unknown road, perhaps without an outlet. Might he not expose himself to the loss of months, perhaps of years, in barren efforts?

M. Dumas insisted. 'I attach,' said he to his old pupil, now become his colleague and his friend, 'an extreme value to your fixing your attention upon the question which interests my poor country. Its misery is beyond anything that you can imagine.'

'But consider,' said Pasteur, 'that I have never handled a silkworm.'

'So much the better,' replied M. Dumas. 'If you know nothing about the subject, you will have no other ideas than those which come to you from your own observations.'

Pasteur allowed himself to be persuaded, less by the force of these arguments than by the desire to give his illustrious master a proof of his profound deference.

As soon as the promise was given and the resolution made to go to the South, Pasteur thought over the method to be employed in the pursuit of the problem. Certainly, amidst the labyrinth of facts and opinions, it was not hypotheses which were wanting. For seventeen years they had been rising up on all sides.

One of the most recent and the most comprehensive memoirs upon the terrible epidemic had been presented to the Academy of Sciences by M. de Quatrefages. One paragraph of this paper had forcibly struck Pasteur. M. de Quatrefages related that some Italian naturalists, especially Filippi and Cornalia, had discovered in the worms and moths of the silkworm minute corpuscles visible only with the microscope. The naturalist Lebert affirmed that they might always be detected in diseased silkworms. Dr. Osimo, of Padua, had even perceived corpuscles in some of the silkworms' eggs, and Dr. Vittadini had proposed to examine the eggs with a microscope in order to secure having sound ones. M. de Quatrefages only mentioned this matter of the corpuscles as a passing remark, being doubtful of its importance, and perhaps of its accuracy. This doubt might have removed from Pasteur's mind the thought of examining the significance of these little corpuscles, but, amid the general confusion of opinions, Pasteur was attracted to the study of these little bodies all the more readily because it related to an organic element which was visible only with the microscope. This instrument had already rendered such services to Pasteur in his delicate experiments on ferments, that he was fascinated by the thought of resuming it again as a means of research.

I.

On June 6, 1865, Pasteur started for Alais. The emotion he felt on the actual spot where the plague raged in all its force, in the presence of a problem requiring solution, caused him at once to forget the sacrifices he had made in quitting his laboratory at the École Normale. He determined not to return to Paris until he had exhausted all the subjects requiring study, and had triumphed over the plague.

In a few hours after his arrival he had already proved the presence of corpuscles in certain worms, and was able to show them to the President and several members of the Agricultural Committee, who had never seen them. The following day he installed himself in a little house three kilometers from Alais. Two small cultures were there going on; they were nearly the last, the cocoons had all been spun. One of these cultures, proceeding from eggs imported that very year from Japan, had succeeded very well. The other, proceeding also from Japanese eggs which had been reproduced in the country, had arrived at their fourth moulting and had a very bad appearance. But, strange to say, on examining with the microscope a number of chrysalides and moths of the group which had so delighted its proprietor, Pasteur found corpuscles almost always present, whereas the examination of the worms of the bad group only exhibited them occasionally. This double result struck Pasteur as very strange. He at once sent messengers into all the neighbourhood of Alais to seek for the remains of backward cultivations. He attached extreme importance to ascertaining whether the presence of corpuscles in the chrysalides or moths of the good groups, and the absence of the same corpuscles in the worms of the bad groups, was an accidental or a general fact. He soon recognised that these results did very frequently occur. But what would happen when the worms of the bad group spun their cocoons? Pasteur found that in the chrysalides, especially in the old ones, the corpuscles were numerous. As regards the moths proceeding from these cocoons, not one was free from them, and they existed in profusion.

Following up the idea that a connection between the disease and the corpuscles might possibly exist, as other observers had previously imagined, Pasteur declared, in a Note presented to the Agricultural Committee of Alais on June 26, 1865, twenty days after his arrival, that it was a mistake to seek for the corpuscle in the eggs or in the worms. Both the one and the other could carry in them the germ of the disease, without exhibiting distinct corpuscles, visible under the microscope. The evil developed itself especially in the chrysalides and in the moths, and it was in them that search should be made. Finally, Pasteur came to the conclusion that the only infallible method of procuring healthy eggs must be by having recourse to moths free from corpuscles.

Pasteur hastened to apply this new method of obtaining pure eggs. Notwithstanding that the malady was universally prevalent, he succeeded, after several days of assiduous microscopic observations, in finding some moths free from corpuscles. He carefully preserved their eggs, as well as other eggs which had proceeded from very corpusculous couples, intending to wait for what these eggs would produce the following year; the first would be probably free from corpuscles, while the latter would contain them. He would thus have in future, though on a small scale, samples of originally healthy and of originally unhealthy cultivations, by the comparison of which with the cultivations of the trade—all more or less smitten with the evil—totally new views might be expected to emerge. Who can tell, thought Pasteur, whether the prosperity of the silk cultivation may not depend on the practical application of this production of pure eggs by means of moths free from corpuscles?

Scarcely had Pasteur made known, first to the Committee of Alais, and then to the Academy of Sciences, the results of his earliest observations and the inductions to which they pointed, when critics without number arose on all sides. It was objected that the labours of several Italian *savants* had established beyond all doubt that the corpuscles were a normal element of certain worms, and especially of all the moths when old; that other authors had affirmed it to be sufficient to starve certain worms to make these famous corpuscles appear in all their tissues; and that Dr. Gaetano Cantoni had already tried some cultivations with eggs coming from moths without corpuscles, and that he had totally failed.

'Your efforts will be vain,' wrote the celebrated Italian entomologist Cornalia; 'your selected eggs will produce healthy worms, but these worms will become sickly through the influence of the epidemic demon which reigns everywhere.'

Anyone but Pasteur would have been staggered, but he was not the man to allow himself to be discouraged by *à priori* opinions, and by assertions which were more or less guesswork. He was resolved not to abandon his preconceived idea until experiment had pronounced upon it with precision. All scientific research, in order to be undertaken and followed up with success, should have, as point of departure, a preconceived idea, an hypothesis which we must seek to verify by experiment. To judge of the value of the facts which Pasteur had just announced, it was necessary to know if there existed the relation of cause and effect between the corpuscles and the disease. This was the great point to be elucidated.

But if, without preliminary groping, he had discovered the way to be pursued, Pasteur subsequently brought to bear his rare prudence as an experimentalist. For five years he returned annually for some months to Alais. The little house nestling among the trees called Pont-Guisquet became at the same time his habitation and his silkworm nursery. It is hemmed in by mountains, up the sides of which terraces rise, one above the other, planted with mulberry trees. The solitude was profound. Madame Pasteur and her daughter constituted themselves silkworm-rearers—performing their part in earnest, not only gathering the leaves of the mulberry trees, but also taking part in all the experiments. The assistants of the École Normale, Duclaux, Maillot, Gernez, and Raulin, grouped themselves around their master. Thus, in an out-of-the-way corner of the Cévennes was formed a colony seeking with ardour the solution of an obscure problem, and the means of curing or preventing a disease which had for so long a time blighted one of the great sources of the national wealth.

One of the first cares of Pasteur was to settle the question as to the contagion of the disease. Many hypotheses had been formed regarding this contagion, but few experiments had been made, and none of them were decisive. Opinions were also very much divided. Some considered that contagion was certain; the majority, however, either doubted or denied its existence; some considered it as accidental. It was said, for example, that the evil was not contagious by itself, but that it became so through the presence and complication of other diseases which were themselves contagious. This hypothesis was convenient, and it enabled contradictory facts to be explained. If some persons had seen healthy worms, which had been mixed up either by mistake or intention with sickly ones, perish, and if they insisted on contagion, others forthwith replied by diametrically opposite observations.

But whatever the divergences of opinion might be, everyone at all events believed in the existence of a poisonous medium rendered epidemic by some occult influence. Pasteur soon succeeded, by accurate experiments, in proving absolutely that the evil was contagious.

One of the first experiments was as follows. After their first moulting, he took some very sound worms free from corpuscles, and fed them with corpusculous matter, which he prepared in the following simple manner. He pounded up a silkworm in a little water, and passed a paint-brush dipped in this liquid over the whole surface of the leaves. During several days there was not the least appearance of disease in the worms fed on those leaves; they reached their second moulting at the same time as the standard worms which had not been infected. The second moulting was accomplished without any drawback. This was a proof that all the worms, those infected as well as the standard lot, had taken the same amount of nourishment. The parasite was apparently not present. Matters remained in this state for some days longer. Even the third moulting was got through without any marked difference between the two groups of worms. But soon important changes set in. The corpuscles, which had hitherto only showed themselves in the integuments of the intestines, began to appear in the other organs. From the second day following the third moulting—that is to say, the twelfth after the infection—a visible inequality distinguished the infected from the non-infected worms. Those of the standard lot were clearly in much the best health. On examining the infected worms through a magnifying glass, a multitude of little spots were discovered on their heads, and on the rings of their bodies, which had not before shown themselves. These spots appeared on the exterior skin when the interior skin of the intestinal canal contained a considerable number of corpuscles. It was these corpuscles that impeded the digestive functions, and interfered with the assimilation of the food. Hence arose the inequality of size of the worms. After the fourth moulting, the same type of disease was noticed as that which was breaking out everywhere in the silkworm nurseries, especially the symptom of spots on the skin, which had led to the disease being called *pébrine*. The peasants said that the worms were peppered. The majority of the worms were full of corpuscles. Those which spun their cocoons produced chrysalides which were nothing but corpusculous pulp, if such a term be allowed.

It was thus proved that the corpuscles, introduced into the intestinal canal at the same time as the food of the worms, convey the infection into the intestinal canal, and progressively into all the tissues. The malady had in certain cases a long period of incubation, since it was only on the twelfth day that it became perceptible. Finally, the spots of *pébrine* on the skin, far from being the disease itself, were but the effect of the corpuscles developed in the interior; they were but a sign, already removed from the true seat of the evil. 'If these spots of *pébrine*,' thought Pasteur, 'were considered in conjunction with certain human maladies in which spots and irruptions appear on the body, what interesting inductions might present themselves to minds prepared to receive them!'

Pasteur was never tired of repeating this curious experiment, or of varying its conditions. Sometimes he introduced the corpusculous food into healthy worms at their birth, sometimes at the second or third moulting. Occasionally, when the worms were about to spin their cocoons, the corpusculous food was given them. All the disasters that were known to have happened in the silkworm nurseries, their extent and their varied forms, were faithfully reproduced. Pasteur created at will any required manifestation of *pébrine*. When he infected quite healthy worms, after their fourth moulting, with fresh corpusculous matter, these worms, even after several meals of corpusculous leaves alternated with meals of wholesome leaves, made their cocoons. It might have been supposed that in this case the contagion had not taken effect. This was but a deceptive appearance. The communication of the disease exhibited itself in a marked degree in the chrysalides and in the moths. Many of the chrysalides died before they turned into moths, and their bodies might be said to be entirely composed of corpuscles. Such moths as were formed, and which emerged from their cocoons, had a most miserable appearance. The disease sometimes went so far as to render breeding and the laying of eggs impossible.

Faithful to the rules prescribed by the experimental method, Pasteur was careful to reproduce these same experiments with the worms of the standard lot, from which all infected worms had been selected. He fed these healthy worms on leaves over which a clear infusion made from the remains of moths or worms exempt from corpuscles had been spread with a paint-brush, instead of leaves contaminated with corpusculous remains. This food kept the worms in their usual health. Could there be a better proof that the corpuscles alone were the real cause of the *pébrine* disease?

These experiments, I repeat, threw a strong light on the nature of the disease, and exactly accounted for what took place in the industrial cultivations. From the malady which attacked the worms at their birth, decimating a whole cultivation, down to the invisible disease that may be said to inclose itself in the cocoon, all was now explained. One of the effects of the plague which had most excited the surprise and thwarted the efforts of cultivators was the impossibility of finding productive eggs, even when they tried to obtain them from the cocoons of groups which had succeeded perfectly well as far as the production of cocoons was concerned. It was proved that almost invariably the following year the eggs of these fine-looking groups were unproductive. Numbers of the agricultural boards, and practitioners, not being able to believe in the existence of the disease in collections that were so satisfactory as regards the abundance and beauty of the cocoons, persisted in thinking that the failures had an origin not connected with the seed itself. This resulted in deception after deception, often even in mistakes that were much to be regretted. Frequently the best husbandmen were known to reserve for the production of eggs some very fine cultivations, not having observed in the worms either spots of *pébrine* or corpuscles even up to the time when the mounting of the brambles had been accomplished; and the year following they had the pain of seeing all the cultivations from these eggs perish. These circumstances, so well calculated to produce discouragement and to give the disease a mysterious character, met with their natural explanation in the facts proved by experimental infection.

Still, as it never occurs to the cultivator to infect the worms directly by giving them food charged with corpusculous débris, it might be asked how, in the industrial establishments, such results can be produced. Pasteur lost no time in solving this difficulty.

In a cultivation containing corpusculous worms these worms perpetually furnish contagious matter, which falls upon the leaf and fouls it. This is the excreta of the worms, which the microscope shows to be more or less filled with corpuscles drawn from the lining of the intestinal canal. It is there that they swarm. It is easy to understand that these excreta, falling on the leaves, contaminate them all the more easily because the worms, by the weight of their bodies in crawling, press the excreta against the leaves. This is one cause of natural contagion. By the excreta of corpusculous worms which he crushed, mixed with water, and spread with a paint-brush over the mulberry leaves intended for a single meal, Pasteur was able to communicate the contagion to as many worms as he liked.

He also indicated another natural and direct cause of contagion. The six fore-feet of the worm have sharp hooks at their ends, by means of which the worms prick each other's skins. Let any one imagine a healthy worm passing over the body of the corpusculous worm. The hooks of the first worm, by penetrating the skin of the second, are liable to be soiled by the corpuscles immediately below that skin; and these hooks are capable of carrying the seeds of disease to other healthy worms, which may be pricked in their turn. To demonstrate experimentally, as Pasteur did, the existence of this cause of contagion, it was only necessary to take some worms and allow them to wound each other. Lastly, infection at a distance, through the medium of the air and the dust it carries, is a fact equally well established. It is sufficient, by sweeping the breeding-houses, or by shaking the hurdles, to stir up the dust of corpusculous excretions and the dried remains of dead worms, and to allow them to be spread over the hurdles of the healthy worms, to cause, after a certain time, contagion to appear among these worms. When very healthy worms were placed in a breeding nursery at a considerable distance from unhealthy worms, they, in their turn, became infected.

After so many decisive experiments it was no longer possible not to see in *pébrine* an essentially contagious disease. Nevertheless, among facts invoked in favour of non-contagion, there was one which it was difficult to explain. There existed several examples of successful cultivations conducted in nurseries which had totally failed from the effects of *pébrine* the year before. The explanation is, as shown by Pasteur, that the dust can only act as a contagion when it is fresh. Corpusculous matter, when thoroughly dried, loses its virulence. A few weeks suffice to render such matter inoffensive: hence the dust of one year is not injurious to the cultivations of the next year. The corpuscles contained in the eggs intended for future cultivation alone cause the transmission of the disease to future generations.

And what can be more easily understood than the presence of corpusculous parasites in the egg? The egg comes into existence during that marvellous phase of the life of a silkworm when, after having spun its cocoon, it sleeps within it as a chrysalis, resolving itself, so to speak, into those kinds of albumen and yelk from which the fully-formed moth will emerge, as a chick emerges from its egg. Let anyone imagine this origin of an approaching life, no longer in its normal purity, but associated with a parasite which will find in the materials surrounding it, so adapted to life and transformation, the elements of its own nourishment and multiplication. This parasite will be present when the eggs of the female moth, tender and soft as albumen, begin to define their outlines. Woe betide those eggs if they then enclose any particles of corpuscle, or of its original matrix. In vain will the envelope of those eggs become by degrees hard and horny; the enemy is within, and later on he will be discovered in the embryo of the silkworm.

Thus this terrible plague is at the same time contagious and hereditary, helping us to understand the evolution of this double character in certain maladies both of men and animals.

II.

The first time Pasteur went to Alais the silkworm epidemic was universally attributed to a single cause—*pébrine*. *Pébrine* was called *the disease*. This word expressed everything. It indicated the existence of a mysterious scourge, the origin and nature of which could not be traced, but which was ready to fall upon all the establishments devoted to the nurture of the worms. Whatever might happen, or whatever might be the cause of ruin in a silkworm nursery, *the disease* was held responsible. One of the most striking proofs that the evil was attributed to *pébrine* alone is found in the fact that a prize of 5,000 florins was offered by the Austrian Government in 1868, as a reward for the discovery of the best remedy for the prevention and cure of *pébrine*—'the epidemic disease which devastates the silkworm.'

A rapid glance at the principles which have just been established suffices to show that *pébrine* might now be regarded as vanquished. Pasteur had demonstrated that moths free from corpuscles never produced a single corpusculous egg; he had proved, moreover, that eggs brought up in a state of isolation, at a distance from contaminated eggs, produce no worms, chrysalides, or moths which are corpusculous. It was easy, therefore, to multiply cultivations free from *pébrine*. The production of silk and the production of eggs was thus secured. To make sure that the eggs were pure it was only necessary to have recourse to the microscopic examination of the moths which had produced them. These observations might be made by women, by young girls, even by children. It was sufficient to crush up a moth in a little water, and to put a drop of this mixture under the microscope, to see the corpuscles clearly, if they existed. It seemed, then, that the plague was got rid of. But Pasteur was not slow in recognising that the general belief in a single malady could not be justified. If the experiments of 1866 had demonstrated to him the full extent of the corpusculous malady, and had established the principles of a treatment proper for its prevention, the method he had adopted had also shown him that *pébrine* was far from being the only cause from which the silk culture suffered.

It was in 1867 that this result was obtained. From an experimental point of view, that year counted double for Pasteur. Influenced by a profound sympathy for the misery which he had witnessed during two successive years, and, at the same time, impatient to find the cause of the scourge, Pasteur, in the months of February, March, and April, in advance of the great industrial cultivations, commenced a series of experiments on worms hatched by artificial heat, and fed with mulberry leaves from a hothouse.

During these forced experiments Pasteur observed that out of sixteen broods derived from non-corpusculous parents, fifteen succeeded, while the sixteenth perished almost entirely between the fourth moulting and the climbing on to the brambles. After having exhibited a most healthful appearance, the worms died suddenly. In a cultivation of 100 worms, ten, fifteen, twenty dead ones were picked up daily: these turned black, and became putrid with extraordinary rapidity, often within the space of twenty-four hours. Sometimes they were soft and flabby, like an empty, crumpled intestine. Consulting the authors who had written upon silkworms, Pasteur could not doubt that he had before his eyes a characteristic specimen of the disease called *morts-flats*, or *flacherie*. Not only were these worms free from all *pébrine* spots, but no corpuscles were to be found in any part of their bodies. A still more significant fact was, that corpuscles were also absent from the chrysalides and the moths of those few worms which were able to spin their cocoons. Although this sample was confined to a single group of eggs derived from parents free from corpuscles, Pasteur continued to entertain doubts as to the existence of only a single disease, and also as to the necessary connection of *pébrine* with *flacherie*.

These suspicions were confirmed by his cultivations of April and May. Numerous cases of *flacherie* presented themselves. Uncertainty was no longer possible as to the mutual independence of the two maladies—*pébrine* and *flacherie*. The cultivations most seriously invaded by the last-mentioned disease came from eggs produced by parents free from corpuscles, and led on to reproducers also free from this parasite. On visiting a multitude of industrial cultivations, Pasteur discerned that what had passed in his own laboratory was of very general occurrence, and that, contrary to the received opinion, two distinct maladies divided between them the cause of all the misfortunes. *Pébrine* was evidently the most widely spread, but *flacherie* had also its share, and a very large share, in the calamity.

Here, once more, the microscope came to Pasteur's assistance. If, at the period of the rearing of the silkworms, when the mean temperature is always rather high, some mulberry leaves are crushed in a mortar and mixed with a little water, the liquid being left to itself, in twenty-four hours it will be found filled with microscopic organisms; some motionless, resembling little rods or spores joined end to end, like strings of beads, others more or less active, flexible, endowed with a sinuous movement like that of the vibrios found in nearly all organic infusions in process of decomposition. Whence come these microscopic organisms? The facts relating to spontaneous generation indicate that the germs of these organisms were on the surface of the pounded leaf, spread in the form of dust over the instruments used to triturate the leaf, possibly on the mortar, the pestle, or in the water added to the pounded leaves.

It is a curious fact, that if the intestinal canal of a worm in full process of digestion be opened, the pounded leaf which fills it from one end to the other will not show microscopic organisms of any kind, but only cells of parenchyma, green granules of the chlorophyl of the leaf, and remains of the air-vessels of the plant. Through the action of the liquids secreted by the glands which line the integuments of the intestinal canal, the germs of organisms are themselves digested or hindered in their development. The digestive functions of silkworms are so active that everything is carried away, destroyed in the same manner as the leaves themselves.

But if from any cause the digestion of the worms be impeded or suspended, then the germs introduced with the food into the intestinal canal will give rise to the multiplication of microscopic organisms which are always found in the artificially bruised leaf when mixed with a little water. How numerous are the causes which may check this digestive function of the worm—a function of such importance to a creature which in the space of one month passes from the weight of half a milligramme to that of five, six, seven, or even eight grammes! Pasteur proved that whenever a worm was attacked with *flacherie*, it always had, associated with the food in its intestinal canal, one or other of the microscopic organisms which are invariably to be met with among crushed mulberry leaves. Summing up in a kind of aphorism a series of observations, Pasteur observes: 'Every *ver flat* is one which digests badly, and, conversely, every worm which digests badly is doomed to perish of *flacherie*, or to furnish a chrysalis and a moth the life of which, through the injury produced by organised ferments, is not normally perfected.'

Thus, as in the case of *pébrine*, the morbid symptoms of *flacherie* are very variable. All depends on the intensity of the evil—that is to say, on the abundance and the nature of the parasites developed in the intestinal canal, and also on the period in the life of the worm when this fermentation begins to show itself. The most dangerous of all these ferments are those of the family of vibrios. If they exist in the first phases of the life of the worm, it dies quickly and very soon becomes putrid, sometimes resolving itself into an infected pus. The disease often manifests itself in a manner particularly distressing and disastrous to the cultivator. The worms have presented the most beautiful appearance up to the time of climbing the heather. The mortality has scarcely been two or three per cent., which is nothing; the moultings have been effected in a perfect manner, when suddenly, some days after the fourth moulting, the worms become languid, crawling with difficulty, and hesitating to take the leaves which are thrown upon their hurdles. If some few have mounted on to the heather, they stretch themselves on the twigs, their bodies swollen with food which they cannot digest. Sometimes they remain there motionless till they die, or, falling, remain suspended only by their false feet. The few moths which have succeeded in piercing their cocoons do not show any corpuscles. They can produce eggs, but these eggs, coming from parents weakened by disease, give rise the following year to a generation threatened with *flacherie*. It is in this sense that the disease may be regarded as hereditary, although the parasites of the intestinal canal to which *flacherie* is due do not transmit themselves to the eggs or to the worms which issue from them. The worms inherit weakly constitutions, and, being without power of resistance against anything that can derange their digestive functions, they are at the mercy of the accidents of their culture.

Too large an assemblage of worms in one nursery; too high a temperature at the time of moulting; a thunderous atmosphere, which predisposes organic matter to fermentation; the use of heated or wet leaves, especially if the wetting be caused by a fog or by the morning or evening dew, which deposits on the leaf the germs suspended in a great mass of air;—these are so many causes calculated to diminish the activity of the digestive functions of the worms, and to produce in consequence a fermentation of the leaf in the intestinal canal— the malady now under consideration. Often also *flacherie* depends upon mistakes committed by the husbandman while tending his precious 'kine,' to use an expression of the sixteenth century.

A Chinese book published on the rearing of silkworms contains a series of little practical counsels. 'The person who takes care of the silkworms,' says this guide to the perfect cultivator, 'ought to wear a simple garment, not lined. He must regulate the temperature of the spinning-house according to the sensation of heat or cold which he experiences; if he feels cold, he may conclude that the worms are cold, and he will increase the fire; if he feels hot, he will conclude that the worms are hot, and he will suitably diminish the fire.'

One point which had been ignored before the experiments of Pasteur was the contagious character of *flacherie*. This contagion may surpass that of *pébrine* itself as regards duration. In *pébrine* the dried corpusculous matter loses all virulence after the lapse of some weeks. The disease cannot, therefore, communicate itself from one year to another by the corpusculous dust of a rearing establishment. The germs, on the contrary, of the microscopic organisms which provoke fermentation in the mulberry leaves, especially the vibrios, retain their vitality for several years. The dust of a silkworm nursery infected by *flacherie* appears under a microscope quite full of cysts or spores of vibrios. These spores or cysts rest, like the sleeping beauty in the forest, until a drop of water falls upon them and awakens them into life. Deposited on the leaves which are to serve as nourishment, these germs of vibrios are carried into the intestinal canal of the worm, develop and multiply themselves, and completely disturb the digestive functions, unless the digestion is so strong that the germs are immediately arrested, and disposed of like the food itself. This is what happens when the worms are in full vigour. It is a struggle for life, in which the worms often gain the victory.

Giving to some very healthy worms a meal of leaves covered with the dry dust of a silkworm nursery, infected the year before by *pébrine* and *flacherie*, Pasteur reproduced *flacherie*, and not *pébrine*. Still more readily did he produce the first of these maladies, when he gave, as food, leaves polluted by the contents of the intestinal canal of worms which had died of the disease. As in the case of *pébrine*, the excreta of the worms attacked by *flacherie*, defiling the leaves, carry the mischief to the healthy worms, or add to the dangerous fermentation in the intestines of those which are already in part attacked.

To preserve silkworms from accidental *flacherie*, hygienic precautions are sufficient. As regards hereditary *flacherie*, or, to speak more correctly, that which develops itself easily on any diminution of vigour in the eggs and in the embryo, Pasteur again found a remedy by having recourse to the microscope. By means of the microscope it is possible to obtain information as to the health of the worms, the chrysalides, and the moths destined to produce the eggs. Every attention should be directed to the complete exclusion of ferments from the intestinal canal of the worms, and from the stomach-pouch of the chrysalides—a little pouch to which the intestinal canal of the worm is reduced, with its contents more or less transformed. But if there is not time to make this examination for parasitic ferments with the microscope, a simple inspection of the worms in their last stage will suffice. Pasteur laid great stress upon the observation of the worms when they climbed on to the heather.

'If I were a cultivator of silkworms,' he wrote in his beautiful work on the diseases of silkworms, 'I would never hatch an egg produced from worms that I had not observed many times during the last days of their life, so as to make sure of their vigour at the moment when they spin their silk. If you use eggs produced by moths the worms of which have mounted the heather with agility, have shown no signs of *flacherie* between the fourth moulting and mounting time, and do not contain the least corpuscle of *pébrine*, then you will succeed in all your cultivations.'

III.

We have now arrived at the end of this long investigation. All the obscurity which enveloped the origin of the diseases of silkworms had now been dispelled. Pasteur had arrived at such accurate knowledge both of the causes of the evil and their different manifestations, that he was able to produce at will either *pébrine* or *flacherie*. He could so regulate the intensity of the disease as to cause it to appear on a given day, almost at a given hour. He had now to carry into practice the results of his laboratory labours.

Since the beginning of the plague, and after some doubts which were soon dispelled, it was clearly seen that all the mischief was to be attributed to the bad condition of the eggs. The remedy of distant explorations for procuring non-infected eggs was both insufficient and precarious. It simply amounted to going very far to seek, and paying very dear, for seed which could not be relied on with certainty. The prosperity of the silkworm culture could only be secured by measures capable of restoring to the native eggs their pristine qualities.

The results obtained by Pasteur were sufficient to solve this problem. The struggle against *flacherie* was easy, but there remained the struggle against *pébrine*. To triumph over this disease, which was so threatening, Pasteur devised a series of observations as simple as they were ingenious.

Here is a crop which has perfectly succeeded. The moultings, and the climbing upon the heather, are all that could be desired. The cocoons are finished, and the appearance of the moths alone is waited for. They arrive, and they pair. Then begins the work of the cultivator, who is careful about the production of his eggs. He separates the couples at the end of the day; laying each female moth by itself on a little linen cloth suspended horizontally. The females lay their eggs. After the laying, he takes each female in turn and secures her by a pin passed through the wings to a folded corner of the little cloth, where are grouped some hundreds of eggs which she has laid. The male moth also might be pinned in another corner of the cloth, but the examination of the male is useless, as it has been found that he does not communicate the *pébrine*. The female moth, after having been desiccated by free contact with the air, is examined at leisure, it may be even in the autumn or winter. Nothing is easier than to ascertain whether there are any corpuscles in its dead body. The moth is crushed in a mortar and mixed with a little water, and then a drop of the mixture is examined by the microscope. If corpuscles be found, the bit of cloth corresponding to the examined moth is known, and it is burnt with all the eggs it contains.

This method of procuring pure eggs is, in fact, only the rational development of the first inductions which Pasteur had submitted to the Agricultural Committee of Alais in June 1865. At that time he hardly ventured to hope that he should be able to find the means of preparing more than very small quantities of healthy eggs for his experiments; but events were so ordered that the starting-point, which seemed to be purely scientific, unfolded a method susceptible of a widespread practical application. This process of procuring sound eggs is now universally adopted. In the Basses-Alpes, in Ardèche, in Gard, in the Drôme, and in other countries, may be met with everywhere, at the time of the cultivation, workshops where hundreds of women and young girls are occupied, with a remarkable division of labour and under the strictest supervision of skilful overseers, in pounding the moths, in examining them microscopically, and in sorting and classifying the little cloths upon which the eggs are deposited.

———————————————

But if Pasteur had brought back wealth to ruined countries, if he had returned to Paris happy in the victory he had gained, he had also undergone such fatigues, and had so overstrained himself in the use of the microscope while absorbed in his daily and varied experiments, that in October 1868 he was struck with paralysis of one side. Seeing, as he thought, death approaching, he dictated to his wife a last note on the studies which he had so much at heart. This note was communicated to the Academy of Sciences eight days after this terrible trial.

A soul like his, possessing so great a mastery over the body, ended by triumphing over the affliction. Paralysed on the left side, Pasteur never recovered the use of his limbs. To this day, sixteen years after the attack, he limps like a wounded man. But what stages had this wounded man yet to travel over, what triumphs were yet in store for him!

———————————————

DECISIVE EXPERIMENTS.

After having dictated this scientific note, which he thought would have been his last, his courage forsook him for a time. 'I regret to die,' he said to his friend, Sainte-Claire Deville, who had hastened to his bedside; 'I should have wished to render more service to my country.' His life was spared, but for several months Pasteur remained entirely paralysed, incapable of the slightest movement. Smitten thus in his full strength at the age of forty-five, he took a sad review of his own state. Even at the height of his attack his mind had always retained its clearness. He had pointed out to the doctor without any faltering of voice the progressive symptoms of the paralysis. Then reproaching himself for having added to the grief of his wife by thus dwelling on the details of his illness, he never allowed another word to escape him about his infirm condition. Sometimes, even when he heard his two assistants,
M. Gernez and M. Duclaux, whose devotion to him during those sad days could only be compared to that of his wife, talking to him of future labours, he entered into these thoughts and appeared to add faith to their hopes. He finished by sharing them.

In January 1869, although it was still impossible for him to drag himself about his room, he was so much excited by the contradictions that his system of culture had aroused that he wished to start again for Alais. 'Aided by the method of artificial cultivation,' he remarked, 'we shall soon annihilate these latest oppositions. There is here both a scientific principle and an element of national wealth.'

His wish could not be opposed, but a terrible and anxious journey it was! At some leagues from Alais, at a place called Saint Hippolyte-du-Fort, where the earliest experiments were made, Pasteur stopped. He installed himself—we might rather say he encamped—with his family and his assistants, in a more than humble lodging, one of those miserable, cold, paved houses of the rural districts. Seated in his arm-chair, Pasteur directed the experiments, and verified the observations which he had made the year before. Each of his predictions as to the destiny of the different groups of worms was fulfilled to the smallest detail. In the following spring he left for Alais, where he followed in all their phases, from the egg up to the cocoon, the cultivations there undertaken, and he had the happiness of proving once more the certainty of his method.

But opposition still continued. The French Government, shaken by the violence and tenacity of the opponents, hesitated to decide upon this process of culture. The Emperor interposed; he instructed Marshal Vaillant to propose to Pasteur to go into Austria to the Villa Vicentina, which belonged to the Prince Imperial. For ten years the silk harvest at this place had not sufficed to pay the cost of eggs. Pasteur accepted with joy the prospect of a great decisive experiment. He traversed France and Italy, reclining in a railway carriage or in an arm-chair, and at last arrived at the Imperial villa near Trieste. Pasteur succeeded in a marvellous manner. The sale of the cocoons gave to the villa a net profit of twenty-six million francs. The Emperor, impressed with the practical value of the system, nominated Pasteur a Senator, in the month of July 1870. But this nomination, like so many other things, was swept away before it had time to appear in the 'Journal Officiel.' Pasteur, however, cared little for the title of Senator. He returned to France on the eve of the declaration of war.

A patriot to the heart's core, he learned with poignant grief the news of his country's disasters. The bulletins of defeat, which succeeded each other with mournful monotony, threw him into deep despair. For the first time in his life he had not the strength to work. He lived at his little house in Arbois as one completely vanquished. Those who went into his room found him often bathed in tears. On January 18, 1871, he wrote, to the Dean of the Academy of Medicine at the University of Bonn, a letter in which all his grief and all his pride as a Frenchman were displayed, requesting him to withdraw the diploma of German doctor which the Faculty of Medicine of the University had conferred upon him in 1868. Whilst he wrote this letter, which was a cry of patriotism, his son, enrolled as a volunteer, though hardly eighteen years of age, was gallantly doing his duty in the Army of the East.

STUDIES ON BEER.

The war was over. Little by little the life of the country was resumed, and with returning hope the desire and necessity for renewed work. After two years of infirmity, Pasteur at length began to feel the recovery of health. It was like a slow and gentle renewal of all things. He wished to return as soon as possible to his laboratory in Paris to put into execution projects of experiments which had long been working in his brain. At the moment when he was preparing to start, the rebellion of the Commune broke out. M. Duclaux, who had become Professor of the Faculty of Sciences in Clermont- Ferrand, offered the use of his laboratory to his old master. Pasteur accepted it. Eager to commence an investigation which would bring him again to the study of fermentation, he attacked the diseases of beer. But it was not only for the purpose of creating a new link between these researches and his former ones that he occupied himself with this subject, he was also influenced by a somewhat patriotic idea. He dreamt of success in an industry in which Germany is superior to France. He hoped by means of scientific principles, by which commerce would largely profit, to succeed in making for French beer a reputation equal, if not superior, to that of Germany.

Beer is much more liable to contract diseases than wine. It may be said that while old wine is often to be found, there is no such thing as old beer. It is consumed as fast as it is made. Less acid and less alcoholic than wine, beer is more laden with gummy and saccharine matters, which expose it to rapid changes. Thus the trade in this beverage is constantly struggling with the difficulties of its preservation.

The manufacture of beer is simple. It is extracted from germinated barley, or malt, an infusion of which is made and gradually heated to the boiling point. It is then flavoured by hops. When the infusion of malt and hops, which is called 'wort,' is completed, it is subjected to a cooling process, and drawn off into tuns and barrels. It is then that alcoholic fermentation sets in. The cooling ought to be performed rapidly. While the wort is at a high temperature there is nothing to fear, it remains sound; but under 70° Centigrade, and particularly between 25° and 35°, it is easily attacked by injurious ferments—acetic, lactic, or butyric. After the wort is cooled, a little of the yeast proceeding from a former fermentation is added to it, in order that the whole mass of the wort should be invaded as soon as possible after its cooling by the alcoholic ferment alone—the only one, properly speaking, which can produce beer. If this wort were treated in the same way as the must of the grape, if it were abandoned to fermentation without yeast—to so-called spontaneous fermentation—this would hardly ever be purely alcoholic, as in the must of grapes, which is protected by its acidity. Most frequently, instead of beer, an acid or putrid liquid would be obtained. Divers fermentations would simultaneously take place in it. When the wort has fermented and the beer is made, there is still the fear of its rapid deterioration, which necessitates its being quickly consumed. This condition is sometimes disastrous to those employed in the beer trade; and the improvements in the manufacture of beer which have been made during the last forty years have all had for their object the removal of this necessity for the daily production, so to speak, of an article of which the consumption is liable to constant variations.

Formerly only one kind of beer was known, the beer of high fermentation. The wort, after having undergone cooling in the troughs, is collected in a large open vat at a temperature of 20°, and yeast is added to it. When the fermentation begins to show itself on the surface of the liquid, by the formation of a light white froth, the wort is transferred to a series of small barrels, which are placed in cellars or store-rooms, kept at a temperature of from 18° to 20° Centigrade. The activity of the fermentation soon causes a foam to rise, which becomes more and more thick and viscous. This is owing to the abundance of yeast which it contains. This yeast, collected in a large trough placed under the casks, is gathered up for future operations. The fermentation lasts for three or four days, then the beer is made and has become clear; the bungs are fixed in the barrels, and they are sent direct to the retail dealer or to the consumer. During the transit, a certain quantity of yeast, fallen to the bottom of the casks, thickens the beer, but a few days of repose suffice to make it again clear and fit to drink, or to be bottled.

This system of 'high' fermentation (so called because it begins at a temperature of 18° to 20°, and is raised one or two degrees higher by the act of fermentation itself) is very commonly practised in the north of France, and to a greater extent in the breweries of England. Ale, pale ale, bitter beer, are all beers from high fermentation.

The 'low' fermentation, which is almost exclusively employed in Germany, and which is spreading more and more in France, consists in a slow fermentation, at low temperature, during which the yeast settles at the bottom of the tubs and casks. The wort, after it has been cooled, is passed into open wooden tuns, and the working of the yeast takes place at a temperature of about 6° Centigrade. This temperature is maintained by means of floats, in the form of cones or cylinders, thrown into the fermenting tuns and kept filled with ice. The fermentation lasts for ten, fifteen, and even twenty days. When the beer is drawn off, the yeast is collected from the bottom of the fermenting tuns. This kind of beer, which is sometimes called German beer, sometimes Strasburg beer, is generally much more esteemed than the other, but it requires certain expensive, or at least inconvenient, conditions. There must be ice-caves, where the temperature is maintained all the year round at a few degrees only above zero. This makes it necessary to have enormous piles of ice. It has been calculated that for one single hectolitre of good beer, from the beginning of the cooling of the wort until the time when it is fit for sale, 100 kilogrammes of ice are required. The 'low' beer, called also *bière de garde*, beer for keeping, is principally manufactured in winter, and is preserved in ice-caves until the summer.

It is not only the taste of the consumers which has favoured the manufacture of beer of low fermentation everywhere except in England; it is also the advantage this beer possesses in being much less liable to deterioration than the other. By employing ice, the brewer may manufacture in winter, or in the beginning of spring, and thus place himself in a position to meet the demands of consumption without fear of seeing his beer attacked by disease.

All the diseases of beer, as Pasteur has shown, are caused exclusively by the development of little microscopic fungi, or organised ferments, the germs of which are brought by the dust constantly floating in the air, or which gets mixed with the original substances used in the manufacture. 'By the expression *diseases* of wort and of beer, I mean,' said Pasteur, 'those serious alterations which affect the quality of these liquids so as to render them disagreeable to the taste, especially when they have been kept for some time, and which cause the beer to be described as sharp, sourish, turned, ropy, putrid.' The wort of beer, after it has been raised to the boiling heat, may, as Pasteur's experiments testify, be preserved indefinitely, even in the highest atmospheric temperatures, when in contact with air free from the germs of the lower microscopic organisms. The must, leavened by the addition of pure yeast, kept free from foreign organisms, contains nothing but the alcoholic ferment, and undergoes no other changes than those due to the action of the oxygen, which does not give rise to acidity, putridity, or bitterness. Since the causes of deterioration are the same in beer as in wine, would it not appear as if the action of heat must be the best preservative? But beer is a drink necessarily charged with carbonic acid, and the application of heat to considerable masses of the liquid would expel this gas. It would be a very complicated business to attempt to preserve this gas, or to introduce it afresh after it had been expelled. This difficulty does not arise when the beer is bottled. At a temperature of 50° to 55°, the process of heating not only cannot take away from the beer all its carbonic acid, but it does not prevent the secondary fermentation from taking place to a certain extent, and this allows of the beer being heated immediately after it is put into bottles. This heating of the beer is practised on a large scale in Europe and in America. In honour of Pasteur the process is called *Pasteurisation*, and the beer *Pasteurised* beer.

But Pasteur was not content with simply destroying the ferments of these diseases, he wished above all to prevent their introduction. At the moment when the wort is raised to the boiling-point, when the germs of disease are destroyed by the heat, if the cooling of the wort is effected in contact with both air and yeast free from exterior germs, the beer may be made under conditions of exceptional purity. Some brewers, taking for their basis Pasteur's principles, constructed an apparatus which enabled them to protect the wort while it was cooling from the organisms of the air, and to ferment this wort with a leaven as pure as possible. At the Exhibition of Amsterdam there might be seen bottles half full, containing a perfectly clear beer, which had been tapped from the time of opening of the Exhibition. This was French beer, manufactured according to Pasteur's principles, by a great brewer of Marseilles, M. Velten. The happy effect of these studies is universally recognised. At Copenhagen, M. Jacobsen has had a bust of Pasteur, by Paul Dubois, placed in the *salle d'honneur* of his celebrated laboratory.

In terminating his *Studies on Beer*, Pasteur recalled to mind the principles which for twenty years had directed his labours, the resources and applications of which appeared to him unlimited. 'The etiology of contagious diseases,' he wrote with a scientific certainty of conviction, 'is on the eve of having unexpected light shed upon it.'

VIRULENT DISEASES.
SPLENIC FEVER (CHARBON)—SEPTICÆMIA.

'He that thoroughly understands the nature of ferments and fermentations,' said the physicist Robert Boyle, 'shall probably be much better able than he that ignores them, to give a fair account of divers phenomena of certain diseases (as well fevers as others), which will perhaps be never properly understood without an insight into the doctrine of fermentations.'

At all times, medical theories, more particularly those which concern the etiology of virulent diseases, have had to encounter the opposition of explanations invented to account for the phenomena of fermentation. When Pasteur in 1856 began his labours on these subjects, the ideas of Liebig were everywhere revived. Like the ferments, so the viruses and processes of disease were considered as the results of atomic motions proper to substances in course of molecular change, and able to communicate themselves to the diverse constituents of the living body.

The researches of Pasteur on the part played by microscopic organisms in fermentation, changed the course of these ideas. The ancient medical theory of parasites and living contagia was revived. A German Professor, Dr. Traube, in 1864, put forward, in one of his clinical lectures, a new doctrine of the ammoniacal fermentation of urine.

'For a long period,' he said, 'the mucus of the bladder was regarded as the agent of the alkaline decomposition of urine. It was supposed that, in consequence of the distension produced by the retention of the liquid, the irritated bladder produced a larger quantity of mucus, and this mucus was regarded as the ferment which brought about the decomposition of urea, by an innate chemical force. This opinion (which was that of Liebig) cannot hold its ground in presence of the researches of Pasteur. This investigator has demonstrated, in the most decisive manner, that alkaline fermentation, like alcoholic and acetic fermentation, is produced by living organisms, the pre-existence of which in the liquid is the *sine quâ non* of the process.' And Dr. Traube, citing some facts which confirmed the doctrine of Pasteur, concluded thus: 'Notwithstanding the long retention of the urine, its alkaline fermentation is not produced by an increased secretion of mucus or of pus; it only begins to develop from the moment when the germs of vibrios find access to the bladder from without.

The opposite doctrines of Liebig and Pasteur are here brought into clear juxtaposition; and thus was their mutual and reciprocal influence established in dealing with the etiology of one of the most serious diseases of the bladder. So far back as 1862, Pasteur, in his memoir on spontaneous generation, had announced, contrary to all the notions then held, that whenever urine becomes ammoniacal, a little microscopic fungus is the cause of this alteration. Later on he established that in affections of the bladder ammoniacal urine was never found without the presence of this fungus; and in order to show how in these studies therapeutic application often runs hand in hand with scientific discovery, Pasteur, having proved, with his assistant, M. Joubert, that boracic acid is antagonistic to the development of the ammoniacal ferment, advised Dr. Guyon, Clinical Professor of Urinary Diseases in the Faculty of Paris, to combat the dangerous ammoniacal fermentation by injection of boracic acid into the bladder. The celebrated surgeon hastened to follow this advice, and with the most happy results. While attributing to Pasteur the honour of this discovery, M. Guyon, in one of his lectures, said:—

'Boracic acid has this immense advantage, that it can be applied in large doses —3 to 4 per cent.—without causing the slightest pain. It has therefore become, in our practice, the agent continually and successfully used for injections. I also have recourse to a solution of boracic acid to produce large evacuations after the operation of breaking up stones in the bladder (lithotrity). I never omit to use this antiseptic agent in operations where breaking up is required, and I never wash the bladders of lithotritised patients with any other substance. I have also had good results from copiously washing the bladders and the wounds of patients on whom lithotomy has been performed with boracic acid. I always finish the operation by prolonged irrigations with a solution of from 3 to 4 per cent.'

It was not only into France and Germany that Pasteur's ideas penetrated; in England, surgery borrowed from Pasteur's researches important therapeutic applications. In 1865 Dr. Lister began in Edinburgh the brilliant series of his triumphs in surgery by the application of his antiseptic method, now universally adopted. In the month of February 1874 in a letter which does honour to the sincerity and modesty of the great English surgeon, he wrote to Pasteur as follows:—

'It gives me pleasure to think that you will read with some interest what I have written about an organism which you were the first to study in your memoir on lactic fermentation. I do not know whether you read the 'British Medical Journal;' if so, you will from time to time have seen accounts of the antiseptic system which for the last nine years I have been trying to bring to perfection. Allow me to take this opportunity of sending you my most cordial thanks, for having, by your brilliant researches, demonstrated to me the truth of the germ theory of putrefaction, thus giving me the only principle which could lead to a happy end the antiseptic system.'

Pasteur followed with lively interest the movement of thought and the successful applications to which his labours had given rise. It was a realisation of the hopes he had ventured to entertain. Already, in 1860, he expressed the wish that he might be able to carry his researches far enough to prepare the way for a profound study of the origin of diseases. And, as he gradually advanced in the discovery of living ferments, he hoped more and more to arrive at the knowledge of the causes of contagious diseases.

Nevertheless, he hesitated long before definitely engaging himself in this direction. 'I am neither doctor nor surgeon,' he used to repeat with modest self-distrust. But the moment came when, notwithstanding all his scruples, he could no longer be content himself to play the part of a simple spectator of the labours started by his studies on fermentation, on spontaneous generation, and on the diseases of wines and beer. The hopes to which his methods gave rise, the eulogies of which they were the object, obliged him to go forward. In February 1876 Tyndall wrote to him thus:—

'In taking up your researches relating to infusorial organisms, I have had occasion to refresh my memory of your labours; they have revived in me all the admiration which I felt on first reading them. It is my intention to follow up these researches until I shall have dissipated every doubt that has been raised as to the unassailable exactitude of your conclusions.

'For the first time in the history of science we are able to entertain the sure and certain hope that, in relation to epidemic diseases, medicine will soon be delivered from empiricism, and placed upon a real scientific basis. When this great day shall come, humanity will recognise that it is to you the greatest part of its gratitude is due.'

Pasteur approached the study of viruses by seeking to penetrate into all the causes of the terrible malady called splenic fever (*charbon*, Germ. *Milzbrand*). Each year this disease decimates the flocks not only in France but in Spain, in Italy, in Russia, where it is called the Siberian plague, and in Egypt, where it is supposed to date back to the ten plagues of Moses. Hungary and Brazil pay it a formidable yearly tribute; and to come back to France, the losses have amounted in certain years to from fifteen to twenty millions of francs. For centuries the cause of this pest has eluded all research; and further, as the malady did not always exhibit the same symptoms, but varied according to the kind of animal that was smitten by it, the disease was supposed to vary with the species that was attacked by it. The splenic fever of the horse was distinct from that of the cow; the splenic fever of horse and cow were again different from that of the sheep. In the latter, splenic fever was called *sang-de-rate*; in the cow, it was *maladie du sang*; in the horse, splenic fever; in man, malignant pustule.

It was not until 1850 that trustworthy data were first collected regarding the nature of the malady, its identity with and difference from other maladies. From 1849 to 1852 a commission of the Medical Association of Eure-et-Loir made a great number of inoculations, applied other tests, and proved that the splenic fever of the sheep is communicable to other sheep, to the horse, to the cow, and to the rabbit; that the splenic fever of the horse is communicable to the horse and to the sheep; that the splenic fever of the cow is communicable to the sheep, to the horse, and to the rabbit. As for the malignant pustule in man, no doubt remained that it must arise from the same cause as splenic fever in animals. What class of men is it that the malignant pustule most frequently attacks? Shepherds, cowherds, cattle breeders, farm servants, dealers in hides, tanners, wool cleaners, knackers, butchers—all who derive their living from domestic animals. In handling contaminated subjects the slightest excoriation or scratch of the skin is sufficient to allow the virus to enter. When others besides the class that we have named become infected, it is because they live in the neighbourhood of herds smitten with splenic fever. There are also certain flies which transport the virus. Suppose one of these flies to have sucked the blood of an animal which has died of splenic fever, a person stung by that fly is forthwith inoculated with the virus.

At the very time (1850) when these first experiments were being made by the Medical Association of the Eure-et-Loir, Dr. Rayer, giving an account in the 'Bulletin de la Société de Biologie de Paris' of the researches he had made, with his colleague, Dr. Davaine, on the contagion of splenic fever, wrote:
—'In the blood are found little thread-like bodies about twice the length of a blood corpuscle. These little bodies exhibit no spontaneous motion.'

This is the date of the first observation on the presence of little parasitic bodies in splenic fever, but, strange to say, no attention was paid to these minute filaments. Rayer and Davaine also paid no attention to them. This indifference lasted for thirteen years; it would have lasted longer still, if the parasitic origin of communicable diseases had not been brought before the mind by each new publication of Pasteur's. From 1857 to 1860 it will be remembered that he had demonstrated lactic fermentation, like alcoholic fermentation, to be the work of a living ferment; in 1861 he had discovered that the agent of butyric fermentation consisted of little moving thread-like bodies, of dimensions similar to those of the filaments discovered by Davaine and Rayer in the blood of splenic fever patients; in 1861 he had announced that no ammoniacal urine existed without the presence of a microscopic organism; in 1863 he had established that the bodies of animals in full health are sealed against the introduction of the germs of microscopic organisms;

that blood drawn with sufficient precaution from the veins and the arteries, and urine taken direct from the bladder, could be exposed to the contact of pure air without putrefaction, and without the appearance of living thread-like organisms of any kind whatever, mobile or immobile. It was all these facts which in 1863 brought back the attention of Davaine, as he himself has acknowledged, to the observation which he had made in 1850.

'M. Pasteur,' said M. Davaine in a communication made to the Academy of Sciences, 'published some time ago a remarkable memoir on butyric fermentation, which consists of little cylindrical rods, possessing all the characteristics of vibrios or of bacteria. The thread-like corpuscles which in 1850 I saw in the blood of sheep attacked with *sang-de-rate*, having a great analogy with these vibrios, I was led to examine whether filiform corpuscles, analogous to or of the same kind as those which determined the butyric fermentation, would not, if introduced into the blood of an animal, equally act the part of a ferment. Thus would be easily explained the alteration, and the rapid infection of the mass of the blood, in an animal which had received accidentally or experimentally into its veins a certain number of these bacteria —that is to say, of this ferment.'

But two summers passed before M. Davaine was able to procure a sheep affected with the *sang-de-rate*. It was only in 1863 that he first recognised the constant presence of a parasite, in the blood of sheep and rabbits which had died from successive inoculations with blood taken after death or in the last hours of life. He further proved that the inoculated animal, in the blood of which no parasites were as yet visible with the microscope, had every appearance of health, and that in these conditions the blood could not communicate splenic fever.

'In the present state of science,' Davaine concluded, 'no one would think of going beyond these corpuscles to seek for the agent of the contagion. This agent is visible, palpable; it is an organised being, endowed with life, which is developed and propagated in the same manner as other living beings. By its presence, and its rapid multiplication in the blood, it without doubt produces in the constitution of this liquid, after the manner of ferments, modifications which speedily destroy the infected animal.' 'For a long time,' he repeated, 'physicians and naturalists have admitted theoretically that contagious diseases, serious epidemic fevers, the plague, &c., are caused by invisible animalculæ, or by ferments, but I do not know that these views have ever been confirmed by any positive observations.'

A few months after the publication of the results obtained by Davaine, two professors of Val-de-Grâce, MM. Jaillard and Leplat, sought to refute the preceding conclusions. After having inoculated rabbits and dogs with various putrefying liquids filled with vibrios, they could not cause the death of these animals. To bring about this result it was necessary to introduce into the blood of these dogs and rabbits several cubic centimeters of very putrid liquid. Again in this case, which only added another example to the experiments of Gaspard and Magendie upon the action of putrid liquids, they failed to generate any virulence in the blood. Davaine had no difficulty in showing that MM. Jaillard and Leplat's experiments were made under conditions totally different from his; that he, Davaine, had not made use of the vibrios or bacteria of unselected infusions, but of bacteria which had been found in the blood of sheep which had died from *sang-de-rate*.

Jaillard and Leplat returned to the charge, and this time with entirely new and unexpected experiments. They inoculated some rabbits, as Davaine desired, with the blood of a cow which had died of splenic fever. The rabbits died rapidly, but without showing before or after their death the least trace of bacteria. Other rabbits, inoculated with the blood of the first, perished in the same manner, but it was still impossible to discover any parasite in their blood. MM. Jaillard and Leplat offered Davaine some drops of this blood. Davaine, taking up the experiments of his opponents, confirmed the exactitude of the facts they had announced, but concluded by saying that these two professors had not employed true splenic fever blood, but the blood of a new disease, unknown up to that time, which Davaine proposed to call the cow disease.

'The blood which we used,' replied MM. Jaillard and Leplat, 'was furnished to us by the director of the knacker's establishment of Sours, near Chartres, and this director is undeniably competent as to the knowledge of splenic fever.'

Full of sincerity and conviction, MM. Jaillard and Leplat recommenced their experiments, using this time the blood of a sheep which had died of splenic fever, and which M. Boutet, the most experienced veterinary surgeon of the town of Chartres, had procured for them. Their results were the same as those obtained with the blood of the cow. Notwithstanding the replies of Davaine, which, however, added nothing to the facts already adduced on one side or the other, it was difficult to pronounce decidedly in such a debate. Unprejudiced minds received from these important discussions the impression that Jaillard and Leplat, in producing facts the exactitude of which were admitted by Dr. Davaine himself, had given a blow to the assertions of the latter, and that the subject required, in every case, new experimental studies.

In 1876, a German physician, Dr. Koch, took up the question. He confirmed the opinion of Davaine, but without in the least producing conviction, since he threw no light upon the facts adduced by MM. Jaillard and Leplat, of which, indeed, he did not even deign to speak. At the very same moment when the memoir of Koch appeared in Germany, the eminent physician Paul Bert came forward to corroborate the opinion of Jaillard and Leplat.

'I can,' said M. Paul Bert, 'destroy the bacteria in a drop of blood by compressed oxygen, inoculate with what remains, and reproduce the disease and death without any appearance of bacteria. Therefore, the bacteria are neither the cause nor the necessary effect of the disease of splenic fever. It is due to a virus.'

This was indeed the opinion of Jaillard and Leplat. Pasteur, in obedience to the necessity he felt to get at the fundamental truth of things, and also in his eager desire to discover some decisive proofs as to the etiology of this terrible disease, resolved in his turn to attack the subject.

Dr. Koch had stated in his memoir that the little filiform bodies, seen for the first time by Davaine in 1850, had two modes of reproduction—one by fission, which Davaine had observed, and another by bright corpuscles or spores. The existence of this latter mode of reproduction Pasteur had already discovered in 1865, reasserted and illustrated in 1870, as being common to the filaments of the butyric ferment, and to all the ferments of putrefaction. Was Dr. Koch ignorant of this important fact, or did he prefer by keeping silence to reserve to himself the advantage of apparent priority?

In order to solve the first difficulty which presented itself to his mind—that is to say, the question as to whether splenic fever was to be attributed to a substance, solid or liquid, associated or not associated with the filaments discovered by Davaine, or whether it depended exclusively upon the presence and the life of these filaments—Pasteur had recourse to the methods which for twenty years had served him as guides in his studies on the organisms of fermentation. These methods, delicate as they are, are very simple. When he wished, for example, to demonstrate that the microbe-ferment of the butyric fermentation was the very agent of decomposition, he prepared an artificial liquid formed of phosphates of potash, of magnesia, and of sulphate of ammonia, added to the solution of the fermentable matter, and in this medium he caused the microbe-ferments to be sown in a pure state. The microbe multiplied, and provoked fermentation. From this liquid he could pass to a second or third fermentable liquid composed in the same manner, and so on in succession. The butyric fermentation appeared successively in each. Since the year 1857 this method was supreme. In this particular research on the disease of splenic fever Pasteur proposed to isolate the microbe of the infected blood, to cultivate it in a state of purity in artificial liquids, and then to come back to the examination of its action on animals. But as, since his attack of paralysis in 1868, Pasteur had not recovered the use of his left hand, and consequently found it impossible to carry on a long series of experiments alone, he was obliged to seek for a courageous and devoted assistant. He found one in a former pupil of his at the École Normale, M. Joubert, now Professor of Physics at the Collège Rollin. If M. Joubert incurred the danger of these experiments on splenic fever, he also shared with Pasteur, in the Comptes- rendus of the Academy of Sciences, the honour of the researches and the triumph of the discoveries.

On April 30, 1877, Pasteur read to the Academy of Sciences, in his own name and in that of his fellow-worker, a note in which he demonstrated, this time in a completely unanswerable manner, that the bacilli called bacteria, bacterides, filaments, rods, in a word the bacilli discovered by Davaine and Rayer in 1850, constituted the only agent of the malady.

A little drop of splenic fever blood, sown in urine or in the water of yeast, previously sterilised—that is to say, rendered *un*putrescible by contact with air free from all suspended germs—produces in a few hours myriads of bacilli or of bacteria. A little drop of this first cultivation sown in a second flask containing the same liquid as the first and prepared with the same precautions as to sterility and purity, shows itself no less fertile. Finally, after ten or twenty similar cultures the parasite is evidently freed from the substances which the initial drop of blood might carry with it; yet, if a very small quantity of the last culture is injected under the skin of a rabbit or a sheep, it kills them in two or three days at most, with all the clinical symptoms of natural splenic fever.

It might be objected that the parasite was associated in the cultivating liquid with some dissolved substance that it had produced during its life and which acted as a poison. Pasteur accordingly transported some cultivating tubes into the cellars of the Observatory, where a temperature absolutely constant reigned, a circumstance which permits of the deposit of all the parasitic filaments at the bottom of the tubes. Inoculating afterwards both with the clear upper liquid and with the deposit at the bottom, he found that the latter alone produced disease and death. It is, then, the bacteria which cause splenic fever. The proof was given and no further doubt remained.

I.

Yes, splenic fever is no doubt produced by bacteria just as itch is produced by acaries and trichinosis by trichinæ. The only difference is that the parasite of splenic fever can only be seen by means of a rather powerful microscope. Here, then, is a disease in the highest degree virulent, due in its first cause to the *infinitely little*. Pasteur laid hold of and isolated this terrible virus. It was in a microscopic parasite, and in it alone, that the virulence of splenic fever resided. A great scientific fact had been gained. A virus might consist not of amorphous matter, but of microscopic beings. The virulence was due to their life.

Liebig, and all the chemists and doctors who had accepted and maintained his doctrine, totally repudiated all vital action in fermentation as well as in contagious and infectious diseases. Dominated by their hypotheses, they allowed themselves to be deceived by false assimilations to facts of a purely chemical kind, which appeared to them to be connected with the phenomena of fermentation and virulence.

Liebig wrote, 'By the contact of the virus of small-pox the blood undergoes an alteration, in consequence of which its elements reproduce the virus, and this metamorphosis is not arrested until after the complete transformation of all the globules capable of decomposition.'

This vague theory of viruses was forced to give way before the multiplied experiments of Pasteur. But before occupying himself with further discoveries, although it had been irrefutably proved that the microscopic parasite was the true contagium, it was necessary to throw light upon the facts, mainly accurate, which had been announced by Jaillard and Leplat, and to bring them into harmony with the facts, not less certain, which had been advanced by Davaine. The rabbits which Jaillard and Leplat had inoculated with a drop of the blood of a cow or sheep stricken with splenic fever, died rapidly, and the blood of these rabbits was shown to be also virulent. It was sufficient to inoculate other rabbits with a very minute quantity to cause their death. But Jaillard and Leplat affirmed that the examination of that blood did not reveal the existence of any microscopic organisms. Paul Bert, on his part, had succeeded in destroying the bacteria by compressed oxygen, and yet the virulence had continued.

Were there, then, two kinds of virus? What escape was there from this darkness? A new light suddenly began to dawn. Pasteur had already some years previously demonstrated that the animal body is sealed against the introduction of lower organisms—that in the blood, the urine, the muscles, the liver, the spleen, the kidneys, the brain, the marrow, and the nerves, in a normal state, no germ is found, or particle of any kind, known or unknown, which could be transformed into bacteria, vibrios, monads, or microbes. The intestinal canal alone is filled with matters associated with a host of germs and living products in process of development, and in divers states of physiological action. Not only is its temperature favourable to the life of infusoria, but it receives incessantly matters charged with the germs of these microscopic organisms. To the upper portions of the canal the air still has access, so that even in the stomach aerobic microbes may be found, but in the lower parts of the intestinal canal oxygen is absent, and only anaerobic microbes can be developed there. Although the life exerted in the mucous surface of the intestines opposes itself to the passage of those little organisms into the interior of the body, this ceases to be the case after death. There is no longer any obstacle to arrest or prevent them from acting according to the respective laws of their evolution and of the decomposing influence which belongs to them. It is by anaerobic organisms, in fact, that the putrefaction of dead bodies is begun. They penetrate into the organs and into the blood as soon as this liquid is deprived of oxygen; and it is not long before this happens, the oxygen fixed in the globules being soon consumed. In the body of an animal which has died of splenic fever, putrefaction is still more rapid, because, through the action of the disease, the blood is already in a great degree deprived of oxygen at the time of death. Nothing is more striking than the rapid inflation and almost immediate putrefaction of animals which have succumbed to splenic fever. Of all the vibrios ready to pass from the intestinal canal into the network of mesenteric veins which surround the canal those which seem to take the foremost place are the septic vibrios. These specially merit the name of vibrios of putrefaction, from the very putrid gases which result from their action upon nitrogenous and sulphurous substances. The others diffuse themselves more or less slowly in the blood, but the septic vibrio takes almost immediate possession of the dead body. Already after twelve or fifteen hours, the blood of the diseased animal, which at the time of its death and during the first following hours contained exclusively the parasite of splenic fever, harbours at one and the same time both the bacillus of splenic fever and the septic vibrio. Then occur the very curious effects arising from the anaerobic nature of these vibrios, and their opposition to the bacillus of splenic fever, which is exclusively aerobic. Diffused in blood deprived of oxygen gas, the splenic bacillus soon perishes. In its place are to be found amorphous granulations deprived of all virulence. The septic anaerobic vibrio, on the contrary, finds itself after death in the most favourable conditions for its life and development. Not only does it penetrate into the blood by the deep mesenteric veins, but also into the liquids which ooze out of the abdomen and muscles.

From the antagonism existing between the physiological peculiarities of the splenic bacilli and the septic vibrio, it results that if, in order to inoculate an animal capable of contracting the fever, a drop of blood be taken from one that has just died of it, and if the operation is performed during the first few hours after death, it is certain to communicate to that animal splenic fever, and splenic fever only. If, on the other hand, the operation is performed after a greater number of hours—say, between twelve and twenty, according to the season of the year—then the inoculation of the blood will communicate, at one and the same time, splenic fever and septicæmia—acute septicæmia, as it may be called, because of the rapid inflammatory disorders that the septic vibrio causes in the inoculated animal. The two diseases may be developed simultaneously in the inoculated animal, but generally one precedes the other. The septic contagium is the quickest in its action; it generally causes death before the splenic fever has had time to develop itself and to produce appreciable effects.

We are now in a position to explain all the contradictory results obtained by MM. Jaillard and Leplat on one side, and by Davaine on the other. In a country which splenic fever had made famous, the Département d'Eure-et- Loir, they had asked for a little splenic fever blood. Now, what takes place in a farm where an animal has died of this disease? The dead body is thrown upon a dungheap, or into some shed or stall, until the knacker's cart happens to pass. The knacker takes his own time, and the body often remains there twenty-four or forty-eight hours. The blood taken from this animal is more or less invaded by putrefaction, and vibrios are mingled with the bacteria of splenic fever, the development of which is arrested the moment the animal dies. In short, it may be easily conceived that an experimenter writing to Chartres to procure some splenic fever blood might, without his knowledge, or the knowledge of his correspondent, receive blood at the same time both splenic and septic. And this septicæmia is sometimes manifold, for a special septicæmia may be said to correspond to every sort of vibrio of putrefaction.

Such were the circumstances which, without their being aware of it, accompanied Jaillard and Leplat's researches upon splenic fever infection. This impression will be derived from reading the successive notes laid by them before the Academy of Sciences. The blood of the cow which had died of splenic fever, sent from the knacker's establishment of Sours, and the blood of the sheep sent by M. Boutet, must both have been taken from the bodies of animals which had been dead a sufficient number of hours to render their blood both splenic and septic; and it was septicæmia, so prompt in its action, that had killed the rabbits of Jaillard and Leplat. As the examination of the blood of these animals showed no signs of bacteria, they had concluded, with great apparent truth, that the inoculation of splenic blood could cause death without any appearance of these organisms, even while the blood used for inoculation was full of them. The presence of *septic* vibrios in the blood of the inoculated rabbits escaped their notice. When Davaine replied that Jaillard and Leplat had not worked with pure splenic blood he had hit upon the truth, but he could not give plausible reasons for it. The contest was carried on by experiments in which, on both sides, truth and error were closely blended.

The work of M. Paul Bert, at the close of 1876, was surrounded with circumstances no less complex. To thoroughly understand them we must call to mind Pasteur's discovery as to the mode of reproducing the anaerobic germs of putrefaction. These vibrios reproduce themselves by spores. In the vibrio of acute septicæmia this is the mode of generation. Short or long jointed filaments show themselves studded with brilliant points, which are precisely the spores of which we speak. Experience proves that these spores resist perfectly the poisonous action of compressed oxygen. Inoculating an animal with blood which is at the same time septic and splenic, after the blood has been compressed, the septic germs, remaining alive, produce death, although neither bacteria nor filaments may be perceptible in its blood at the moment of death. It was likewise from Chartres that M. Paul Bert obtained his supply of splenic fever blood. The blood he had received was without doubt not only splenic but also septic. The filaments of bacteria and the filaments of septic vibrios had perished under the influence of the compressed oxygen; but the spores were there, and the great pressure of oxygen gas had not affected them. The new contagium which had appeared, and which had killed the inoculated animals, was due to these spores.

As regards the proof that this virulence in the blood of the body of an animal which has died of splenic fever is really the effect of the septic vibrio, Pasteur, assisted by Joubert and a new assistant, M. Chamberland, has given that proof, as he did in the case of the bacterium of splenic fever, by resorting to the method of successive cultivations in an artificial medium. These cultivations, however, of the septic vibrio require very special precautions and conditions. They should be carried on in as perfect a vacuum as it is possible to obtain, or in contact with carbonic acid gas without the presence of air. In contact with air the cultivations of septic vibrios would prove sterile, because the vibrio is exclusively anaerobic and air kills it. If a spore of this organism could germinate in contact with the air, the product of the germination would be at once arrested and would perish by the action of the oxygen. It is exactly the contrary with the bacilli of splenic fever, which prove sterile in a vacuum or in presence of carbonic acid gas. If one of the spores of the splenic fever bacillus (for it also produces spores) could germinate, the product of the germination, deprived of free oxygen, would at once perish. And, to mention in passing a very ingenious experiment of Pasteur's, we thus obtain a means of separating by culture the bacillus of splenic fever from the septic vibrio when they are temporarily associated together. If this mixture of pathogenic organisms is cultivated in contact with the air, the bacilli of splenic fever alone will be developed. If this same mixture is cultivated without air, either in a vacuum or in carbonic acid gas, the septic vibrio alone will be developed. This device of culture is one of the best which can be employed to demonstrate that the blood of a body dead from splenic fever possesses immediately after death a single contagium, that of splenic fever, and that twenty-four hours after death, on the contrary, there are two contagia, that of splenic fever and that of septicæmia.

Some months ago a very hot discussion arose between Pasteur and a commission formed principally of professors of the veterinary school in Turin, regarding the facts above mentioned. One experiment, in the success of which Pasteur was extremely interested, had been made at this school. Instead of employing pure splenic fever blood, free from all contagium, the Italian professors, whether from ignorance of the preceding facts or from inadvertence, employed the blood of a diseased sheep, which, from their own showing, had been dead more than twenty-four hours. Pasteur immediately wrote, pointing out that the commission had done wrong in using blood which must have been at the same time splenic and septic. The Turin professors grew angry, and affirmed that this assertion of Pasteur's was incorrect; that this sheep's blood had been studied with care, and that no filaments had been found in it except those of splenic fever; and it would, moreover, be marvellous, they added ironically, that Pasteur from the depths of his laboratory in Paris should be able to assert that this blood was mixed with septic poison, whilst they, good observers, armed with a microscope, had had this sheep's blood under their eyes. Pasteur contented himself with replying that his assertion rested upon a principle, and that he was perfectly able, without having seen the blood of the sheep, to affirm that under the conditions in which it had been collected that blood was septic. A public correspondence ensued, but no understanding could be come to. Pasteur then offered to go himself to Turin, in order to demonstrate upon as many bodies of sheep dead of splenic fever as they would like to give him, that the blood of these dead bodies—at the end of twenty-four hours if in the month of March, and in twelve or fifteen hours if in the month of June, would be found to be both splenic and septic. Pasteur also proposed, by appropriate cultures, to withdraw at pleasure the splenic fever poison or the septic poison, or the two together, at the choice of the Italians. The Italians, however, shrank from Pasteur's proposal to pay them a visit in order to convince them of their error.

The clearness and certainty of Pasteur's assertions are celebrated, but what gives such authority to all that he advances is, as M. Paul Bert once said, that Pasteur's boldness of assertion is only equalled by his diffidence when he has not experiment to back him up. He never fights except on ground with which he has made himself familiar, but then he fights with such resolution, and sometimes with such impetuosity, that one might say to his adversary, whoever he be, 'Je vous plains de tomber dans ses mains redoutables.'

'Take care!' said a member of the Academy of Sciences to a member of the Academy of Medicine, who a short time after the incident just related was proposing scientifically to 'strangle' Pasteur, 'take care! Pasteur is never mistaken.'

One day, in 1879, a professor attached to a faculty of medicine in one of the provinces announced to the Academy of Sciences that he had found, in the blood of a woman who had died in a hospital after two weeks' illness from severe puerperal fever, a considerable number of motionless filaments, simple or jointed, transparent, straight, or bent, which belonged to the genus Leptothrix. Engaged in studies on puerperal fever, and having never met with a fact of this kind in his researches, Pasteur wrote at once to this professor to ask him for a specimen of the infected blood. The blood arrived at the laboratory, and some days after Pasteur wrote to the doctor, 'Your leptothrix is nothing else than the bacterium of splenic fever.'

This answer perplexed the doctor very much. He wrote to Pasteur that he did not dispute the affirmation, but that he proposed to control it; that if he found he had been in error he would publish it.

Pasteur offered to send him guinea-pigs which had been inoculated with splenic fever. 'You will receive them still living; they will die under your eyes. You will make the autopsy and you will yourself recognise your leptothrix.' The doctor accepted the test. Pasteur inoculated three guinea-pigs, had them placed in a cage and sent by rail to the professor. They arrived the following morning and died twenty-four hours afterwards under the doctor's own eyes. The first had been inoculated with the infectious blood of the dead woman, the second with the bacterium of splenic fever blood from Chartres, the third with the blood of a cow which had died of splenic fever in the Jura. At the autopsy it was impossible to discover the slightest difference in the blood of the three animals. Not only the blood but the internal organs, and especially the spleen, were in exactly the same condition.

Then, in the most honourable manner, the doctor hastened to state, in a communication to the Academy of Sciences, that he regretted doubly not having known about splenic fever the year before, as he might have been able, on the one hand, to diagnose the formidable complication which had manifested itself in the woman who died on April 4, 1878, and, on the other hand, to have traced out the mode of contamination which now eluded him. He had, however, succeeded in learning a few details regarding the unhappy woman. She was a charwoman, and lived in a little room adjoining the stables of a horse-dealer. Through these stables a large number of horses passed continually.

But to return to our septic vibrios. If air destroys them, if their culture is impossible in contact with air, how can septicæmia exist, since air is everywhere present? How can blood exposed to the air become septic from particles of dust on the surface of objects or which the air holds in suspension? Where can the septic germs be formed? The objection seems a serious one, but it disappears before a very simple experiment. Take some serum from the abdomen of a guinea-pig which has died of acute septicæmia. It will be found full of septic vibrios in process of generation by fission. Let this liquid be then exposed to the contact of air, with the precaution of giving a certain depth to the liquid—say, a centimeter of depth. In some hours, if examined with the microscope, the following curious spectacle will be witnessed: In the upper layers the oxygen of the air is absorbed, which is manifested by the already changed colour of the liquid. There the filamentous vibrio dies, and disappears under the form of fine amorphous granulations deprived of virulence. At the bottom of this layer of one centimeter in thickness, on the contrary, the vibrios, protected from the approach of oxygen by those of their own kind which have perished above them, continue to multiply by fission until by degrees they pass into the state of spores; so that instead of moving threads of all dimensions, the length of which sometimes even extends beyond the field of the microscope, nothing is now seen but a dust of brilliant isolated specks, upon which the oxygen of the air has no action. It is thus that a dust of septic germs can be formed even in contact with air. And thus it becomes possible to understand how anaerobic organisms may be sown in putrescible liquids by the dust suspended in the atmosphere. Thus also may be explained the permanence of putrid diseases, even of those which are caused by anaerobic microbes, that cannot live in the atmosphere and which escape destruction by becoming spores.

By means of these experiments, as unexpected as they were conclusive, Pasteur had demonstrated that Jaillard and Leplat had not really inoculated their rabbits with an amorphous virus, liquid or solid, but with a virus constituted of a living microscopic organism—in other words, with a true ferment. By the side of the parasite of splenic fever we have thus a fresh example of a living animated virus, with germs forming dust. And the extraordinary thing is that among the microbes of special maladies—which they produce by penetrating and multiplying in the bodies of animals—are to be found aerobies like the bacilli of splenic fever, and anaerobies like the vibrios of acute septicæmia.

II.

In these two virulent maladies, then, splenic fever and septicæmia, the researches of Pasteur had clearly established the parasitic theory. A grand and novel opening was made for future studies on the origin of diseases. Yet, judging from the surprising differences which separate septicæmia and splenic fever, we can foresee that should the future, copying the past, in regard to this and still more recent discoveries, have in store, as it no doubt has, the knowledge of new microbes of disease, the specific properties of these microscopic organisms will demand, for each new exploration, ceaselessly repeated efforts, not only to make the existence of these organisms evident, but also to furnish decisive proofs of their morbific power. But the question which may be considered as already solved is the non-spontaneity of these infectious microbes. By what is called spontaneous disease is meant parasitic disease. But in the present state of science spontaneous disease has no more existence than spontaneous generation. Such aphorisms, however, are not allowed to pass without occasional contradictions, all the more vehement from their rarity. At the International Medical Congress held in London, August 1881, Dr. Bastian, who practises in one of the principal hospitals of London, declared that though he was unable to deny the existence of parasitic diseases, yet, in his opinion, the microbes were the effect and not the cause of these diseases.

'Is it possible,' cried Pasteur, who was present at the meeting, 'that at this day such a scientific heresy should be held? My answer to Dr. Bastian will be short. Take the limb of an animal and crush it in a mortar; let there be diffused in this limb, around these crushed bones, as much blood, or any other normal or abnormal liquid as you please. Take care only that the skin of the limb is neither torn nor laid open, and I defy you to exhibit on the following day, or during all the time the malady lasts, the least microscopic organism in the humours of this limb.'

After the example of Liebig in 1870, Dr. Bastian did not accept the challenge.

But if a disease like splenic fever is carried by a microbe, this microbe is under the influence of the medium in which it finds itself. It does not develop everywhere. Easily inoculable and fatal to the ox, the sheep, the rabbit, and the guinea pig, splenic fever is very rare in the dog and in the pig. These must be inoculated several times before they contract the disease, and even then it is not always possible to produce it. Again, there are some creatures which are never assailable by it. It can never be taken by fowls. In vain they are inoculated with a considerable quantity of splenic blood; it has no effect upon them. This invulnerability had very much struck Pasteur and his two assistants, Joubert and Chamberland. What was it in the body of a fowl that enabled it to thus resist inoculations of which the most infinitesimal quantity sufficed to kill an ox? They proved by a series of experiments that the microbe of splenic fever does not develop when subjected to a temperature of 44° Centigrade. Now, the temperature of birds being between 41 and 42 degrees, may it not be, said Pasteur, that the fowls are protected from the disease because their blood is too warm—not far removed from the temperature at which the splenic fever organism can no longer be cultivated? Might not the vital resistance encountered in the living fowl suffice to bridge over the small gap between 41-42, and 44-45 degrees? For we must always allow for a certain resistance in all living creatures to disease and death. No doubt, life to a parasite in the body of an animal would not be as easy as in a cultivating liquid contained in a glass vessel. If the inoculating microbe is aerobic, it can only be cultivated in blood by taking away the oxygen from the globules, which retain it with a certain force for their own life. Nothing was more legitimate than to suppose that the globules of the blood of the fowl had such an avidity for oxygen that the filaments of the splenic parasite were deprived of it, and that their multiplication was thus rendered impossible. This idea conducted Pasteur and his assistants to new researches. 'If the blood of a fowl was cooled,' they asked, 'could not the splenic fever parasite live in this blood?'

The experiment was made. A hen was taken, and, after inoculating it with splenic fever blood, it was placed with its feet in water at 25 degrees. The temperature of the blood of the hen went down to 37 or 38 degrees. At the end of twenty-four hours the hen was dead, and all its blood was filled with splenic fever bacteria.

But if it was possible to render a fowl assailable by splenic fever simply by lowering its temperature, is it not also possible to restore to health a fowl so inoculated by warming it up again? A hen was inoculated, subjected, like the first, to the cold-water treatment, and when it became evident that the fever was at its height it was taken out of the water, wrapped carefully in cotton wool, and placed in an oven at a temperature of 35 degrees. Little by little its strength returned; it shook itself, settled itself again, and in a few hours was fully restored to health. The microbe had disappeared. Hens killed after having been thus saved, no longer showed the slightest trace of splenic organisms.

How great is the light which these facts throw upon the phenomenon of life in its relation to external physical conditions, and what important inferences do they warrant as to the influence of external media and conditions upon the life and development of living contagia! There have been great discussions in Germany and France upon a mode of treatment in typhoid fever, which consists in cooling the body of the patient by frequently repeated baths. The possible good effects of this treatment may be understood when viewed in conjunction with the foregoing experiment on fowls. In typhoid fever the cold arrests the fermentation, which may be regarded as at once the expression and the cause of the disease, just as, by an inverse process, the heat of the body arrests the development of the splenic fever microbe in the hen.

FOWL CHOLERA.

If fowls are naturally impervious to the infection of splenic fever, there is a disastrous malady to which they are subject, and which is commonly called 'fowl cholera.' Pasteur thus describes the disorder:—'The bird which is attacked by this disease is without strength, staggering, the wings drooping. The ruffled feathers of the body give it the shape of a ball. An overpowering somnolence takes possession of it. If forced to open its eyes, it appears as if it were awakened out of a deep sleep. Very soon the eyelids close again, and generally death comes without the animal changing its place, or without any struggle, except at times a slight movement of the wings for a few seconds.' The examination after death reveals considerable internal disorders.

Here, again, the disease is produced by a microscopic organism. A veterinary surgeon of Alsace, M. Moritz by name, was the first who suspected the presence of microbes in this disease; a veterinary surgeon of Turin, M. Peroncito, depicted it in 1878; a professor of the veterinary school of Toulouse, M. Toussaint, recognised it, in his turn, in 1879, and sent to Pasteur the head of a cock which had died of the cholera. But, however skilful they were, these observers had not succeeded in deciding the question of parasitism. None of them had hit upon a suitable cultivating medium for the parasite, nor had they reared it in successive crops. This, however, is the only method of proving that the virulence belongs exclusively to a parasite.

It is absolutely necessary, in the study of maladies caused by microscopic organisms, to procure a liquid where the infectious parasite can grow and multiply without possible mixture of other organisms of different kinds. An infusion of the muscles of the fowl, neutralised by potash, and rendered sterile by a temperature of 110 to 115 degrees, has proved to be wonderfully appropriate to the culture of the microbe of fowl cholera. The facility of its multiplication in this medium is almost miraculous. In some hours the clearest infusion begins to grow turbid, and is found to be filled with a multitude of little organisms of an extreme tenuity slightly strangulated at their centres. These organisms have no movement of their own. In some days they change into a multitude of isolated specks, so diminished in volume that the liquid, which had been turbid to the extent of resembling milk, becomes again almost as clear as at first. The microbe here described belongs to a totally different group from that of the vibrios. It is ranged under the genus called 'micrococci.' 'It is in this group,' said Pasteur on one occasion, 'that the microbes of the viruses which are yet unknown will probably be one day found.'

In the cultivation of the microbe of fowl cholera, Pasteur tried one of the cultivating liquids which he had previously made use of with most success—the water of yeast—that is to say, a decoction of yeast in water rendered clear by filtration and then sterilised by a temperature of over 100 degrees. The most diverse microscopic organisms find in this liquid suitable nourishment, particularly if it has been neutralised. When, for example, the bacterium of splenic fever is sown in the liquid, it assumes in a few hours a surprising development. Now, it is remarkable that this medium is quite unsuited to the life of the microbe of fowl cholera. Not only does it not develop, but the microbe perishes in this liquid in less than forty-eight hours. May we not connect this singular fact with that which is observed when a microscopic organism proves innocuous in an animal which has been inoculated with it? It is innocuous because it cannot develop itself in the body of the animal, or because, its development being arrested, it cannot attain the vital organs.

The decoction extracted from the muscles of the fowl is the only medium which really suits the microbe of fowl cholera. It suffices to inoculate the fowl with the hundredth, even the thousandth, part of a drop of this mixture, to produce the disease and cause death. But here is a strange peculiarity. If guinea-pigs are inoculated with this little parasite they are hardly ever killed by it. Guinea-pigs of a certain age generally exhibit only a local lesion at the point of inoculation, which ends in an abscess more or less prominent. After opening spontaneously, the abscess closes again and heals, while the animal preserves its appetite and its appearance of health. These abscesses sometimes last several weeks. They are surrounded by a pyogenic membrane and filled with a creamy pus, in which the microbe swarms side by side with the pus globules. It is the life of the microbe inoculated under the skin which causes the abscess. The abscess, with the membrane which surrounds it, becomes for the little organism a sort of closed vessel, which it is even easy to tap without sacrificing the guinea-pig. The organism is mixed with the pus in a state of great purity, and although it is localised its virulence is extreme. When fowls are inoculated with the contents of the abscess they die rapidly, while the guinea-pig, which has furnished the virus, gets well without the least suffering. A curious instance this is of the local evolution of a very virulent microscopic organism, which produces neither internal disorders nor the death of the animal upon which it lives and multiplies, but which can carry death to other species inoculated with it. Fowls and rabbits living among the guinea-pigs suffering from these abscesses might in a moment be smitten and perish, while the health of the guinea-pigs remained unchanged. To produce this result it would suffice that a little of the discharge from the abscess of a guinea-pig should get smeared over the food of the fowls and rabbits. An observer witnessing such deaths without apparent cause, and ignorant of this strange dependency, would no doubt be tempted to believe in the spontaneity of the disease. He would be far from supposing that the evil had originated in the guinea-pigs, which were all in good health. In the history of contagia what mysteries may some day be cleared up by even more simple solutions than this one!

When some drops of the liquid containing this microbe are placed on the food of fowls, the disease penetrates by the intestinal canal. There the little organism increases in such great abundance that inoculation with the excrements of the injected fowls produces death. It is thus easy to account for the mode of propagation of this very serious disease, which depopulates sometimes all the poultry yards in the country. The only means of arresting the contagion is to isolate, for a few days only, the fowls and the chickens, to remove the dung heaps, to wash the yard thoroughly, especially with water acidulated with a little sulphuric acid, or carbolised water with two grammes of acid to the litre. These liquids readily destroy the microbe, or at least suspend its development. Thus all causes of contagion disappear, because, during their isolation, the animals already smitten die. The action of the disease, in fact, is very rapid.

The repeated cultivation of the infectious microbe in the fowl infusion, passing always from one infusion to the next following, by sowing in the latter an infinitely small quantity, so to speak, of the virus—as much, for example, as may be retained on the point of a needle simply plunged into the cultivation— does not sensibly lessen the virulence of the microscopic organism. Its multiplication inside the bodies of fowls is quite as easy with the last as with the first culture. In short, whatever may be the number of the successive cultures of the microbe in the fowl infusion, the last culture is still very virulent. This proves the microbe to be the cause of the disease—a proof the same in kind as that which had already enabled Pasteur to show that splenic fever and septicæmia are produced by specific microbes.

Like the bacillus of splenic fever, the microbe of the fowl cholera is an aerobic organism. It is cultivated in contact with the air, or in aerated liquids. At the same time, though it is entitled to be called an aerobic organism, it differs essentially in certain respects from the parasite of splenic fever. If splenic fever blood filled with filaments of the parasite be enclosed in a vessel protected from the air—say, in a tube closed at its two extremities—in a few days, eight or ten at the most, and much fewer in summer, the parasite disappears, or rather is reduced to fine amorphous granulations, and the blood loses all its virulence. If the same system of shutting out the air be employed with the blood of a fowl charged with the microbe of fowl cholera, this microbe will be preserved with its virulence for weeks, months, even years.

Pasteur has been able to keep for three years tubes thus sealed, a drop of blood from which when cultivated in fowl infusion, sufficed to infect the birds in the poultry yard with cholera. And not only is the microbe preserved thus in the blood contained in the tube; the same occurs if fowl infusion be put into tubes and then sealed by the flame of a lamp.

When, in course of time, such tubes lose their virulence, it is because the vitality of the organism is extinct. The moment the contents of the tube cease to be virulent, it is a sign that the contagium is dead. It is useless, then, to attempt to cultivate it: the microbe cannot be revived.

Here, then, is a third virulent disease, also produced by a microscopic organism. The characteristics of fowl cholera are very different from those of splenic fever and acute septicemia, and these three microbes do not in the least resemble each other. But, glancing back over Pasteur's work, are not the diseases of silkworms, pébrine and flacherie, also virulent diseases? Thus, in so many things, through so many studies, the same connection holds good. Each discovery of Pasteur's is linked to those which precede it, and is the rigorous verification by experimental method of a preconceived idea.

'Nothing can be done,' said he one day, 'without preconceived ideas; only there must be the wisdom not to accept their deductions beyond what experiments confirm. Preconceived ideas, subjected to the severe control of experimentation, are the vivifying flame of scientific observation, whilst fixed ideas are its danger. Do you remember the fine saying of Bossuet? "The greatest sign of an ill-regulated mind is to believe things because you wish them to be so." To choose a road, to stop habitually and to ask whether you have not gone astray, that is the true method.'

It is this method which conducted him in 1880 to that wonderful discovery, the attenuation of contagia. What certain of these contagia are, we have already seen. We shall now learn what they become in the hands of Pasteur.

THE ATTENUATED VIRUS, OR VACCINATION OF VIRULENT DISEASES.
THE VACCINE OF FOWL CHOLERA.

Among the scourges which afflict humanity there are none greater than virulent diseases. Measles, scarlatina, diphtheria, small-pox, syphilis, splenic fever, yellow fever, camp typhus, the plague of the East—what a terrible enumeration! I pass over some, such as glanders, leprosy, and hydrophobia. The history of these diseases presents extraordinary circumstances. The most strange, assuredly, is that which has been from all time established with a great number of these diseases, that they are non-recurrent. As a general rule, notwithstanding some rare exceptions, man can only have measles, scarlet fever, plague, yellow fever once. What explanation, even hypothetically, can be given of such a fact? Still more difficult is it to explain how vaccination, which is itself a virulent though benign disease, preserves from a more serious malady, the small-pox? Has there ever been a discovery more mysterious in its causes and origin, standing, as it does, alone in the history of medicine, and for more than a century defying all comparison?

After dwelling long on Jenner's discovery this question arose in Pasteur's mind: If contagious maladies do not repeat themselves, why should there not be found for each of them a disease different from them, but having some likeness to them, which, acting upon them as cow-pox does upon small-pox, would have the virtue of a prophylactic? A chance occurrence, one of those chances which not unfrequently occur to those who are steadfastly looking out for them, opened out to Pasteur the way to a discovery which may well be called one of the greatest discoveries of the age.

In causing the microbe of fowl cholera to pass from culture to culture, in an artificial medium, a sufficient number of times to render it impossible that the least trace of the virulent matter from which it originally started should still exist in the last cultivation, Pasteur gave in an absolute manner the proof that infectious microbes are the sole authors of the diseases which correspond to them. This culture may be repeated ten, twenty, a hundred, even a thousand times: in the latest culture the virulence is not extinguished, or even sensibly weakened. But it is a fact worthy of attention that the preservation of the virulence in successive cultures is assured only when no great interval has been allowed to elapse between the cultures. For example, the second culture must be sown twenty-four hours after the first, the third twenty-four hours after the second, the hundredth twenty-four hours after the ninety-ninth, and so on. If a culture is not passed on to the following one until after an interval of several days or several weeks, and particularly if several months have elapsed, a great change may then be observed in the virulence. This change, which generally varies with the duration of the interval, shows itself by the weakening of the power of the contagium.

If the successive cultures of fowl cholera, made at short intervals, have such virulence that ten or twenty inoculated birds perish in the space of twenty- four or forty-eight hours, a culture which has remained, say, for three months in its flask, the mouth of which has been protected from the introduction of all foreign germs by a stopper of cotton wool, which allows nothing but pure air to pass through it—this culture, if used to inoculate twenty fowls, though it may render them more or less ill, does not cause death in any of them. After some days of fever they recover both their appetite and spirits. But if this phenomenon is extraordinary, here is one which is surely in a different sense singular. If after the cure of these twenty birds they are reinoculated with a very virulent virus—that, for instance, which was just now mentioned as capable of killing its hundred per cent. of those inoculated with it, in twenty- four or forty-eight hours—these fowls would perhaps become rather ill, but they would not die. The conclusion is simple; the disease can protect *from* itself. It has evidently that characteristic of all virulent diseases, that it cannot attack a second time.

However curious it may be, this characteristic is not a thing unknown in pathology. Formerly it was the custom to inoculate with small-pox to preserve from small-pox. Sheep are still inoculated to preserve them from the *rot*; to protect horned cattle from peripneumonia they are inoculated with the virus of the disease. Fowl cholera offers the same immunity; it is an additional scientific acquisition, but not a novelty in principle.

The great novelty which is the outcome of the preceding facts, and which gives them a distinct place in our knowledge of virulent diseases, is that we have here to do with a disease of which the virulent agent is a microscopic parasite, a living organism cultivated outside of the animal body, and that the attenuation of the virulence is in the power of the experimenter. He creates it, he diminishes it, he does what he wishes with it; and all these variable virulences he obtains from the maximum virulence by manipulation in the laboratory. Looked at in juxtaposition with the great fact of vaccination for small-pox, this weakened microbe, which does not cause death, behaves like a real vaccine relatively to the microbe which kills, producing a malady which may be called benign, since it does not cause death, but is a protection from the same malady in its more deadly form.

But for this enfeebled microbe to be a real vaccine, comparable to that of cow-pox, must it not be fixed, so to speak, in its own variety, so that there should be no necessity for having recourse again to the preparation from which it was originally derived? Jenner, when he had demonstrated that cow- pox vaccination preserved from small-pox, feared for some time that it would be always necessary to have recourse to the cow to procure fresh vaccinating matter. His true discovery consisted in establishing that the cow-pox from the cow could be dispensed with, and that inoculation could be performed from arm to arm. Pasteur made his enfeebled microbe pass from one cultivation to another. What would it become? Would it resume its very active virulence, or would it preserve its moderate virulence?

The virulence remained enfeebled and, we may say, unchanged. This showed it to be a real vaccine. Some veterinary surgeons and farmers, on the announcement of this discovery, applied to Pasteur for a vaccine against the disease which was so disastrous among their poultry. Some trials were made, and all succeeded beyond expectation. To preserve this vaccine it must be secured from contact with the air, the cultures being enclosed in tubes, the extremities of which are sealed by the flame of a blowpipe.

What takes place during that interval of time intentionally placed between two successive cultivations of the cholera microbe—that interval which is employed in effecting the attenuation and producing the vaccine? What is the secret of this result? The agent which intervenes is no other than the oxygen of the air. Here is the proof. If the cultivation of this microbe is carried on in a tube containing very little air, and if the tube is then closed by the flame of a lamp, the microbe, by its development and life, quickly appropriates all the free oxygen contained in the tube, as well as the oxygen dissolved in the liquid. Thus, completely protected from contact with oxygen, the microbe does not become sensibly weakened for months, sometimes even for years.

The oxygen of the air, then, appears to be the cause of modification in the virulence of the microbe.

But how, then, is the absence of influence on the part of the atmospheric oxygen, in the successive cultures which are practised every twenty-four hours, to be explained? There is, in Pasteur's opinion, but one possible explanation; it is that the oxygen of the air in this latter case is solely employed in the life of the microbe. A culture has a duration of some days; in twenty-four hours it is not terminated. The air which comes in contact with it is then entirely employed in nourishing and largely reproducing the microbe. During the longer intervals of culture, the air acts only as a modifier, and at last there arrives a moment when the virulence is so much weakened as to become nil.

This very extraordinary fact is, then, established that the virulence may be entirely gone while yet the microbe lives. The cultures offer the spectacle of a microbe indefinitely cultivable, yet, on the other hand, incapable of living in the bodies of fowls, and in consequence deprived of virulence. May not this domesticated microbe, as M. Bouley calls it, be compared to those inoffensive microbes of which there are so many in nature? May not our common microbes be those organisms which have lost their former virulence? But may not these harmless microbes, become infectious in some particular circumstances? And if there are fewer virulent maladies now than there were in times past, might not the number of these maladies again increase?

Questions multiply as the facts relating to the attenuation of a virus suggest inductions, awaken ideas, and throw new lights upon a problem which, until within these last few years, has remained so obscure. Formerly it was believed that these viruses were morbid entities. A virus was a unity. This opinion has still its declared upholders. According to Pasteur a virus has different degrees of virulence; it can pass from the weakest virulence to the maximum. Modifying, at will, the virus of fowl cholera, Pasteur inoculates some hens, for instance, with a virus too attenuated to protect from death, but which nevertheless is effectual in securing them against a virus stronger than itself. The second virus will preserve them from the attacks of a third virus, and thus passing from virus to virus they end by being guaranteed against the most deadly virulences. The whole question of vaccination resolves itself into knowing at what moment a certain degree of virus attenuation is a guarantee of protection against the mortal virus.

It seems that between small-pox and cow-pox facts of a similar kind take place. It is probable that vaccination rarely gives perfect security against the infection of a very malignant small-pox; moreover, during epidemics of small-pox many persons who have been previously vaccinated are attacked, and some even die of the disease.

As regards the practice of vaccinating fowls against the cholera peculiar to them—which, though it certainly is not of the same importance as human vaccination, is a scientifically *capital* fact—we may hope that whatever the differences of receptivity in different races, or in different individuals of the same race, there will be found vaccines to suit them all, special care being taken to resort to the employment of two successive vaccines of unequal power, employed after an interval of ten or fifteen days. The first vaccine may always be chosen of a degree of weakness which will not in any case cause death, and yet of sufficient strength to prevent dangerous consequences from the second vaccine, which would in some cases be fatal if employed at once, and to enable it to act as a vaccine against the most virulent virus.

With regard to the preparation of vaccines, and the ascertaining of their proper strength, it is necessary to make trials upon a certain number of fowls, even at the risk of sacrificing a few in these preliminary experiments. Beyond such questions of manipulation there remains still a scientific question. How are the effects of vaccination to be conceived? What explanation can be given of the fact that a benign disease can preserve from a more serious and deadly one? Pasteur long sought for the solution of this problem. Without flattering himself that he has unravelled the difficulty, he has nevertheless amassed facts which, amid these physiological mysteries, permit us to frame a hypothesis which can satisfy the mind. Pasteur believes, for example, that the vaccine, when cultivated in the body of the animal, robs the globules of the blood, for example, of certain material principles which the vital actions take a long time to restore to the system, and which to the most deadly contagium is a condition of life. The impossibility of action of the progressive virus and of the deadly virus is thus accounted for.

When Pasteur communicated to the Academy of Sciences these important and unforeseen facts, they were at first received with hesitation. It was not without some surprise that the word vaccination, hitherto exclusively reserved for Jenner's discovery, was heard applied to fowl cholera. At the International Medical Congress held in London in August 1881, Pasteur, in the presence of 3,000 doctors of medicine from all parts of the world, who received him with an enthusiasm which reflected glory on France, justified the name that he had given to his prophylactic experiments.

'I have lent,' he said, 'to the expression vaccination an extension that I hope science will consecrate, as a homage to the merit and immense services rendered to humanity by one of the greatest men of England—Jenner.'

Still, while rendering homage to the sentiment which induced Pasteur to efface himself in favour of Jenner, we may be permitted to say that there is no likeness between the two discoveries. Great as was the discovery of Jenner, it was but a chance observation, which had no ulterior development; and for a whole century, medicine has not been able to derive anything from it beyond its actual application, which is the one result achieved. 'Vaccination is vaccination,' an opponent of Pasteur's, who was driven hard, was obliged to say. The opponent found no other answer, and he could not have found any other. The cow-pox is a malady belonging exclusively to a race of animals. Man can only observe it; he cannot produce it. Suppress cow-pox and there will be no more vaccination. In the French discovery, on the contrary, it is the deadly virus itself which serves as a starting point for the vaccine. It is the hand of man which makes the vaccine, and this vaccine may be artificially prepared in the laboratory, in sufficient quantity to supply all needs. What a future is presented to the mind in the thought that the virus and its vaccines are a living species, and that in this species there are all sorts of varieties susceptible of being fixed by artificial cultivation! The genius of Jenner made a discovery, but Pasteur discovered a method of genius.

'This is but a beginning,' said M. Bouley on the day when Pasteur announced these facts to the Academy of Sciences. 'A new doctrine opens itself in medicine, and this doctrine appears to me powerful and luminous. A great future is preparing; I wait for it with the confidence of a believer and with the zeal of an enthusiast.'

THE VACCINE OF SPLENIC FEVER.

We have seen how the facts have been established with regard to the microbe of fowl cholera. Immunity against a virulent disease may be obtained by the influence of a benign malady which is induced by the same microbe, only weakened in virulence. What a future there would be for medicine if this method could be applied to the prevention of all virulent diseases! As splenic fever was at that time being studied in the laboratory of the École Normale, it was upon this fever that the research was first attempted. But the success of this research, said Pasteur, can only be hoped for if the disease is non-recurrent. It is only in this case that inoculation with the weakened microbe can protect from the deadly splenic fever. Unfortunately, human medicine is dumb as regards this question of non-recurrence. The man who is smitten with malignant pustule rarely recovers. If there are any cases of recovery— and there are some authentic ones—he who has so narrowly escaped death could not confidently count upon his chance of protection from the disease in future. In order to acquire such a sense of security he would have to expose himself to experiments of direct inoculation, which he would hardly care to do. Animals alone offer the possibility of solving this problem. Yet it is not to all species of animals that we can have recourse. Every sheep inoculated with splenic fever infection is a sheep lost; but the ox and the cow have more power of resistance. Among them there are frequent cases of cure. An incident occurred which enabled Pasteur to push very far this experimental study.

In 1879 the Minister of Agriculture appointed him to give judgment upon the value of a proposed mode of cure for cows smitten with splenic fever, which had been devised by M. Louvrier, a veterinary surgeon of the Jura. Choosing M. Chamberland as his assistant to watch the application of M. Louvrier's remedy, Pasteur instituted a series of comparative experiments. Some cows were inoculated, two and sometimes four at a time, with the virulent splenic fever virus. Half of these cows were treated by M. Louvrier's method; the other half were left without treatment. A certain number of the cows under M. Louvrier's care resisted the disease, but an equal number of those not under treatment recovered also. The inefficacy of the remedy was demonstrated as well as the cause of the inventor's illusions. But one precious result remained from the trial of this remedy. Pasteur and Chamberland had thus at their disposition several cows which had recovered from splenic fever, and which had experienced in their attack all the worst symptoms. At the places of inoculation enormous swellings were formed, which extended to the limbs, or under the abdomen, and which contained several quarts of watery fluid. The fever had been intense, and at one time death had appeared imminent. When these cows recovered they were reinoculated with great quantities of virulent virus. Not the least trace of disease showed itself, even in cases where the inoculation was performed after an interval of more than a year.

The question was solved; splenic fever, like most of the virulent diseases which it has been possible to study, was non-recurrent. The immunity obtained has a long duration. With that valiant ardour which always urges him on, Pasteur next proposed to examine the vaccine of splenic fever. In view of these new investigations, which would require long and careful labours, and which necessitated a certain amount of medical knowledge, Pasteur associated with himself, in addition to M. Chamberland, a young savant, now a doctor of medicine, M. Roux.

Following the rigorous course of his deductions, Pasteur naturally turned to the oxygen of the air in his attempts to modify the virulence of the splenic microbe. But a difficulty presented itself at the outset. Between this microbe and the microbe of fowl cholera there exists an essential difference. The microbe of fowl cholera, as is the case with a great number of microscopic organisms, reproduces itself only by fission. The parasite of splenic fever, on the contrary, has another mode of generation; it forms spores, nothing analogous to which is found in the microbe of cholera.

In the blood of animals, as in the cultures at the beginning, the splenic fever microbe appears at first in transparent filaments, more or less divided into segments. Up to that point, the resemblance between the microbe of splenic fever and the microbe of cholera is complete. But this blood, or the cultures exposed to the free contact of the air, instead of continuing this first mode of generation, frequently exhibit, even in the course of twenty-four hours, spores distributed more or less regularly along the length of the filaments. All around these corpuscles the matter of the filaments is absorbed, in the manner formerly illustrated by Pasteur in the diagrams of his work on the diseases of silkworms, when treating of the bacilli of putrefaction. Little by little, all cohesion between the spores disappears, and the whole collection soon forms nothing more than a dust of germs. But—and here lies the great difficulty which experimenters encountered in applying to splenic fever the method of gradual attenuation which was practised with the microbe of cholera—these germs of splenic fever may be exposed for years to the air without losing their virulence, always ready to reproduce themselves without any appreciable change, and to manifest their effects in the bodies of animals. How can it be hoped to discover a vaccine of splenic fever by the method used with the contagium of fowl cholera, since the splenic fever virulence, at the end of twenty-four hours, is concentrated in a spore? Before the oxygen of the air has had time to attenuate the contagium, the virulence of the parasite would be encased in these spores. Yet this objection did not appear insuperable to Pasteur. Since (said he to himself), under its filamentous form, the microbe of splenic fever is quite analogous to the microbe of fowl cholera, may not the problem of exposing the splenic microbe to the air be reduced to the following one: to determine the conditions which would prevent the production of spores? The difficulty would thus be surmounted; for, once we have got rid of the spores, the splenic filaments might be maintained in contact with air for any length of time, and we might then no doubt fall back upon the conditions which had produced the attenuation of the cholera microbe.

Pasteur and his two assistants gave themselves up to this research. Days passed and experiments were multiplied. Pasteur became more and more engrossed: he had, what his daughter called, 'the face of an approaching discovery.'

'Ah! what a grand thing it would be,' he was heard from time to time to murmur to himself with a suppressed voice, 'if one could arrive at that—if the fact that the attenuation of the microbe of fowl cholera proved not to be an isolated one!' But if anyone ventured to ask him a timid question as to the phase his experiments were going through, he would reply, 'No, I can tell you nothing. I dare not express aloud what I hope.'

At last one day he came up from his laboratory with a triumphant face. His joy was such that tears stood in his eyes. I have never seen a more radiant expression of the highest and most generous emotions than emanated from his countenance.

'I should never console myself,' he said while embracing us, 'if a discovery such as my assistants and I have just made were not a French discovery.'

And with the clearness which is the charm of this powerful mind, he related to us the most recent discoveries of his laboratory.

In neutralised chicken infusion the splenic microbe can no longer be cultivated at a temperature of 44 or 45 degrees. Its cultivation, on the contrary, is easy at 42 or 43 degrees; and in these conditions the microbe produces no spores. At this latter temperature, therefore, and in contact with pure air, we can maintain a culture of filamentous parasites of splenic fever, deprived of all germs. In some weeks the crop dies—that is to say, when this culture is sown in fresh broth the sterility of the broth remains complete. But during the preceding days life exists in the cultivating liquid. If after two, four, six, or eight days of exposure to the air and to heat, the contagium is tried upon animals, its virulence is found to be continually changing with the time of its exposure to the air, and, consequently, it represents a series of attenuated contagia. From the moment when the formation of the spores of the splenic fever bacillus is prevented, all becomes substantially the same as in the case of the microbe of fowl cholera. Moreover, as in the cholera microbe, each of these states of attenuated virulence can be reproduced by cultivation. Finally, splenic fever not being recurrent, each of these splenic fever microbes constitutes a vaccine for the more virulent microbe.

In order to apportion the virulence of the vaccine to the species it is desired to vaccinate, it must be tried on a certain number of individuals of the same species. If some vaccinated animals are inoculated with the virulent virus, and none of them perish, the vaccine is good. Among individuals of the same species, however, the difference of receptivity is in general great enough to make it prudent, and even necessary, to have recourse to two vaccines, one weak and the other stronger, with an interval of from 12 to 15 days between the two inoculations.

It was on February 28, 1881, that Pasteur communicated to the Academy of Sciences, in his own name, and in those of his two fellow workers, the exposition of this great discovery. Loud applause burst forth with patriotic joy and pride. And yet so marvellous were these results that some colleagues could not help saying, 'There is a little romance in all this.' All this reminds one, in fact, of what the alchemist of Lesage did to the demons which annoyed him. He shut them up in little bottles, well corked, and so kept them imprisoned and inoffensive. Pasteur shut up in glass bulbs a whole world of microbes, with all sorts of varieties which he cultivated at will. Virulences attenuated or terrible, diseases benign or deadly, he could offer all. Hardly had the journals published the *compte-rendu* of this communication when the President of the Society of Agriculture in Melun, M. le Baron de la Rochette, came, in the name of the Society, to invite Pasteur to make a public experiment of splenic fever vaccination.

Pasteur accepted. On April 28 a sort of convention was entered into between him and the Society. The Society agreed to place at the disposal of Pasteur and his two young assistants, Chamberland and Roux, sixty sheep. Ten of these sheep were not to receive any treatment; twenty-five were to be subjected to two vaccinal inoculations at intervals of from twelve to fifteen days, by two vaccines of unequal strength. Some days later these twenty-five sheep, as well as the twenty-five remaining ones, were to be inoculated with the virus of virulent splenic fever. A similar experiment was to be made upon ten cows. Six were to be vaccinated, four not vaccinated; and the ten cows were afterwards, on the same day as the fifty sheep, to receive inoculation from a very virulent virus.

Pasteur affirmed that the twenty-five sheep which had not been vaccinated would perish, while the twenty-five vaccinated ones would resist the very virulent virus; that the six vaccinated cows would not take the disease, while the four which had not been vaccinated, even if they did not die, would at least be extremely ill.

As soon as the agricultural and scientific press had published this programme, and recorded Pasteur's prophecies, several of his colleagues at the Academy of Sciences, startled by such boldness in reference to a subject which had hitherto been enveloped in such profound obscurity, and fearing to see the illustrious company somewhat compromised by these affirmations in relation to problems of physiology and pathology, addressed some observations to M. Pasteur on what they called 'a scientific imprudence.'

'Take care,' they said to him, 'you are committing yourself without possibility of retreat. Your experiments in the laboratory hardly authorise you to attempt experiments like those at Melun.'

'No doubt,' Pasteur answered, 'we have never had in our experimental studies so many animals at our disposition to inoculate; but I have full confidence. What has been already done in my laboratory is to me a guarantee of what can be done.'

And M. Bouley, confident also in the assurances of his illustrious friend, and arranging to meet him, to witness these audacious experiments, said to his anxious colleagues, 'Fear nothing; he will come back triumphant.'

The experiments began on May 5, 1881, at four kilometers' distance from Melun, in a farm of the commune of Pouilly-le-Fort, belonging to a veterinary doctor, M. Rossignol, secretary-general of the Society of Melun. At the desire of the Society of Agriculture, a goat had been substituted for one of the twenty-five sheep of the first lot. On the 5th of May they inoculated, by means of the little syringe of Pravaz—that which is used in all hypodermic injections—twenty-four sheep, the goat, and six cows with five drops of an attenuated splenic virus. Twelve days after, on May 17, they reinoculated these thirty-one animals with an attenuated virus, which was, however, stronger than the preceding one.

On May 31 very virulent inoculation was effected. Veterinary doctors, inquisitive people, and agriculturists formed a crowd round this little flock. The thirty-one vaccinated subjects awaiting the terrible trial stood side by side with the twenty-five sheep and the four cows, which awaited also their first turn of virulent inoculation. Upon the proposal of a veterinary doctor, who disguised his scepticism under the expressed desire to render the trials more comparative, they inoculated alternately a vaccinated and a non-vaccinated animal. A meeting was then arranged by Pasteur and all other persons present for Thursday, June 2, thus allowing an interval of forty-eight hours after the virulent inoculation.

More than two hundred persons met that day at Melun. The Prefect of Seine-et-Marne, M. Patinot, senators, general counsellors, journalists, a great number of doctors, of veterinary surgeons, and farmers; those who believed, and those who doubted, came, impatient for the result. On their arrival at the farm of Pouilly-le-Fort, they could not repress a shout of admiration. Out of the twenty-five sheep which had not been vaccinated, twenty-one were dead; the goat was also dead; two other sheep were dying, and the last, already smitten, was certain to die that very evening. The non-vaccinated cows had all voluminous swellings at the point of inoculation, behind the shoulder. The fever was intense, and they had no longer strength to eat. The vaccinated sheep were in full health and gaiety. The vaccinated cows showed no tumour; they had not even suffered an elevation of temperature, and they continued to eat quietly.

There was a burst of enthusiasm at these truly marvellous results. The veterinary surgeons especially, who had received with entire incredulity the anticipations recorded in the programme of the experiments, who in their conversations and in their journals had declared very loudly that it was difficult to believe in the possibility of preparing a vaccine capable of triumphing over such deadly diseases as fowl cholera and splenic fever, could not recover from their surprise. They examined the dead, they felt the living.

'Well,' said M. Bouley to one of them, 'are you convinced? There remains nothing for you to do but to bow before the master,' he added, pointing to Pasteur, 'and to exclaim—

"I see, I know, I believe, I am undeceived."'

Having suddenly become fervent apostles of the new doctrine, the veterinary surgeons went about proclaiming everywhere what they had seen. One of those who had been the most sceptical carried his proselytising zeal to such a point that he wished to inoculate himself. He did so with the two first vaccines, without other accident than a slight fever. It required all the efforts of his family to prevent him from inoculating himself with the most virulent virus.

An extraordinary movement was everywhere produced in favour of vaccination. A great number of agricultural societies wished to repeat the celebrated experiment of Pouilly-le-Fort. The breeders of cattle overwhelmed Pasteur with applications for vaccine. Pasteur was obliged to start a small manufactory for the preparation of these vaccines in the Rue Vauquelin, a few paces from his laboratory. At the end of the year 1881, he had already vaccinated 33,946 animals. This number was composed of 32,550 sheep, 1,254 oxen, 142 horses. In 1882, the number of animals vaccinated amounted to 399,102, which included 47,000 oxen and 2,000 horses. In 1883, 100,000 animals were added to the total of 1882.

From the commencement of the practical application of this new system, the results were topical. Among flocks where half had been vaccinated and the other half not vaccinated—all the animals continuing to live together—the mortality from splenic fever in 1881 was ten times less in the vaccinated sheep than in the non-vaccinated, being 1 in 740 as against 1 in 78; and in cows and oxen fourteen times less, being 1 in 1,254 against 1 in 88. In 1882 also, the mortality was ten times greater among the non-vaccinated than among the vaccinated animals.

In 1883 it was proved that the duration of the immunity generally lasted longer than a year. It is, however, prudent to vaccinate every year, and to select for performing the operation a period when splenic fever has not yet become developed—in March and April. If the vaccinating is postponed until the fever is in the sheepfolds, there is the risk of attributing to vaccination the losses which in reality belong to the natural disease. Just as human vaccination cannot preserve from small-pox a patient who is already under the influence of small-pox, so the splenic vaccinations are powerless against a fever already in process of incubation.

It must not be assumed that the duration of immunity to animals after splenic vaccination cannot be compared with the duration of immunity from small-pox after Jennerian vaccination. Jenner and his contemporaries believed that vaccination was able to preserve from small-pox during the whole life. That illusion disappeared long ago, and now ten years has been fixed as the average duration of that immunity and of the interval which ought to separate successive vaccinations. This interval, moreover, is too long for a certain number of individuals. Besides, in order to judge of the immunity of antisplenic vaccination, we must not lose sight of the formidable trial which vaccinated animals have to undergo when inoculated with the most virulent virus. What doctor would dare to subject a vaccinated child to inoculation from virulent small-pox a year after its vaccination? Finally, taking into consideration the commercial and economic view of the life of a sheep—if such an expression may be used—the average scarcely exceeds three years. The duration, then, of the immunity that vaccination confers is about a third of the duration of the animal's life.

THE RETURN TO VIRULENCE.

After having reduced the microbes of fowl cholera and splenic fever to all degrees of virulence, and brought them to a point where they could no longer multiply in the bodies of animals inoculated with them, and fixed them in media appropriate to their life, Pasteur asked himself whether it would not be possible to restore to these attenuated microbes—weakened to such a degree as to have lost all virulence—a deadly virulence, and to render them again capable of living and multiplying in the bodies of animals.

Experiment soon confirmed this mental prevision. An attenuated splenic fever virus which could cause no danger of disease or death to guinea-pigs of a year, or a month, or even a week old, could kill a little guinea-pig just born, or one or two days old. The attenuated microbe could multiply itself in the blood of so young an animal. We can well imagine that in an animal, scarcely formed, the power of oxygenation of the blood globules is not as yet capable of preventing the aerobic microbe from turning to its own account the oxygen of the blood. The disease does its work and death supervenes.

After all, there is nothing surprising in the fact that the vital resistance of a newly-born guinea-pig should differ from that of an adult one. But what is very remarkable is, that if an older guinea-pig be inoculated with the blood of one a day old; if a third, still older, be inoculated with the blood of the second; and so on; the virulence of the microbe will be gradually reinforced—that is to say, the usual habit of this parasite to develop itself in the body of the animal will be restored. The process may be likened to that of an animal or vegetable species, passing by successive stages and long sojourns, from one region to another very distant one, subjected to quite new conditions of climate, and gradually becoming acclimatised to the last one. How great, then, must be the importance of the medium of cultivation, with regard to the virulence of the microbes of communicable diseases! Cultivating the microbe by passing it from one guinea-pig to another, we soon arrive at a strength capable of killing guinea-pigs of a week, a month, or several years old, until at last the smallest drop of the blood of these guinea-pigs suffices to kill a sheep; and from the sheep we may pass on to the ox.

The same is the case with the microbe of fowl cholera. When it has ceased to have any effect upon fowls, its virulence can be restored by inoculating small birds. Blackbirds, canaries, sparrows, all die, if the virus has not been too much attenuated; and the effect is similar on young chicks. Thus by several successive transitions from bird to bird a virulence may be fostered capable of destroying full-grown fowls.

These facts suggested to Pasteur certain inductions which may be well founded. Is not the attenuation of the virus by the influence of the air one of the factors in the extinction of great epidemics? And may not the reappearance of these scourges be accounted for by the reinforcement of the virulence?

'The accounts which I have read,' Pasteur remarked some months ago, 'of the spontaneous appearance of the plague in Benghazi in 1856 and in 1858 tend to prove that this outbreak could not be traced to any original contagion. Let us suppose, guided by the facts now known to us, that the plague, a malignant disease belonging to certain countries, has germs of long duration. In all these countries its attenuated virus must exist, ready to resume its active form whenever the conditions of climate, of famine, of misery present themselves afresh. The condition of long duration in the vitality of the germs of evil is not even indispensable; for, if I may believe the doctors who have visited these countries, in all places subject to the plague, and in the intervals of the great outbreaks of the epidemic, cases may be met with of people attacked with boils, not fatal, but resembling those of the deadly plague. Is it not probable that these boils contain an attenuated virus of the plague, and that the passage of this virus into exhausted bodies, which abound only too freely in periods of famine, may restore to it a greater virulence?

'The same may be the case with other maladies which appear suddenly, like typhus in armies and in camps. Without doubt, the germs which are the authors of these diseases are everywhere scattered around, but attenuated; and in this state a man may carry them about him or in his intestinal canal without great damage. They only become dangerous when, by conditions of overcrowding, and perhaps of successive developments on the surfaces of wounds, in bodies enfeebled by disease, their virulence is reinforced.'

ETIOLOGY OF SPLENIC FEVER.

M. Pasteur had triumphed over splenic fever with as much rigour as precision. But he considered that he had still to make one further investigation. He had established the effects of the pest; he had discovered a preventive method with which to combat it: he now wished to know the origin of the evil. Whence comes splenic fever? Why is it endemic in certain departments of France, in certain parts of Russia, Germany, Austria, Italy, Spain, and America? How is it sustained? It was for a long time believed that splenic fever was born spontaneously under the influence of various accidental causes. M. Bouley has related, in his learned work on the 'Progress of Medicine by Experimentation,' that in 1842 the Minister of Agriculture, M. Cunin-Gridaine, at the request of the deputies of the departments that were ravaged by the epidemic, entrusted to M. Delafond, a professor of the school at Alfort, the task of investigating this malady, commonly called the 'blood disease,' in the districts in which it was raging. He was to search out its causes, and ascertain whether they did not result from the system of cultivation prevalent in the country.

M. Delafond arrived in Beauce. One fact struck him—namely, that almost all the animals attacked by the disease were young, fine, and vigorous: those, in short, that gave the best promise. Viewing the richness of the soil and the abundance and quality of the crops in conjunction with this observation, Delafond at once elaborated a speculative theory. 'The blood disease,' said he, 'is nothing but an overfulness—an excess of blood circulating in the vessels, and especially the predominance in that liquid of red globules.'

Starting from this idea, his one object was, by means of logical deduction, to trace everything to this fundamental error. He analysed the soil, and demonstrated to what extent it was fitted to furnish crops that were rich and abounding in nutritive properties. He analysed the plants. He then complacently referred the richness of blood of the Beauce sheep to the richness in nitrogenous principles of the substances on which they were fed. He examined the lesions of the diseased animals, and concluded that they were the consequence of the blood containing too large a proportion of the organic elements, called globules, fibrine, albumen, and too small a proportion of water.

'Reduce the proportion of nutritious elements,' he wrote as his advice to the agriculturists, 'mix roots with all that is too rich in nitrogenous principles, and you will reduce in proportion the losses caused by the excess of the ultra-nutritious substances with which you supersaturate your cattle.'

'Such is the very logical conclusion to which Delafond was led,' adds M. Bouley, ridiculing these observations, based on a method of reasoning, instead of on the experimental method. 'And as a fresh proof of his theory he mentions the fact that the disease decreases as you descend the country towards the Loire. On the right bank of that river—in Sologne, for instance, which is a low, sandy, damp district—blood disease is unknown. In the arrondissements of Gien and Montargis and in parts of those of Orleans and Pithiviers it prevails but little. There, Delafond imperturbably remarks, the soil is sandy and the herbage not nearly so rich as in the Beauce plateau; and there the blood disease is consequently less common.'

When we consider that such opinions could be written unchallenged only forty years ago, that they could even borrow a scientific character from the inspiration that gave them birth, we can see the progress that has since been made, and can realise how great were the obscurity and uncertainty which have been dispelled by the experimental method.

The presence of a parasite having been brought to public notice in the blood of animals suffering from splenic fever, at the very time when Pasteur had shaken the belief in spontaneous generation, people grew accustomed to the idea that the stricken animals might have contracted the germs of the malady from the outer world, without any spontaneous birth, strictly so called, of the disease. This opinion was strengthened by a knowledge of the spores of the splenic bacillus. Pasteur, aided by Messieurs Chamberland and Roux, commenced experiments with a view to solving this difficult etiological question. The first experiments took place in the fields of a farm at the village of St. Germain, near Chartres. Several groups of sheep were fed on lucern grass which had been sprinkled with artificially-reared splenic fever bacteria, or with their germs or spores. Although all the sheep of the same group absorbed an immense number of the spores of the parasite, many survived, even after being visibly affected. Those that died showed all the symptoms of what is called spontaneous splenic fever. The period of incubation lasted as long as eight or ten days, although, in its latter stages, the disease exhibited those startling features which have caused a belief that the incubating period is a very short one—short, that is to say, for those conditions of contagion where the parasite is not deposited in its pure state under the animal's skin.

But if prickly plants (notably the pointed ends of dried thistle leaves, or beards of barley blades cut into little bits about a centimeter in length) were added to this infected food, the mortality increased to a striking extent. On examination after death, the lesions of these animals were found to be similar to those observed in sheep which were attacked by splenic fever in sheds, or which died of the disease in the open fields.

From that time forward, the idea which had been predominant in the minds of Pasteur and his fellow-workers during all their inquiries, was materially strengthened. They were convinced that the animals which died of blood disease in the department of Eure et Loire had been infected by germs or spores of the splenic microbe contained in their food; but the question remained, Whence came these germs?

From the moment when all belief in the spontaneous generation of the parasite is rejected, attention is naturally drawn to the possible consequences which may arise from burying in the earth animals which have died of splenic fever. In the greater number of cases, when the knacker's establishment is too far off and the dead animal is of little value, a trench is dug on the spot, at a depth varying from half a meter to a meter. If the animal dies in a field, it is buried where it falls; if it dies in a shed the body is carried into a neighbouring field. There it is buried, and putrefaction sets in; and since all the splenic fever filaments of the blood are destroyed by putrefaction, it was thought that no dissemination of the germs of splenic fever, after the animal had been buried, could occur. Pasteur showed that this opinion rested on a superficial observation. Even when the animal is not cut up, blood spreads itself outside of the body in more or less abundance. Is it not an habitual characteristic of the disease, that at the time of death blood issues from the nostrils and the mouth, and that the urine is often bloody? All around the corpse, therefore, the earth is polluted with blood. Moreover it takes several days for the splenic fever microbe to resolve itself into harmless granulations by the action of gases, other than oxygen, which putrefaction generates. During this time, the excessive inflation of the dead body causes the liquids of the interior to issue from all the natural apertures. How often also, a rent in the skin or the tissues increases this flow. The blood and other matters, mixed with the surrounding aerated soil, are no longer in the conditions of putrefaction, but rather in those which form a suitable medium of cultivation for the microbe. Experiments confirmed these views. Adding some splenic fever blood to earth sprinkled with the water of yeast, or with urine, at summer temperature, or at the temperature which the fermentation of a dead body keeps up around it, as in a dung heap, in less than twenty-four hours the splenic fever filaments deposited with the blood had multiplied and resolved themselves into spores. These spores were afterwards found in their state of latent life, ready to germinate and to communicate splenic fever, after remaining in the earth for months, and even years.

These experiments, curious as they were, were only, so to speak, laboratory experiments. It was necessary to investigate what happened in the open country with all the variations of dryness, of damp, and of cultivation. A happy inspiration came to Pasteur and his assistants. They had buried in the midst of summer, in an isolated corner of the farm of St. Germain, near Chartres, a sheep which had died of natural splenic fever, and of which they had made the autopsy. Ten months afterwards, and again fourteen months afterwards, the idea occurred to them of collecting some of the earth from this grave. After having examined it, and established the presence of the spores of the microbe, they produced, by the inoculation of guinea-pigs, the splenic disease and death. But the circumstance which deserves the greatest attention, is that the same experiment was successfully made with the earth on the *surface* of the grave, though this earth had not been disturbed during the interval. Some experiments were afterwards made on the earth of some trenches dug in a meadow of the Jura, where some cows which had died of splenic fever had been buried at a depth of two meters. Two years afterwards, by successive washings of the earth on the surface of the graves, deposits were extracted which at once produced splenic disease. At three trials within these two years the same surface earths produced splenic fever, while, away from the graves, the earth exhibited nothing of the kind. Finally, Pasteur and his assistants proved that on the surface of the earth which covered the buried animals, the germs were again found, after all the operations of ploughing, sowing, and reaping.

But how, it will be asked, can the earth, which is so powerful a filter, allow the germs of microscopic organisms to rise again to its surface? Is one not tempted here to quote Pasteur against himself, since, in his joint researches with M. Joubert, Pasteur had proved that the waters of springs issuing from the earth, even at a shallow depth, are entirely free from germs? Such waters, nevertheless, being supplied from the earth's surface, which is constantly washed by rain, the effect must be to carry down the finest particles to the springs. But these latter, notwithstanding conditions so conducive to their pollution, remain perfectly pure. Can there be a better proof that earth of a certain thickness will arrest all solid particles, even the most minute? Nevertheless, in these experiments on splenic fever, we hear of microscopic germs, starting from the depths and coming up to the surface—that is to say, in a direction contrary to the flow of the rain. This is an enigma.

The explanation will cause surprise. The earth-worms transport the germs, and bring up, from the depths where they lie buried, the terrible microbes. In the tiny cylinders of earth which the worms deposit on the surface of the soil, after the dews of the morning or after rain, the splenic germs are to be found. It is easy to prove this directly. If in earth, with which spores of the microbe have been previously mingled, we place some worms, and at the end of several days open the bodies of these worms, with all necessary precautions, so as to extract from them the earthy matter which fills their intestinal canals, we find in them large numbers of splenic fever spores. It is, then, absolutely proved, that if splenic fever germs exist, as they often do, in the light earth which covers the pits in which animals dead of that disease lie buried, these germs result from the disintegration by rain of the little excremental cylinders deposited by the earth-worms. The dust of this disintegrated earth spreads itself over the grasses on a level with the soil, and thus it is that animals come to find on the pasture-field, and in particular kinds of forage, the germs of splenic fever by which they are infected.

'In these results,' said Pasteur a short time ago at the Academy of Medicine, 'what outlooks are opened to the mind in regard to the possible influence of earths in the etiology of diseases, and the possible danger of the earth of cemeteries!'

The earth-worms also bring to the surface other germs, which, while they are as harmless to the worms as the splenic germs, are nevertheless bearers of diseases to which animals are liable. All sorts of germs are found in them, and the germs of splenic fever are in fact always associated with those of putrefaction and septicæmia.

———————————————

'And now,' concluded Pasteur, when laying before the Academy a rapid survey of the etiology of splenic fever, 'is not the remedy naturally indicated? We should never bury animals in fields destined either for cultivation, for forage, or for sheep pasture. When it is possible a sandy soil should be chosen for the purpose, or any poor calcareous soil, dry, and easily desiccated—in a word, soil not suited to the existence of earth-worms.' M. Tisserand, Director of Agriculture, has remarked that splenic fever is unknown in the region of the Savarts of Champagne, although it is surrounded by countries invaded by the disease. If the conditions of commerce introduce splenic fever, it is but a passing accident. Must not this be attributed to the fact that in these poor soils, such as that of the camp at Châlons, where the thickness of arable soil is only from 4 to 5 inches, superposed upon chalk, the worms cannot live? In such a soil the burial of a splenic fever animal will give rise to great quantities of germs, which, owing to the absence of earth-worms, will abide in the depths of the soil and remain harmless. Finally, it has been proved that the countries subject to splenic fever have an argillaceous-calcareous soil, and that the disease is unknown in schistose and granitic soils. The contrast of the results, in relation to such differences of soil, is seen sometimes in the Department of the Aveyron, between the right and left side of one and the same road or watercourse.

May we not now in all confidence assert that, if the cultivators choose, splenic fever may soon be a thing of the past among their animals, their shepherds, and among the butchers and the tanners of the towns, because splenic fever and malignant pustule are never spontaneous? The disease exists only where it has been sown, or where it has been diffused by the unconscious instrumentality of the earth-worm.

The progress of vaccination will also contribute to the disappearance of splenic fever; for this preventive, if extensively used, as there is no doubt it will be, must end by establishing a race of domestic animals which, having all sprung from vaccinated parents, will in consequence be more resistant to the disease in its worst form. It will be with them in relation to splenic fever as it is with ourselves in relation to small-pox. It is a well-known fact that the ravages of small-pox are much less considerable in our days than when it first appeared in Europe. It is difficult not to attribute this, at least in part, to the prevalence of vaccination.

In the populations where small-pox is introduced for the first time it has an exceptional intensity. Some months ago a significant fact of this nature occurred in Paris. A whole family of Esquimaux perished from small-pox in the 'Jardin d'Acclimatation.' They had never been vaccinated, nor had their ancestors. They were new to the attacks of small-pox, which did not spread beyond them.

METHOD OF DISCUSSION AND CONTRADICTIONS.

Every new discovery produces a revolution in general ideas; a revolution gladly hailed by some, but opposed by others as disturbing their habits of thought and reasoning. Those also who are thrown out in their calculations, while engaged in working out a problem in any way similar to the one that has been solved, too often atone for their dilatoriness by furious denial of the newly asserted truth. The great fact of the attenuation of virus, the artificial production of the vaccines of chicken cholera and of splenic fever, the importance of their employment for the preservation of animals from these diseases, excited throughout the world a surprise and enthusiasm which passionate critics soon sought to disparage. The fiercest attack was from Germany. It commenced immediately after Pasteur's triumph at the International Congress of Medicine held in London in 1881. The German doctor Koch and his colleagues, MM. Gaffki and Lœffler, published in Berlin, in the report of the German Sanitary Office, a kind of scientific tirade against the discovery of virus vaccine, and the possibility of utilising it in the large operations of cattle-breeding.

At the London Congress Dr. Koch had said to a French physician that the possibility of attenuating virus was a thing too good to be true. The whole question was therefore reopened by Dr. Koch and his disciples. At first Pasteur let the torrent flow; but, not being the man to give way before an adversary, he at last declared that the attacks of the German savants must be repelled at Berlin itself. Continual applications for splenic vaccine were made to him from different parts of Germany. M. Pasteur replied that, seeing that the discovery was so formally contested in Prussia, it would be well, before sending any vaccine abroad, to institute a great demonstrative experiment, as had been done at Pouilly-le-Fort.

Dr. Roloff, head of the Veterinary School of Berlin, hastened to take the initiative, by an application to the German Minister of Agriculture. The minister at once nominated a Commission to follow the experiments in vaccination and to draw up a report for the German Government. M. Pasteur entrusted the conduct of the vaccinations to his new colleague, Louis Thuillier, who accepted with deep and silent joy the management of an experiment that was to test a French discovery. He was always ready for anything, this brave Thuillier, who was destined to die, a martyr to the cause of science, in the full promise of his youth, and in the full hope of glory. His courage and his work were alike great and silent. In the laboratory he would spend days, even weeks, without speaking, bent over his microscope with tenacious resolution, endeavouring to follow Pasteur in all his investigations: proud to live near his illustrious master, happy to be his disciple and to be loved by him almost as a son. What a vacancy he has left in the laboratory! What a place he might have held in science!

The composition of the German Commission, over which M. Beyer, member of the Superior Council of Government, presided, showed clearly the importance attached by Germany to the investigation of this French discovery. Among its members was the famous Professor Virchow.

The experiments were carried out on the estate of Pakisch. The minutes and reports of the Commission left no doubt as to the correctness of the facts announced by Pasteur. But, as the negations of Dr. Koch and his colleagues embraced questions beyond that of the prophylaxy of splenic fever, Pasteur did not rest content with this initial success; he sought for a fresh opportunity of convincing his opponents. This opportunity occurred in September 1882, when an International Hygienic Congress was held at Geneva. Thither went Pasteur, hoping to meet Dr. Koch at the sittings; and he was not disappointed. Dr. Koch was there, surrounded by his disciples. From the tribune of the Congress, Pasteur refuted his criticism, exposed his errors, and challenged him to a discussion in the presence of competent judges. There was an instantaneous salvo of applause, and everyone awaited Dr. Koch's reply. But he declined all debate, reserving his case for careful and deliberate statement in the press.

It took three months for Dr. Koch to bring out a small pamphlet, and these three months had borne their fruit. The discovery of the attenuation of virus, which had been so vehemently attacked only a year before in the report of the Sanitary Office, was now extolled by Dr. Koch as a discovery of the first importance. Being, however, unwilling absolutely to stultify himself, he continued the attack by denying its efficacy in practical agriculture.

The clear, direct style of argument, which goes straight to its point, was invariably adopted by Pasteur.

'Contradictions may retard, although they cannot ultimately prevent, the recognition of truth,' he once remarked to me when walking in the gardens of the École Normale; 'that is why it is so important to remove the obstacles which temporarily clog and hamper it. In scientific discussions, it is not as in politics,' he added with a smile, 'where demonstration is often difficult. In the natural sciences, doctrines must be based on an assemblage of results, of observations, and of experiments. If a doctrine is challenged, it seldom happens that its truth or falsehood cannot be established by the application of some crucial test. Even a single experiment will often suffice either to refute or consolidate the doctrine.'

Reviewing the labours of the past forty years, Pasteur then called to mind the numerous controversies in which he had been engaged. Not only had he been attacked by Pouchet and Joly on the question of spontaneous generation, by Liebig on the subject of fermentation, by Germans and Italians regarding the attenuation of virus, but every one of his assertions had been met with such passionate opposition that, from sheer weariness, he had invariably ended by referring the matter to some authorised commission, only asking it to put an end to all strife by coming to some definite decision.

The upshot was at times somewhat amusing. For instance, when Pasteur described to the Academy of Medicine how, simply by lowering the temperature of a hen, he had made her susceptible to inoculation with splenic fever, the facts were at once denied by M. Colin, a professor of the school of Alfort. Pasteur immediately requested that a commission might be named, which should include both himself and his opponent among its members. This was on a Tuesday, one of the Academy days of sitting. The following Saturday, in presence of the whole commission, Pasteur produced four hens that had died of splenic fever. M. Colin himself conducted the autopsy. It was clear to everyone that their blood was full of the filaments of the splenic fever parasite. The *procès-verbal* was drawn up and signed by all the members of the commission, necessarily including M. Colin. The following Tuesday it was read at the sitting of the Academy. To cover his retreat M. Colin now contended that the hens had taken splenic fever not because they had been subjected to a chilling process, but because, so as to keep them in the water, the poor creatures had had their wings and feet tied to planks. This sentimental objection was disposed of by comparative experiments that had been made on hens similarly tied and inoculated, but not chilled. The latter had in no case taken the disease.

At the Academy of Sciences, some days later, a mine was sprung upon Pasteur by a posthumous publication of Claude Bernard's. He again submitted this abruptly raised question to the decision of the Academy. A series of experiments had been found among Bernard's papers, having as their object the inauguration of a new method of spontaneously generating the substance which causes the fermentation of the must of the grape.

'I will start for the Jura,' said Pasteur. 'In the midst of my vineyard, which,' he proudly added, 'is ten meters square, I will cover over some stocks with an improvised frame. These stocks will go on living and bearing grapes, which will ripen. It is now July. At this time of year, as I have already declared, the germs of the cellules which form the ferment of the grape in the vats do not yet exist, either on the green grapes, on the bunches, or on the vine leaves. I will envelop the bunches of the stocks that are underneath the frame with a layer of cotton wool that has been raised to a temperature of 150 degrees Centigrade. This done, I will come back to Paris with the keys of the frame in my pocket, not returning to the Jura until the vintage season, at the beginning of October. I predict to the Academy, that the grapes wrapped in cotton wool under the frame, and which will have grown ripe, may be crushed in the open air, and that the juice coming from them will not be capable of fermentation.'

This prediction was fulfilled. In October, Pasteur returned to the Jura, plucked off several of these stocks, laden with ripe bunches, and brought them with the utmost care to Paris. He had at last the satisfaction of depositing them intact on the table of the Academy of Sciences. He then invited M. Berthelot (editor of Bernard's pamphlet), and all his colleagues, to cut off as many bunches as they pleased. 'Only crush them in contact with pure air,' said he, 'and I defy you to produce fermentation.'

How often was Pasteur obliged to return to facts already proved, not only at the Academy of Sciences, but at the Academy of Medicine, where M. Jules Guérin, at the age of eighty, challenged him to a duel as his scientific ultimatum! If M. Pasteur at times pleaded his cause with too much passion, it was the passion of truth, the burning desire to convince, which lent such power and defiance to his vibrating voice. He could not endure his work to be attacked—not from pride, none was more modest than he—but from irritation at the denial of positive facts; facts of which he was a thousand times assured, and which all the world might verify. No one now remembers these discussions. Time has passed, and opposition has been overthrown. It has been granted to Pasteur to see, everywhere around him, the beneficent results of his discoveries. From all parts, from his own as well as from foreign countries, such proofs of admiration and gratitude have been showered upon him as are usually granted only to those whose death has atoned for their genius. He has opened up such sources of wealth to industry and agriculture that, as the learned English professor Huxley has truly said, 'Pasteur's discoveries suffice, of themselves, to cover the war indemnity of five milliards of francs paid by France to Germany.' His investigations of contagious diseases have revealed immense possibilities in prophylaxy. But Pasteur considered these marvellous discoveries as a mere beginning. 'You will see,' he often said, 'how it will all grow by-and-by. Would that my time were longer!'

THE LABORATORY OF THE ÉCOLE NORMALE.
VARIOUS STUDIES. HYDROPHOBIA.

Since the day when a minister told Pasteur, that there were not 1,500 francs in the budget to allow for the expenses of his laboratory, science has obtained a little more consideration. At the present time she has nothing to complain of: her sovereignty is recognised; her schools are becoming palaces; she has an amply sufficient civil list: she is rich enough, in short, to pay for her researches. M. Pasteur's laboratory has had its full share of the well-bestowed generosity of the State. The municipal council of Paris even wished to attach vast dependencies to this laboratory. The old garden of the ancient Collège Rollin was placed at the disposal of Pasteur; who at once hastened to build stables for lodging horses attacked by glanders, stalls for sheltering splenic fever sheep, and kennels for the reception of mad dogs. But, while taking advantage of these hospitable premises, Pasteur still retained, in the basement of his laboratory in the Rue d'Ulm, a whole population of animals under experiment. Isolated in round cages which impart some sense of security, are the rabid dogs; some attacked with furious madness, biting their bars, devouring hay, uttering doleful howls which those who have once heard can never forget; others carrying the germ of this terrible disease, still fawning with a humble look of tenderness, as if imploring attention. Hens and chickens pass their heads through the wooden bars of their coops. From time to time a cock from the bottom of his den crows 'a gloomy dawn.' Rabbits eat peaceably, while little families of guinea-pigs cluster together, and at the least alarm utter a frightened cry. All these animals are destined to be shortly inoculated. Each morning a round of inspection is made in this little hospital of condemned animals. The dead are taken out, carried to one of the upper rooms, and placed on the dissecting-boards.

It is also to such boards that living animals are fastened when it is necessary to experiment upon them. Certainly when one sees a dog lying with a forlorn look, its feet tied, its body trembling from fright, on the point of undergoing, though in full health, a bloody operation, one cannot suppress the feelings of pity. But a single visit to a physiological laboratory suffices to reveal vivisection in its only and true light; that of the interest it offers to science, and the results it may have in store for the benefit of humanity. Moreover, in Pasteur's laboratory, every dog subjected to vivisection is chloroformed. The persons who take up the controversy about vivisection are careful that the outside world shall see only the suffering and anguish of the animal, where the solution of a problem should be the object kept in view. Would the English physiologist Harvey have discovered the circulation of the blood, if he had not practised vivisection on deer in the park of Charles I.? Would Claude Bernard have been able, without vivisection, to demonstrate the glycogenic function of the liver? If Pasteur had not sacrificed some fowls and sheep, would the great scientific fact of the attenuation of virus have been discovered? If 500 dogs had to perish, what would that be, compared with the discovery tomorrow of the cause of hydrophobia, and of the means of protecting humanity against this frightful scourge?

On one occasion, in presence of a large assembly, Pasteur made an experiment on atmospheric oxygen. He placed under a glass bell a bird, which in a short time, after having consumed the oxygen contained in the bell, gathered itself up into a ball, opened its beak, and shut its eyes, as if it were going to die. At this moment Pasteur introduced a second sparrow, which, passing directly from the ordinary air into the bell, without any gradual preparation, immediately fell, asphyxiated. There was a little exclamation of horror and a movement of pity in the audience. While the firstsparrow, which had gone through the ordeal unharmed, was set free, and gradually revived, Pasteur turned towards the assembly and said—

'I never had the courage to kill a bird in sport, but when it is a question of experiment I am deterred by no scruple. Science has the right to assert the sovereignty of its aims.'

<hr>

But to return to the animals of the laboratory: From the little white mice, which hide themselves in a packet of wadding, to the dogs which bark furiously in their iron cages, all are devoted to death. But it is not only the inmates of the laboratory which daily succeed each other upon the operating and dissecting tables. From divers parts of France, hampers full of fowls which have died of cholera, or of some other disease, are sent to Pasteur. Here is an enormous basket packed with straw containing the dead body of a pig which had died of measles. This fragment of lung, packed in a tin box, belonged to a cow which died of peripneumonia. Other packets are still more precious. Since Pasteur went to Pauillac two years ago, to watch for the return of a ship which was to bring back some passengers attacked with yellow fever, he sometimes receives from a distant country a bottled dose of *vomito negro.*

Everywhere, on the work tables, are to be seen tubes filled with blood, microscope slides carrying little drops. In the stoves are ranged the cultivating flasks, which resemble little flasks of liqueur. The point of a needle dipped into one of these flasks is sufficient to cause death. Enclosed in their glass prison, millions upon millions of microbes live and multiply.

It is really a curious spectacle this workshop of research and discovery. How numerous and varied are the subjects which are being studied, and with what energy and patience does Pasteur attack them! It is not only to the most dreaded diseases that he has applied the germ theory. He has extended it to certain common disorders. Everything to him is a subject for experiment. In May 1879, a person who was working in the laboratory was troubled with boils, which reappeared, as usually happens, at short intervals, sometimes on one part of the body, sometimes on another. Pasteur, whose mind was constantly dwelling on the part played by microscopic organisms, asked himself if the pus of the boils did not contain a parasite, the presence and development of which, and its accidental transport here and there in the body, might be the cause of the local inflammation and of the formation of the pus. The constant reappearance of the evil would be thus accounted for.

The pus of the first boil, which was situated on the nape of the neck, was collected in great purity; some days afterwards, the pus of a second boil, then of a third boil, was collected. The pus, or the blood-stained lymph of the red swelling which preceded the formation of the pus, were sown in a sterilised infusion, and each time a microbe, formed of little spherical points connected in pairs, frequently united in small clusters, was seen to develop itself. The cultivating liquid was sometimes infusion of fowl, sometimes of yeast. In the infusion of yeast the little grains are suspended in pairs throughout the liquid, which is uniformly thickened with them. In the fowl infusion, the grains are united into little clusters, which cover the sides of the vessels, the liquid remaining clear as long as it is not shaken.

New observations were made upon a series of boils, in the case of a man sent to Pasteur by Dr. Maurice Raynaud. The same parasite was again found—a unique parasite, distinct from all others. At the Hospital Lariboisière, a woman whose back was covered with boils, offered another opportunity for experiment, and with the same result. It appears certain, then, that every boil contains a microscopic aerobic microbe, and that to it are due the local inflammation and the consequent formation of pus.

When guinea-pigs or rabbits are inoculated with the cultivating liquids, little abscesses are formed, which, however, quickly disappear. As long as the cure of these little abscesses is not quite completed, one can extract from them the microscopic organism which has formed them. When the little parasite is sought for in the general blood of those attacked with boils it is not found. The cause of this, no doubt, is that an aerobic parasite has always some difficulty in developing itself in the blood. The blood corpuscles appropriate, and do not willingly give up to a foreign organism, the oxygen which they require. There is a struggle for life, and in the struggle against the boils the victory is not doubtful. It might be thought, then, that the little organism of boils does not exist in the blood, but there is no doubt that if, instead of a small drop of blood, one could put several grammes or more into cultivation fruitful results would follow. The little parasite is no doubt conveyed by the blood at one time or other. It is transported from a boil, in the process of development, to another point of the body, where it may be fortuitously arrested, there to cultivate itself and form a new boil.

'It is to be wished,' said Pasteur, 'that a patient would submit to a number of punctures on different parts of the body, distant from boils already formed or in process of formation, and that with the blood thus taken from the general circulation a multitude of cultivations might be carried on. I am persuaded,' he added, 'that, among these cultivations, we should find some fruitful in the little organism of the boils.'

But whilst Dr. Maurice Raynaud gave Pasteur the means of studying boils, Dr. Lannelongue enabled him to investigate that serious disease of the bones and marrow called 'osteomyelitis.' In February 1880 that skilful surgeon, who has published a highly esteemed work on osteomyelitis, and on the possibility of its cure by trepanning the bone, followed by washings and antiseptic dressings, conducted Pasteur to the Hospice Trousseau. A little girl twelve years of age, attacked with this cruel malady, was about to be operated upon. The right knee was much swollen, as was also all the leg to below the calf, and a part of the thigh above the knee. After having chloroformed the child, Dr. Lannelongue made a long incision below the knee, from which pus flowed abundantly. The bone of the tibia was laid bare for a considerable length. Three trepanning perforations were then made in the bone, from each of which the pus issued in great quantities. Pasteur carefully collected, with all the conditions necessary to the preservation of their purity, the pus of the exterior and the pus of the interior of the bone, and, returning to his laboratory, he examined them attentively. The direct observation, by a microscope, of the two specimens of pus was extremely interesting. It was obvious that they contained, in large quantities, an organism like that of boils, in pairs of two or four, and also in parcels, some with a clearly defined outline, others scarcely visible, and with very faint outlines. The external pus showed an abundance of pus globules, but that of the interior did not show any. It was like a paste entirely composed of microbes, so numerous and fertile that, in less than six hours after sowing them in the cultivating liquid, the development of the little microbe had commenced, and was rendered visible to the naked eye by a slight but general turbidity of the liquid.

Its close resemblance to the organism of the boil might lead to the assertion that they are identical, if it were not known how great are the physiological differences that may exist between microscopic parasites of the same appearance and the same dimensions.

I.

As Pasteur advanced in these studies, he found at the Academy of Medicine some fellow labourers, who being keenly interested in such researches did all they could to promote them. Thus M. Villemin, the chief medical officer of the Val de Grâce (who had with so much sagacity discovered the contagion of tuberculosis) when typhoid fever was raging in Paris two years ago, never allowed a case of the fever to pass through his hands without informing Pasteur, who habitually went himself to collect specimens of the blood of those who had died. How numerous were the drops of blood thus enclosed in little tubes, and how frequent the attempts at cultivation, as yet without result, in the hope of finding the cause of a disease which claims so many victims! There is another malady to which Dr. Hervieux especially called Pasteur's attention, and by which so many women are attacked—puerperal fever. He went with M. Hervieux to the Maternity Hospital, to visit a woman under his charge who had contracted puerperal fever some days after her confinement. By means of a pin a prick was made in the forefinger of the left hand, which had been washed previously with dilute alcohol and carbolic acid, and dried with singed linen. The drop of blood taken in this way was sown in an infusion of fowl. For some days the cultivation remained sterile. Next day blood was taken from a fresh puncture, and this time it proved fertile. The woman died three days after. The blood, therefore, already at the time when Pasteur had taken it, three days at least before death, contained a microscopic parasite capable of cultivation. Eighteen hours before this woman died, some blood taken from the left foot had been sown, and, like the former, it had proved productive; but—and this fact deserves to be noted—while the first productive cultivation only contained a microbe resembling that of boils, the other cultivation contained long flexible chaplets clustered together like tangled strings of beads.

At the post-mortem examination of this woman large quantities of pus were found in the peritoneum and the uterus. This pus was sown with all due precaution. Some blood taken from the basilic and femoral veins was likewise sown. It was everywhere easy to recognise the long chaplets in little tangled parcels, and always without admixture of other organisms, except in the cultivation of the peritoneal pus, which, besides the long strings of grains, showed also the little pyogenic vibrios to which Pasteur had already assigned the name of the pus organism.

From the Maternity Hospital Pasteur went to the Hôpital Lariboisière, where he had been informed that another woman had just died of the same fever. From a puncture in the peritoneum he collected some pus which was found there in great abundance. He sowed this, as well as some blood taken from a vein in the arm. The culture of the pus furnished the long strings of grains and the little pyogenic vibrio. The culture of the blood exhibited only the long strings quite pure.

Pasteur made many other observations of the same kind in cases of puerperal fever. He arrived at the conclusion that, under the name of puerperal fever, diseases of different symptoms were classed, but which all appear to be the result of the invasion of common organisms, which develop themselves on the surface of wounded parts, and from thence spread themselves, in one form or another, by the medium of the blood or of the lymphatics, over different parts of the body. Here the various morbid symptoms are determined by the nature of the parasite and the general constitution of the patient. Pasteur is convinced that, with the possible exception of cases where, by the presence either of internal or external abscesses, the body, before confinement, contains microscopic organisms, the antiseptic treatment ought to be infallible in preventing puerperal fever from declaring itself. The employment of carbolic acid may be of great service; but its smell, and often the melancholy association of ideas which it awakens, might render it unsuitable for women in labour. There is not the same objection to concentrated solutions of boric acid, which, at the ordinary temperature, contain from thirty to forty grammes of acid to one litre of water.

'Would it not be very useful,' said Pasteur one day, when developing his ideas and observations before the Academy of Sciences, 'to place always by the bedside of each patient the concentrated and warm solution of boric acid, with compresses to be very frequently renewed, after having been soaked in the solution, these applications being begun immediately after the confinement? It would also be prudent, before using the compresses, to put them into a hot- air stove, at a temperature of 150 degrees, which is more than sufficient to kill all the germs of common organisms.

'I have,' he added, 'represented the facts as they have appeared to me, and I have hazarded the interpretation of them; but I do not disguise from myself that, in the domain of medicine, it is difficult to withdraw oneself entirely from a pre-existing subjective bias; neither do I forget that the medical and veterinary studies are foreign to myself: therefore I earnestly desire judgment and criticism. While I am little tolerant of frivolous contradiction or of prejudice, despising as I do that vulgar scepticism which would erect doubt into a system, I honour that militant scepticism which makes doubt the basis of a method, whose motto is "More light."'

Since these ideas have penetrated further into practice; puerperal fever, I was told lately by a distinguished medical man, is hardly known in the Maternity Hospital. The employment of a solution of one to a thousandth of corrosive sublimate, which is one of the best antiseptics, gives excellent results, and keeps off all danger. May it not be permitted to hope that puerperal fever will soon disappear in the same way that purulent infection has disappeared in hospitals, since the introduction of Lister's dressings?

II.

In 1882, a new malady occupied the attention of the laboratory of the École Normale, a malady the name of which was not even known in Paris, but which made great ravages in the country—namely, swine fever (*rouget*). Here, again, it is a microbe which causes the disorder. This microbe was first perceived by Thuillier, in a little commune of the Département de Vienne, when examining the blood and humours of pigs which had died of the fever. Experiments were at once set on foot in the laboratory, with the view of proving that the microbe was really the cause of the disease. The microbe was cultivated in a sterilised infusion of veal. This cultivation was passed on to a succeeding one, a small drop of the preceding cultivation being always taken for seed. Inoculations from these last cultivations produced the fever in certain breeds of pigs. The proof was thus given that the microbe was really the origin of the disease.

Pasteur then, accompanied by Thuillier and a young assistant, M. Loir, went, in his turn, to study the disease in the Department of Vaucluse. He remained more than a month in the canton of Bollène, in the house of a veterinary surgeon, M. Maucuer, who took him to all the pigsties in the arrondissement. After having had recourse to the oxygen of the air to attenuate the virulence of the microbe, Pasteur made some experiments in vaccination. Some pigs which had been vaccinated remained in the canton of Bollène, under the supervision of M. Maucuer, the owners having pledged themselves to keep their vaccinated pigs for at least a year. In the ensuing September, when swine fever raged everywhere in the canton of Bollène and in the arrondissement of Orange, not a single vaccinated pig was attacked. 'They are all flourishing,' wrote M. Maucuer. An address of thanks was sent to Pasteur by the municipal council of Bollène.

But, notwithstanding these happy results, the question of the application of vaccines to different breeds requires still further investigation, before the vaccination of pigs can become general.

Soon afterwards a method, different from that of the atmospheric oxygen, for weakening the virulence of the fever virus, was tried in the laboratory.

Pasteur had proved that viruses are not morbid entities, that they can assume numerous forms, and especially physiological properties, dependent on the medium in which they live and multiply. The virulence belongs to living microscopic species, but is at the same time essentially modifiable. It may be weakened or intensified, and each of these states is capable of being made permanent by culture. A microbe is virulent in an animal, when it has the power of swarming in the body of that animal, after the manner of a parasite, and of producing, by the renewal of its own life, disturbances which cause disease and death. If this microbe has lived in any species of animal—that is to say, if several times over it has passed from the body of one individual into that of another of the same kind, without having been subjected to any sensible exterior influence during its passage—we may consider that the virulence of this parasite has reached a fixed and maximum state for the individuals of that race. The splenic fever parasite pertaining to sheep, for instance, varies little from one subject to another or from one year to another in the same country; this must be attributed, doubtless, to the fact that, in its successive passages through the sheep, the habit of the parasite to live in sheep has, so to speak, attained a definite state. It is thus with the virus of the Jennerian vaccination. But the virulence of a virus which is not at its maximum may be essentially modified by its passage into a succession of individuals of the same race. It will be remembered how, when Pasteur and his assistants wished to increase progressively the virulence of the virus of chicken cholera and splenic fever, so as to bring them at last to their maximum intensity, these viruses were first inoculated into young subjects, and from them successively into older ones.

'The Academy remembers, without doubt,' said Pasteur in a recent communication, 'that, some time ago, we discovered a microbe virus in the saliva of hydrophobia. This microbe, though very virulent for rabbits, is shown to be harmless for adult guinea-pigs, but it kills rapidly guinea-pigs only some hours or days old. In following out this inoculation from young guinea-pigs, we have seen the virulence increase, and easily arrive at the point of causing death to older guinea-pigs. There was even at last a marked difference in the lesions. The increase of virulence, by successive passages through individuals of one race, was clearly shown.

'But the new and unexpected result that I wish to point out to the Academy consists in this: that the microbe, after having increased its virulence by successive passages through the bodies of guinea-pigs, shows itself to be less virulent in relation to rabbits than it was before.

'In these new conditions, it gives to the rabbit a disease which is spontaneously curable; and, moreover, having once gone through the malady, the animal becomes refractory in regard to the microbe which is deadly to rabbits. From this arises the all-important consequence, that the habit of living in one species (the guinea-pig) at a definite corresponding degree of virulence, can change this virulence in relation to another species (the rabbit), so much diminishing its effects as to cause it to become a vaccine for this latter species.

'The importance of this result cannot fail to be perceived by everyone, for it contains the secret of a new method of attenuation, which can be applied to some of the most virulent viruses. We will give an example and an application of it.

'If a pigeon be inoculated in the pectoral muscle with the microbe of swine fever, the pigeon dies in an interval of six or eight days, after having shown the apparent exterior symptoms of fowl cholera.

'When a second pigeon is inoculated with the blood of the first, a third with that of the second, and so on in succession, the microbe acclimatises itself to the pigeon. The symptoms of forming itself into a ball, and of somnolence, which are the habitual characteristics of the disease, appear in a much shorter time than with the first pigeons of the series. Death likewise comes on more rapidly. Finally, the blood of the last pigeons exhibits much more virulence in the pig than even the most infectious products of a pig that has died of what is called spontaneous fever.

'The passage of the swine fever microbe through rabbits leads to quite a different result. Rabbits inoculated with the infectious products of a pig that has died of the fever, or with the cultivations of them, are always made ill and most frequently die.

'When the virus is inoculated from rabbit to rabbit, the microbe acclimatises itself to the rabbit. All the animals die, and death comes in a very few days. The cultures of the blood of these rabbits in sterilised media become progressively easy and more abundant. The microbe itself changes its aspect somewhat, grows rather larger than in the pig, and appears in the form of an 8, without the filiform lengthening out characteristic of certain other cultures.'

'When pigs are inoculated with the blood of the last rabbits, and the results compared with those obtained from the first of the series, it is found that the virulence has been progressively diminishing from the first rabbit to the following ones. Very soon the blood of the rabbits ceases to cause death in the pigs, though it renders them ill. On recovery they are proof against the deadly swine fever.'

III.

But in the midst of these investigations undertaken by Pasteur, there is one which is paramount over all the others, one on which for three years all his efforts, as well as those of his pupils, have been concentrated, and this is Hydrophobia. Mysterious in its incubation, alarming in its symptoms, Pasteur's attention had for a long time been drawn to it, when in 1880 he finally attacked it. Besides the attraction which an obscure problem had for him, he felt that if he succeeded in discovering the probably microbean etiology of such a disease, he would carry all minds with him into the current of these new ideas. He had been very often struck, if not with the opposition, at least with the prudent and circumspect reserve, shown in the examination of his doctrine, by a considerable number of physicians who, possessed by the idea that the moral element could cause modifications in the symptoms and development of a malady in man, are not disposed to recognise the least assimilation between human diseases and those of the animal species. No doubt the emotional qualities, grave family cares, the terror of approaching death, the dread of the great unknown, may modify the course of the evil in man, may aggravate it, even hasten it; but, whilst recognising—for never was there a man more a creature of sentiment than he—what there is of deep truth in this opinion, Pasteur could not help thinking that the first origin, the cause of every contagious malady, is physiologically the same in the two groups, and that our bodies, notwithstanding our superior moral qualities, are exposed to the same dangers, to the same disorders, as the bodies of animals.

To overcome these resistances, it was necessary, as in the great experiments on splenic fever, to attack a disease common both to men and animals—one in which experimentation, the only, but great, strength of Pasteur, was supreme. Hydrophobia offered these conditions.

Again, it was Dr. Lannelongue who introduced Pasteur to his first case of hydrophobia. On December 10, 1880, a child of five years old, who had been bitten in the face a month previously, was dying in the Trousseau Hospital. Devoured at the time by a raging thirst, and seized with a horror for all liquids, he approached with his lips the spout of a closed coffee pot, then suddenly started back—the throat contracted—a prey to such fury that he insulted the nursing sister who was attending on him. He was at the same time attacked by aerophobia to a prodigious degree. At a certain moment, the heel of one of his feet protruded from the bed. An assistant blew on it. The child had not seen the assistant, and the breath of air was so light as to be almost imperceptible. The poor child flew into a rage, and a violent spasm seized him in the throat. The next day delirium began, a frightful delirium. The frothy matters which filled his throat suffocated him.

Four hours after his death, the mucus from the palate of the child was collected. It was diluted with a little water, and two rabbits were inoculated under the skin of the abdomen. The rabbits perished in less than thirty-six hours. The saliva of these dead rabbits also transmitted the disease to fresh rabbits. Did it not seem as if one had got hold of an inoculation of hydrophobia? Such was in fact the conclusion of Dr. Maurice Raynaud, who, having been informed, at the same time as Pasteur, of the illness of the child, had made, on his own account, some experiments on rabbits. His rabbits were dead. Already a year previously M. Maurice Raynaud had announced the transmission, by the saliva, of rabies from man to rabbits. 'We are, then, in the presence of a new fact of this kind,' he said, 'and we really believe, until a proof to the contrary is given us, that these latter rabbits died of hydrophobia.'

With his habitual prudence, and trusting more to the results of experiment than to medical observation alone, Pasteur was not in a hurry to form such positive conclusions. He began by doing what Dr. Maurice Raynaud had neglected to do. He examined with the microscope the tissues and the blood of the rabbits inoculated in the laboratory; he discovered, both in those that were dead, and in those which were on the point of death, the presence of a special microbe, easily cultivable in a pure state and of which the successive cultures caused the death of other rabbits. Invariably, the same microbe appeared in the blood. As one or two days sufficed to cause death, hydrophobia could not have had time to make its appearance. Pasteur, moreover, found this same microbe in the saliva of children who had died of common maladies, and even in the normal saliva of healthy adults. It was a new microbe, causing a disease unknown up to that time. To Pasteur it seemed, in the case of the experiments made with the mucus from the child's palate, to be simply an accompaniment of the rabic virus.

This microbe of the saliva is very easily cultivated in sterile infusions—that of veal, for example—and successive cultures can be made in the usual way. The virulence continues. Could the virulence be attenuated, asked Pasteur, by the action of the oxygen of the air? This would, by a new example, go to establish the generalisation of the method of attenuation by oxygen. The attempt succeeded. When care is taken, as with the attenuation of the fowl cholera contagium, not to allow more than some hours' interval to elapse between one cultivation and the succeeding one, the virulence of the successive cultivations of the microbe of the saliva is preserved in some sort indefinitely. In other words, if it be arranged that the cultures succeed each other every twelve hours, the rabbits inoculated from the last cultures die as quickly as those inoculated from the first. Thuillier had had the patience to make, in this manner, eighty cultures in contact with air, and eighty cultures in a vacuum; the microbe of the saliva being both aerobic and anaerobic. The eightieth culture killed as quickly as the first. But by allowing the successive cultures to remain for some time in contact with the air, before passing from one culture to the following one, the virulence of the cultures becomes enfeebled. Thus, then, as in fowl cholera, attenuated cultures of the microbe can be obtained. Unlike what happens with cholera, however, the cultures of the microbe of the saliva, exposed to the contact of air, perish very quickly. Two or three days of keeping suffice for the parent cultivation to lose all virulence. The seed, taken in any quantity from it, does not fertilise a new cultivation. But, before perishing, this culture passes through very different degrees of progressively weakened virulence, and it is easy with these cultivations to render rabbits ill without causing their death. Once cured, they resist all inoculation which would be mortal for others. The oxygen of the air is manifestly the transformer of this virulent virus into vaccine virus; for, if the virulent blood or cultivations remain inclosed in their tubes, sealed from all entrance of the air, they retain not only for some hours, but for months, their life and their original virulence.

But though these results were as new as they were unexpected, and though one cause of confusion in the study of this terrible problem was removed, yet these first researches were not marked by any progress in the etiology of hydrophobia. The question remained wholly unsolved.

Impatient with the length of time required for the incubation of the disease, and with the obligation of waiting whole months for the result of an experiment, when the subject demanded such numerous ones, Pasteur began to seek some means of producing hydrophobia with certainty and of making it appear more rapidly. Notwithstanding the assertion of a professor of the veterinary school at Lyons that the saliva of the rabid dog alone contained the virus of the disease, and that he had failed in every attempt to inoculate, whether with the substance of the brain or with the spinal marrow of rabid dogs; Pasteur, with due care as to purity, introduced under the skin of some rabbits and some dogs, divers parts of the brain of a dog which had died in a rabid state. Hydrophobia declared itself in both dogs and rabbits, with a duration of incubation about equal to that which followed the ordinary bite of a dog. Although it was necessary still to submit to this long uncertainty with regard to the incubation, one great result was obtained: hydrophobia *could* be inoculated with other matter than saliva. Not only is the saliva always impure, containing a saliva microbe, which is endowed with a special virulence of its own, but it presents other inconveniences. It is necessary, in these researches, to have a supply of material constantly at hand. Now, the saliva loses its rabic virulence in twenty-four hours. The existence of the rabic virulence in the brain substance placed, on the contrary, at the disposal of the experimenter, an abundance of the virus, in a state of great purity and capable of long preservation.

The idea then occurred to Pasteur and his assistants, to inoculate the virulent rabic matter in its pure state under the *dura mater* on the surface of the brain of a dog. Why not carry the virus, said Pasteur, directly to the place of its activity and development? After having trepanned the skull of a chloroformed dog, a little bit of the medulla of an animal which had died of hydrophobia was deposited on the surface of the brain. As soon as the influence of the chloroform was dissipated, the dog recovered its healthy appearance. It ate its food that same evening. But after some days the symptoms of hydrophobia appeared. The animal became dejected and restless; it tossed its litter about, refused all nourishment. A doleful, sharp howling was the first indication of the rabic voice, which is but one long cry of suffering and appeal, mingled with barkings from hallucinations. The stomach became depraved; the dog swallowed hay and straw. It soon grew furious, agitated with violent convulsions; finally, after a last fit, it died. During all this time there was great rejoicing in the laboratory. They were at last in possession of a method for singularly shortening the period of incubation, and for communicating the disease with certainty. The experiments were multiplied; all the dogs which were trepanned, and which received on the surface of the brain a little of the medulla of the rabid animal, succumbed to the disease, with very rare exceptions, within a period of twenty days. Did not the method pursued demonstrate, among other things, that hydrophobia is a disease of the brain; that the seat of the rabic virus, far from being exclusively in the saliva, belongs, above all, to the cerebral matter?

Other results, in addition to this one, were not slow in revealing themselves. It was established that not only the brain, but the spinal marrow, along its whole length, may be rabic, and that the nerves themselves throughout their whole system, from the centre to the periphery, may contain the virus of hydrophobia. If there exists a microbe of hydrophobia, its medium of cultivation in the body is, *par excellence*, the brain, the spinal marrow, and the nerves. It was also established that there were localisations of virus in certain parts of the mucous system, and that the very considerable differences of rabic symptoms which exist in different cases of hydrophobia, must be sought for in this fact. At the moment of death the medulla oblongata is always rabic. Finally, it was established that hydrophobia could be given (and almost as rapidly as by trepanning) by inoculating rabic nervous matter into the circulation of the blood by a vein.

In presence of such facts it is easy to account for what takes place in the case of a bite from a mad dog. The circulation of the blood carries the virus to the surface of the brain, or to the surface of the spinal marrow; there it houses itself in particular spots, and, little by little, invades the nervous matter. This last would be progressively attacked throughout, if death from the medulla oblongata did not almost always supervene before the propagation of the virus can become general.

The saliva glands are often rabic, doubtless because the virus oozes into them, little by little, from the nerves which enter these glands. Thus may the presence of this virus be explained in the saliva of mad dogs, where, at all times since the disease was first known, it has been found to exist. When the first point attacked by the virus is the spinal marrow, or certain portions of it, a general paralysis often precedes death. In this case the howling and biting symptoms are for the most part absent, and the dog continues to be caressing until it dies.

In a thesis written by M. Roux, Pasteur's laboratory assistant, last July, we read the following:—'If we examine with care a little of the pulp taken freshly from the brain of a rabid animal, and compare it with the same substance from the brain of a healthy animal, it is difficult to distinguish any difference between the two. In the rabic pulp, however, besides the granulations which are found in profusion in the healthy pulp, there seem to exist little grains of extreme minuteness, almost imperceptible even with the strongest microscopes. In the cephalo-rachidic liquid so limpid in appearance, it is possible with great attention to detect similar little grains. Can this be the microbe of hydrophobia? Some do not hesitate to affirm that it is. For ourselves, as long as the cultivation of the microbe outside of the organism has not been effected, and that hydrophobia has not been communicated by means of artificial cultures, we shall abstain from expressing a definite opinion on the subject.'

But the grand problem in regard to hydrophobia is, not so much the isolation of the microbe, as the finding of a means of preventing this frightful disease.

***

Even now the experiments are in full swing. Biting dogs and bitten dogs fill the laboratory. Without reckoning the hundreds of mad dogs that have died in the laboratory during the last three years, there never occurs a case of hydrophobia in Paris of which Pasteur is not informed. Not long ago a veterinary surgeon telegraphed to him, 'Attack at its height in poodle-dog and bull-dog. Come.' Pasteur invited me to accompany him, and we started, carrying six rabbits with us in a basket. The two dogs were rabid to the last degree. The bull dog especially, an enormous creature, howled and foamed in its cage. A bar of iron was held out to him: he threw himself upon it, and there was great difficulty in drawing it away from his bloody fangs. One of the rabbits was then brought near to the cage, and its drooping ear was allowed to pass through the bars. But, notwithstanding this provocation, the dog flung himself down at the bottom of his cage and refused to bite.

Two youths then threw a cord with a slip loop over the dog, as a lasso is thrown. The animal was caught and drawn to the edge of the cage. There they managed to get hold of him and to secure his jaws; and the dog, suffocating with fury, his eyes bloodshot, and his body convulsed with a violent spasm, was extended upon a table and held motionless, while Pasteur, leaning over his foaming head, at the distance of a finger's length, sucked up into a narrow tube some drops of the saliva. In the basement of the veterinary surgeon's house, witnessing this formidable *tête-à-tête*, I thought Pasteur grander than I had ever thought him before.

***

FOOTNOTES:

[1] 'Vernis des maîtres.'

[2] Art. 'Vitality,' *Fragments of Science*, 6th edit., vol. ii. p. 50.

[3] In Faraday's *induced* dissymmetry the ray, having once passed through the body under magnetic influence, has its rotation doubled, instead of neutralised, as in the case of quartz, on being reflected back through the body. Marbach has discovered that chlorate of soda produces circular polarisation in all directions through the crystal, while in quartz it occurs only in the direction of the axis. Marbach also discovered facets upon his crystals, resembling those of quartz.

[4] It was late in the day when the Royal Society made him a foreign member.

[5] These words were uttered at a time when the pythogenic theory was more in favour than it is now.

[6] The work on *Diseases of Silkworms* was dedicated to the Empress of the French.

[7] [M. Pasteur appears to use the word *devenir* as a substantive in a sense equivalent to the German *Werdende*.]

[8] [A millimeter is 1/25th of an inch.]